THE LOST MADONNA

Isabelle Holland

Rawson, Wade Publishers, Inc. · New York

Library of Congress Cataloging in Publication Data
Holland, Isabelle.
The lost Madonna.
I. Title.
PS3558.03485L6   813'.54   80–5996
ISBN 0–89256–170–X   AACR2

Published simultaneously in Canada by
McClelland and Stewart, Ltd.
Composition by American–Stratford
Graphic Services, Inc.,
Brattleboro, Vermont
Printed and bound by Fairfield Graphics,
Fairfield, Pennsylvania
Designed by Gene Siegel

First Edition

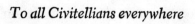

To all Civitellians everywhere

Acknowledgment

I wish to express my appreciation to James Franz of the Metropolitan Museum of Art and to Robert J. Anthony, representing the Perkin Elmer Corporation, for their very helpful advice on scientific techniques used in the authentication of works of art. I would also like to thank Gerald Rupp for his advice on legal technicalities, and Francis Russell and Marilena Sorbello for their generous assistance.

Isabelle Holland

THE LOST
MADONNA

PROLOGUE

She always walked in the garden before breakfast. Awaking before six, she plugged in the electric kettle, which was steaming by the time she returned from a brief visit to the bathroom. Back in bed, she sipped the strong, instant espresso, thick with cream and sugar, and watched the dawn come up over the eastern gate of the castle grounds. Then she bathed and dressed in a wraparound cotton skirt and sweater, slid a bulky white envelope from the top of her bureau into her skirt pocket and in tennis shoes made her way down the silent stone corridors and two flights of steps to the square courtyard.

In the days of her husband, the late Conte di Monaldi, the chapel would be open, and she would sometimes stop in for a few minutes, sitting bolt upright in the hideously uncomfortable high seat considered suitable for the noble owner, her eyes on the red sanctuary light that burned there every night and day of the year, except, of course, for the two days between the last mass of Maundy Thursday and the first mass of Easter. But the contessa had never really liked the chapel. Brought up in a Northern European Protestant country, she despised the porcelain images, the dust-catching bric-a-brac of the passionately visual Italians, and, at the first reasonable excuse after the count's death, had the chapel closed except for the occasional special mass.

Now, coming out of the open half-door in the castle's immense entrance, she paused, sorry for the first time in more than twelve years that the chapel was not open for her to go into.

The contessa, nominally Catholic, had never been entirely sure what she believed, or whether she believed anything at all about the spiritual life, or even whether she cared. What she had loved with all her fierce nature was here on earth to be seen, heard and felt. Now, standing on the entrance steps in the square courtyard, looking towards the chapel door across and to the right, she felt a sudden shiver. Everything that had come to her through her senses had always been so blazingly real, there had never been room in her heart or her intellect for anything else. But, for the first time, she was suddenly overwhelmed with the fact that she was old, that the life of the senses was mortal: that it would soon be over. Very soon.

"What on earth's the matter with me?" she thought, pulling around her a stretched and stained woollen shawl she'd snatched up from a hook behind the door. The sky, a lemony blue, promised a glorious summer day, but up here in the Umbrian hills it was still chilly. For a moment, as she continued to stand, staring at the chapel door, her eyes straying to the *campanile* above and then back again, she almost yielded to an impulse to go back upstairs to the big hall drawer where she kept the ancient, cumbersome keys, find the chapel key, and come down, open it and go in.

But her most ancient enemy, pride, held her. In the marvelous and creative decade since her husband died, she had not much troubled her mind or her conscience with the things of God. So to go to Him now simply because she felt, for a moment, depressed and frightened, seemed poor-spirited, even craven.

4

"Yes, my dear, but you do remember, don't you, that one of the things He said was blessed are the poor in spirit?"

Shocked, she turned around. It was Marcello's voice, and it was certainly the kind of thing he would have said in that charming, amused voice of his that had won her so many years before. Despite her own Italian heritage, she had spent most of her growing up years in a very different culture, and had assumed that the majority of Italians took their Catholicism lightly and cynically. It was therefore something of a shock to find, after her marriage, that her husband, a widower some fifteen years her senior when they married, was a profoundly religious man who lived his faith on a day-to-day basis. This was the only aspect of their extremely happy years together that she was never able to share, and he never once tried to influence her.

But he was trying to influence her now. She could feel it—how, she could not have described, even to herself. Nonetheless, he was there, pushing her to open the chapel and go in.

But nearly eighty years of pride and stubbornness kept her feet on the steps. By osmosis, she had absorbed the parables of the Prodigal Son and the workers hired at the eleventh hour. Nevertheless she could not accept such magnanimity. That was one reason. There was another, but she did not wish even to think about it, such was her anger of the moment. It was an anger that had kept her awake most nights for a fortnight, flowing through her like a corrosive acid, disfiguring every memory it touched. She would, instead, go to the rose garden and pick some roses for the breakfast table before the guests started trailing in to breakfast.

Pulling the shawl tighter, she crossed the courtyard away from the chapel, picked up a flat basket lying inside the stone passageway, and, using the passageway, went down into the garden that lay below the castle.

The six-hundred-year-old castle, its houses, farms and

5

crops were the creation of the Monaldis, who had been powerful in the area since the early fourteenth century. But the garden was hers and its pride was the rosebushes that had become, in their modest way, almost as famous as the family itself, supplying the guest rooms with blooms both fragrant and beautiful, and keeping the contessa's winter quarters in London sweet-smelling with the potpourri that she herself made up. Because it was her own creation, and because she had always had an almost sensual link with flowers of all kinds, she always found peace in her garden that she could find nowhere else. Often she would go in the garden with insoluble problems gnawing her consciousness, and emerge, an hour or so later, with workable answers. That was all she asked of solutions: not that they be perfect, but that they be workable.

But the only answer to the problem that had destroyed her peace, though workable, would be devastating to her, to everything she had created and to others. But there was no other answer. She knew that. A little while among her beloved roses would not change that, she thought. But perhaps it would bring her acceptance of what had to be done. . . .

Moving among the bushes, her white hair and still-beautiful profile rising high above them, she plucked here, snipped there, and touched continually and lightly, deriving satisfaction and comfort from the velvety surfaces. The sun, throwing its long morning shadow across the sundial, was now bright and warm on her shoulders and hands. Two bees on a nearby bush droned and buzzed. The garden magic was beginning—a little—to work. The task that lay in front of her was unpleasant in the extreme, the most unpleasant she had ever had to confront. But perhaps, possibly, it would not be quite as dreadful as she had envisioned. A twig near her snapped, but in her beginning peace she paid no attention to it.

Then suddenly the chill she had felt on the castle steps

6

came back, only much stronger. Stricken with terror, she thought, *it's like death,* and knew, in the last fraction of a moment of her life, before the blow went through her skull, that that was what had been beside her all morning: death.

ONE

The letter from my stepgrandmother filled me with the curious blend of pleasure and fury that her letters nearly always brought: pleasure because I liked going to Italy, liked visiting her at her castle and, despite everything and underneath all our quarrels, liked her: fury because she didn't suggest or invite, she commanded. There was something she had to talk over with me at once, and would I please present myself at the castle as soon as possible?

Just like that.

I'll be damned if I will, I thought, putting the envelope on the mantelpiece in my flat. It was ridiculous to behave so childishly, and I knew it. What I should do, I thought, is to pick up the telephone and call Gianetta and, in a reasonable fashion, talk over the fact that I couldn't think of leaving the gallery for at least three weeks. Rupert would be back by then and I could get away. After fussing, and acting very much the grande dame for a few minutes, Gianetta would agree that she had been preemptory and I would find out that I could really get away in ten days. In other words, we'd negotiate. Her pride versus mine. And because of the Monaldi Museum, Gianetta's creation established as a memorial to her husband, and the solid American fortune behind it, Rupert Carmichael, my employer, who owned and ran the gallery where I worked, and who usually acted like a direct descendent of Ebenezer Scrooge, would grudgingly let me off for a little holiday. This would be accompanied by a sardonic look and polite messages of good wishes to both La Contessa and Oliver Landau, whose brains put the museum together.

But around twelve-thirty at the gallery, when I was munching a sandwich at my desk, I received a telephone call that changed everything.

"Hello," I said, picking up the receiver in my small office off the main ground floor gallery.

"Julia? This is Oliver. Gianetta is dead."

The mind doesn't take in things like that immediately. I found myself as preoccupied with the break in his normally suave voice as with what he was saying. Then, suddenly, the shock hit. "Gianetta?" I said dully, stupidly. "Dead?"

"Killed. In a fall. Oh God." His voice really cracked at that.

"How?" I finally managed to ask. "How did it happen?"

"God knows. She was by herself. Maria found her."

But my mind wouldn't take that in. I was still grappling with Gianetta's death, trying to accept it. I heard then, over the other end of the telephone, something that sounded like a gasp, an indrawn breath of pain. "I'm sorry, Oliver." I spoke gently as I could. Since her husband Marcello's death, there was no doubt in the world who loved Gianetta most: Oliver Landau. And why not? In the professional sense of the word, she had made him, although the concept of the Monaldi Museum had been originally his.

"Where are you calling from?" I said then.

"My flat. I'd been out. When I came in my answering service said someone from Civitella had called, so I rang back."

Suddenly everything he'd said struck me with full force. I saw, in my mind, the regal old lady with her tall white head, elegant profile and narrow body. And then, as though

9

it were taking place on a screen in front of me, I watched her body fold in the middle and start to fall, blood, the color of the roses near her, spurting from her head onto a white blouse and blue cotton skirt. It was gone in a second, but it was appallingly vivid. "Oh!" I said, and for a moment put a hand over my face. But I knew as I did so that I had seen something, something that I couldn't quite remember, that hadn't made the journey to my conscious mind. Or had I imagined it? "You said she was in the rose garden, didn't you?"

There was a moment's silence, then Oliver, his voice back under control, said, "Did I? I suppose I did. Or did they get in touch with you first?"

"No." The moment I'd said that I wish I had lied.

"Then—?"

Another silence. Then he said, "For someone who hasn't deigned to visit her recently, that was a pretty accurate guess."

Oliver and I were back to normal, making slightly edgy comments to each other. "We've been through this before, Oliver. You know she and I have—had—our problems." And then the fact that she was dead hit me again, and I felt a terrible sadness that I hadn't seen her, that we hadn't made up, that I hadn't even answered her last letters. It was inconceivable that she, Gianetta di Monaldi, was dead, because she was one of the most intensely, if irritatingly, alive people I had ever known.

"Oliver," I said. "Are you going over there?"

"Of course. I'm catching the three o'clock plane and I've arranged to have a car meet me at the airport."

"If I can get hold of Rupert I'll come with you."

"It would help. At least you're a relative."

"Not really. Only step."

"You're still family."

"All right. Tell me your flight number and so on, and if I can reach Rupert and have somebody hold the fort, I'll

10

make a reservation. In any case, I'll call you."

Reaching Rupert was not easy. It was late July, and Rupert, who was xenophobic in the extreme, ostentatiously left London on July 1st because, he claimed, it became a foreign city in July and August. He disliked all foreigners, but his degree of dislike increased with the distance from which the foreigners came, except, of course, for visitors from the Dominions, who could be counted on to have a comfortably British view of things.

"And what about Americans?" I once said, somewhat belligerently, being one.

"I haven't made up my mind about them," Rupert said.

"Let me know when you do."

None of this prevented him from traveling extensively on the continent. When I pointed out this inconsistency, he explained that he did not in the least mind foreigners on their own turf. After all, he could leave whenever he wished. What he minded intensely was when they invaded his territory.

I called various cities, leaving messages with business associates and friends, and he finally rang back from Geneva.

"What is it?" he said, with all his accustomed charm.

"Gianetta died," I replied bluntly. And the truth and horror of it struck me all over again.

There was silence. Then, "I'm sorry. What happened?"

"According to Oliver, who called me, she fell. He was pretty upset."

"I imagine he would be." The dryness in his tone was marked.

"There's no need to be nasty about him."

"I'm not being nasty. It's a perfectly obvious fact."

I knew it was; yet around Rupert I was always defensive about Oliver, with whom, at the age of nineteen, I'd fallen passionately in love and who taught me most of what I

11

knew about art. "Anyway," I said, making up my mind. "I'm leaving this afternoon to go with Oliver to Rome. We're taking a car up to Civitella. Who do you want me to get to hold the fort until you can get here?" I hadn't planned to put it on such a take it or leave it basis, but Rupert's comment, coming when it did, irritated me.

"There is no one, as you well know, whom I would trust to take care of the gallery with both of us away. I must ask you to wait until I get back. I can be there tomorrow."

Afterwards, I wondered why I became, at that moment, so unreasonable. It was true I was upset, and Rupert, always brusque, was being, even for him, thick-skinned. But there was more to it than that. A strong urgency was pushing me towards Italy and Civitella. In a way that I could not have explained I felt it imperative that I leave immediately, that I go with Oliver. But instead of explaining this in a rational manner, I proceeded to put on one of my more virulent performances of pigheadedness.

"I can't wait, Rupert. I have to leave this morning. I'll lock the gallery and leave the alarm on. It will be up to you how long you want to leave it closed." As I spoke I knew I was, in fact, deserting my job in an irresponsible fashion. In addition to that, visions of rent due and bills coming in wafted across my mind. I pushed them aside. Then, furious at myself for doing so, wondered if Gianetta had left me any money. I thrust that away, too. "I have to leave with Oliver," I said.

"*Cela va sans dire*," he replied icily. "Aren't you being a little irresponsible? It's not as though you had even bothered to answer Gianetta's letters lately."

Because it was true it made me feel worse. In a remote, detached corner of my mind, I wondered why I seemed to be compulsively doing everything I could to make Rupert fire me. "You mean if I leave without your permission I needn't come back."

12

Pause. "That's about it," Rupert said.

"It will be a pleasure, Rupert. Even for you, spiritual clone of Ebenezer Scrooge, to fire me at this time is definitely scaley. You have the soul of a reptile. Goodbye." And I hung up.

Anyone else, I thought, whipping up my self-justification as I cleaned out papers, letters, tissues, pens, a couple of snapshots and two notebooks filled with notes, would have put up a show of sympathy, simply for form's sake, if nothing else. I brushed aside Rupert's "I am sorry," as too trivial to consider. What else could he say? "Congratulations"?

Maggie, my assistant, came in. "What are you doing, Julia?"

"What does it look like I'm doing?"

"It looks like you're clearing out your desk."

"Ten out of ten for you. That's exactly what I'm doing." I glanced up. "You play your cards right, Maggie, and you can have my job."

"From where I stand on the sidelines, that doesn't look like such a huge temptation. Did you leave in a huff, or did he fire you?"

"Both. By the way, I said I was going to close the gallery. Sorry about that."

Maggie, who worked only part time, sighed. "Never mind. It's no big thing. And it's not as though I were losing huge sums of pay. Who knows, perhaps I can find a better-paying job."

"Almost any job would pay better."

"Why is he so mean with money? It isn't as though he didn't have any."

"It's just his sweet nature. Does Rupert know where to get in touch with you when he comes back, because if not, you'd better leave him a note."

Maggie sighed again and went off. I collected the last of my things, and, nostalgically, looked around the gallery.

It was a mistake. Rupert, who even I had to admit had an eye for new painters, had recently discovered one whose line and color were incomparable, unmatched among contemporary artists.

"Who is he?" I had asked wonderingly, when Rupert brought his first canvases into the gallery several months before.

"He calls himself Andrea, as you can see by the signature."

"Yes. I can see that. Andrea who?"

"Smith."

I stared at Rupert's thin, cynical, but not unattractive, face. "Of course. Andrea Smith. It goes together."

Rupert's rare smile flickered across his mouth, changing him briefly into another man, a man I hardly knew. "He says he has an Italian mother," he said vaguely. Rupert put the canvas on an easel and backed off. "He's good, isn't he?"

"As you very well know, he's marvelous. Where on earth did you find him?"

"Around."

"Are you afraid I'm going to steal him with fair promises and start a gallery of my own?"

"It's been done."

I stared at my boss for a minute. Most of the time, I thought, he looked exactly like the banker he had once been: thin, conservative, boring and stuffy. From his pin-striped suit to his short hair he had the expression of someone whose every instinct was to turn down a loan, except, of course, for somebody who didn't need it.

"You should have stayed in banking."

"I sometimes think that myself. But there's more money to be made in this line. And thirty-nine's more than old enough to start a new career."

"Is that the only reason you opened the gallery? Is that all that art means to you?"

"Spare me the romantic agony. Art is a big business."

"But you don't believe in sharing the profits."

"This is not a charitable organization or a worthy foundation. Which reminds me, do you think your grandmother, the contessa, would be interested in Andrea for her museum?"

"It may be her museum, but it's Oliver who finds the things to put in it."

"That's possibly true. But your grandmother's a forceful lady. I don't see her hiding her light—or her opinions—under a bushel. Landau was curator of what amounted to a second-rate oversized gallery until her money enabled him to start buying up the works of Mantori, Jacopo della Quercia, La Spagna and other notables."

"I think you're jealous."

"Of that bogus lapdog! I thank you."

I was surprised (and delighted) to have got under his skin. Rupert had made it obvious from the start that he hired me only because of my connection with Gianetta. "It's too bad he got there first."

He looked at me out of his light gray eyes. "It's not remarkable you haven't married," he said. "Even with today's liberation a man would have to have a marked death wish to take up permanent residence with you."

It was a nasty hit and he knew it. I was twenty-eight and, as he said, unmarried. And while marriage was no longer considered the *sine qua non* for a woman who wanted to be considered successful, it was, unfortunately, well known that David Brownson, the popular writer, had eventually, and rather publicly, decided not to marry me. After living in my apartment off and on for four years, he had gone back to his wife. That happy event had taken place six months previously. When I returned from a business trip to New York I found his clothes gone and his letter to me on the hall table. Even while reading it, with a hand closing over my midriff, I gave a grim smile. How things come around! Always before in song and story it had been the woman who had left the note on the pincushion.

"You are a foul man with a foul instinct," I had said to Rupert after his comment on my unmarried state. "I hope all your swans turn out to be geese."

He grinned. "They won't."

And they hadn't. Even before the advent of Andrea whoever he was, Rupert had had an eye for rising young painters who also seemed to have more than a touch of popular appeal. Before Andrea there was Tom Letchwick, whose strange, haunted winter landscapes were sold before they'd been up two weeks; and Jeffrey Roth with his finely crafted, unsentimental but sensitive portrayal of children and animals; and Mary O'Connor, who painted houses, preferably small, city houses, bathed in an odd, golden light that seemed to add almost a psychic dimension. All three of them now could command staggering prices, and their works had become collectors' items. They not only paid the gallery's rent, they paid for the renovations of the crumbling, higgledy-piggledy former farm building that Rupert had inherited and that he loved more than any living creature, human or otherwise, except, perhaps, for Bothwell. A large unattractive dog of dubious ancestry and bad habits, Bothwell lay snoring at the back of the gallery whenever Rupert was there, and was given to growling at rich customers.

"Your disgusting hound is going to bite one of the carefully cultivated clients one of these days," I said to him once, as Bothwell bared his teeth at Lady Welles.

"He's got good taste, Bothwell does."

"Lady Welles came in to buy something, in case you hadn't noticed," I said bitterly. If I sold a painting, I received a minute commission, an unusual custom in a gallery, and only instituted by Rupert as a slight sop to compensate for his rotten wages. "She was on the point of saying yes when Bothwell showed his true charm."

"I wouldn't want her to have that Roth anyway. She'd

probably put it next to some nonobjective horror that she was told ten years ago was fashionable. She'd never know for herself. Somebody must have told her that Roth was now in and to get in on the ground floor. Stupid old hag."

"Thanks a lot. Anything to save a commission."

But it was wasted breath. Rupert grinned. "I'm not Scots for nothing."

That exchange still rankled, and I now took considerable satisfaction in turning the gallery lights out, switching on the alarm and firmly locking the door after Maggie and me.

"Serves him right," I said, pulling the key out.

"You'll have to send the key back to him," Maggie pointed out.

I hadn't thought of that. It would have to go by registered mail and that would take more time than was available this morning. I had to hurry home, throw some things in a suitcase and get to the airport to see if I could arrange a ride on Oliver's plane. Rupert and his key would have to wait.

I made the plane by the skin of my teeth, and wouldn't have managed that if Oliver hadn't had the forethought to reserve the seat for me and order the ticket so that everything was waiting when I ran through passport control down Heathrow's corridors towards the right gate. The passengers were filing through the gate as I panted up. Oliver, his salt-and-pepper head rising above most others, was waiting at the end of the line, his dark eyes rimmed by black shadows fixed on the hallways from which I was coming.

"I thought for a moment you wouldn't make it," he said. "Run over to the desk there. They've got your ticket and boarding pass."

"How come we're going Alitalia?" I asked in a few minutes, still panting as we buckled ourselves into our seat belts. "I thought you traveled British Airways."

"That's the kind of sweeping statement based on practically no evidence that you're always making."

I opened my mouth to make a comeback in kind, when I noticed how strained and tired and miserable he looked. He should be granted license for nerves at this point. "Okay, okay," I said, uncharacteristically docile. "I guess I was wrong."

London to Rome is approximately two hours, but because Rome is in a later time zone, our two-fifty-five flight was scheduled to get in, not at five, but at six-fifteen. Oliver had taken the window seat and during takeoff and for the first half hour afterwards, he stared out at the almost cloudless sky. After a while I said, "Who actually telephoned you, Oliver? Paolo?" Paolo Ruggoni was the *fattore*, or land agent, who lived in one of the two houses across the courtyard from the castle entrance, and who managed the farms with their three annual crops: wheat, olives and wine.

Oliver replied without turning his head, "No, Maria."

I sat quietly for a while and thought about that. Maria Natale started out life as Mary Fletcher, from Barnes, in Southwest London, on the south bank of the Thames. But her mother had been Italian, and when the young Gianetta had advertised for a dual-language personal maid, to go with her to Italy, Mary Fletcher had instantly applied. She had never been to Italy before, because her working-class family had never got enough money together for Mary and her mother to go. And her mother died without ever seeing again her native Umbria. So Mary, hard-headed product of cockney London that she was, would have gone with Gianetta for almost no pay. But Gianetta, sole heir to an immense fortune, had always been as generous as she was demanding, and the two had been together ever since. Mary's name had become, over the years in Italy, Maria, and her surname became Italian when she married Giuseppe Natale, who owned the largest farm near the castle. It was a second marriage for Giuseppe, who died three years later. Maria took their little son, Ludovico, and returned to permanent residence with the Monaldis. She had continued as Gianetta's maid whenever Gianetta was in residence in the castle, coming down the cypress drive, through the castle gate and around to the courtyard shortly after dawn each day, to the indignation of her husband who thought she should remain home. But Maria never made any bones about where her first loyalty lay: it was with Gianetta. Giuseppe and even little Ludo, as he came to be called, had to take second and third place.

After Giuseppe's death, Maria and Ludo spent the winters in Perugia at the Monaldi's palazzo, where they had quarters of their own and from where Ludo attended local schools. During the summers they were in Civitella, but long before the conte's death, Ludo had grown up and gone off on his own and it occurred to me now that I had no idea where he was or what he was doing. I had never met him and couldn't even remember anyone mentioning him, except Gianetta when she had, in passing during my first visit, referred to him and I learned of his existence. After her husband's death, Gianetta had moved her winter quarters to a flat in London's Cadogan Place, and Maria had gone with her. In all, she and Gianetta had been together some forty years. So finding Gianetta dead must have been, for Maria, a devastating experience.

"Didn't you say Maria found her?"

"Yes. Apparently Maria had spent the night in the village with friends and didn't arrive at the castle until after breakfast. The guests were each going about their business and no one had missed Gianetta because people straggled in to breakfast at different times and everyone assumed she'd eaten at some other time. You know how it is there. So Maria didn't begin to wonder for an hour or two. Then she started looking and, not finding her anywhere else, went to the rose garden, where she knew

19

Gianetta walked early in the morning. She found her there. Then she called me."

Oliver, as the person known to be closest to Gianetta, was the obvious person to call. Yet, for a moment, I found myself a little surprised. The late count had relatives, admittedly somewhat distant ones, living in Perugia. Wouldn't they be the ones to inform first? Especially when you considered that Maria had never been that fond of Oliver. It was well known and something of a family joke, because the grudging quality of her acceptance was reciprocated by Oliver. It was so plainly jealousy and an overdeveloped sense of rivalry between two devoted attendants that it afforded everyone else—and Gianetta herself, I often strongly suspected—a certain wry amusement.

But, when I thought about it, I knew that the sturdy English Mary Fletcher would consider it her duty to inform her beloved mistress's closest associate.

"What—how had she fallen?" I asked.

There was a silence. Then, "Do you mind if we don't talk about it now. Later, perhaps."

I glanced quickly at him, and saw him fish a handkerchief out of his pocket and blow his nose.

"Sorry, of course."

And there I was, I reflected grimly, sitting dry-eyed, her almost-granddaughter, the one whose education had been paid for and whose art training had been subsidized by Gianetta, whose summers at Civitella had been taken for granted by me and my father, as well as by Gianetta and my grandfather Marcello. Why wasn't I battling grief?

I couldn't really answer that, or rather, the only answer that made sense was so unpalatable and struck such a chill in my heart, I preferred to pretend it was a mystery. The truth was, I hadn't grieved for my father, either, Marcello's American son-in-law. My mother, Isabella Monaldi, Marcello's daughter by his first wife, had come one autumn to Cambridge, Massachusetts, to take a psychology course at Radcliffe. The young man who taught the course was a Fellow at Harvard working on his doctorate. His name was Joshua Winthrop, and in the style of the best, if old-fashioned, romances, they fell in love and got married in the face of total opposition on the part of everyone in both families except Gianetta, my mother's stepmother. My mother, whom I barely remembered, died in a car accident when I was a small child. My father installed a housekeeper, and kept on being one of the most brilliant psychologists in the country—a man in constant demand at universities everywhere, author of several authoritative texts on behavioral psychology, and a miserable parent. I had spent my early childhood adoring him from a distance, dressed up by my current nanny and waiting for him to come home from some triumphant lecture tour, waiting for him to notice me, to notice how nicely I was dressed and how much I looked like him, until, finally, half famished with hunger I would be borne off for the solitary dinner in the kitchen or morning room, instead of dinner à deux. Because, attractive and charming, he could not resist the dinner invitation that would somehow be offered by someone (usually female) between the time he left his last stop and the time he got into the car or taxi to come home. Sometimes he would burst into the duplex apartment on Fifth Avenue, flowers at the ready. "Darling, forgive me. An unavoidable business appointment. I can't wait for us to be together!" . . . . And he would be off two days later, or locked in his study reading proofs on his latest book.

Somewhere between eleven and fourteen I gave up waiting for him to put me just once ahead of his work, his lectures, his admiring (female) fans, his television appearances and, of course, his seminars. And then, suddenly, around fourteen, I got very angry. He didn't even

21

notice for some weeks. Then, when he came home from a series of lectures, I was out. When I returned I made no effort to kiss him. Instead, I asked to be sent to boarding school, a request that he was glad to comply with.

I loved boarding school and was a tremendous success at it. For the first time I was in a close-knit community of my peers, and realized within the first week why I had always been lonely. When I discovered how much I loved boarding school, I forgave my father. We became, not parent and child, not even good friends, but, on the rare occasions when we were together, pleasant companions.

"If you're such a hotshot psychologist," I asked once, "how come you're such a rotten father?" I saw a flicker of pain on his handsome face.

"I didn't mean to hurt your feelings." I said unrepentently. "But surely you know that about yourself?"

"Yes, well, you've heard about the cobbler's children going unshod?" He looked uncomfortable. "The truth is, Julie, I've never liked people that much."

"Then why did you go in for psychology?"

"*Behavioral* psychology. It's pretty theoretical. At least the part that interests me is."

"Rats running the maze," I said.

He didn't reply.

The vacations were a problem, until Gianetta wrote one June and asked me to spend the summer at the castle with her and some other young people from England she had invited. Marcello was still alive then. I had, of course, met them many times in New York, and had been invited to the castle to which they moved in June for the four summer months. But I was too involved in camp and in staying with friends. But the summer I was sixteen, I went, and since my grandfather died the following November, I was always glad I'd done so, although I preferred Gianetta, my stepgrandmother, to him, or, for that matter, anyone else.

Looking down at the Italian coast as the plane circled

22

towards the airport outside Rome, my mind came back to the subject from which it had recoiled: why I was sitting dry-eyed and ungriefstricken next to Oliver, who, though holding himself in control, was plainly devastated.

There go his professional ambitions, my nasty inner self said. But it was much more than that, and I knew it. He really cared for her. And I?

In my fashion. But my fashion was so hedged about and well defended, so adept at putting distance between myself and others, that it could rarely be mistaken for anything that could remotely be called love. And that was undoubtedly why, in the long run, I got along so well with Gianetta. On a one-to-one basis, she was a fairly distant customer herself. After Marcello's death, only Oliver had broken through the first layers or barriers. She was generous and demanding. And I resented both. What was it David had said before I had left on that last trip during which he had returned to his wife? "You're so busy fighting border wars, Julie, you don't have time, or energy, to love properly."

I was not only furious, I was dumbfounded. I had fallen in love with David when I first saw him across the gallery during an opening cocktail party. He was there with his exquisitely beautiful, exquisitely aristocratic and exquisitely wealthy wife. But when his eyes met mine a lightning bolt crackled between us. Three months later he had left his wife. The marriage, he had assured me, had been to all intents and purposes dead for years. As soon as it was feasible he would somehow get a divorce. It never became feasible. And as it became more and more obvious that this was something that he could not bring himself to do, the relationship between us became more and more difficult. As David said, I became given to fighting border wars. . . . Everything boiled down to a kind of proof that he didn't love me enough. . . .

The wheels of the plane hit Italian soil with a thump.

I glanced at Oliver, who was already, and against the counsel given by the flight attendants in both English and Italian, unbuckling his seat belt. And, as always happened when I saw Oliver's profile and remembered the first time I'd seen it, I felt a slight lurch in my midriff. Oliver remained the handsomest man I had ever known in my life. At forty-seven his hair had only just started to gray at the temples. Half Italian, half French, brought up in England, he seemed to have derived the best from all his worlds. He looked more French than Italian, but had the freedom and security to express his emotions that no Northern Europeans ever seem to be able to acquire.

I was in love with Oliver for several years, beginning with the wonderful summer that I was nineteen, when, instructed by Gianetta to do something about my abysmal ignorance of Italian art, he took me through churches, museums and palazzos, up and down and across Italy. By the end of that glorious three months, I had seen every major and most minor works of Italian art still in the country. Any tourist, of course, could have covered the same distance in a far shorter time. What made those weeks an unforgettable experience was Oliver, who was an incomparable teacher. It was both magnificent and painful—magnificent because I received riches nothing could ever take away from me, painful because by summer's end I was deeply in love. Oliver somehow combined within himself the father I hadn't had—one who took time and trouble to give me something of himself—and the lover I was ready for. That our love was entirely one-sided, and our love scenes wholly in my head did not (for me, anyway) make the passion less.

That summer never happened again. I saw Oliver every time I went to Civitella. I met him occasionally in London. He was always a witty and delightful companion—when I allowed him to be. Sometimes the only way I could bear to be with him was to conduct small skirmishes. Somewhere early I had decided that when a kiss was out of the question (for whatever reason) a fight would do almost as well. At least—or so I told myself—being prickly and difficult was better than falling into the arms of a man who didn't want me. Eventually, of course, I grew out of my one-sided passion. There were other men. And then I met David. On the surface he and Oliver were polar opposites, which was perhaps why David had such attraction for me. He was fair-haired, very English, very practical and notably successful. After Oliver's brilliant erraticisms and vague ambiance of failure, David was a powerful relief. And, not to be forgotten, he loved me back. . . .

Now Oliver said, "I ordered the car and hope to heaven it's there."

It was true: Things seemed to fall through, with no explanation given, more in Italy than in England. But the car was there and waiting, and after dealing with the necessary papers at *Roma Autos*, the car rental desk tucked in a corner of the terminal, I followed Oliver's tall, handsome figure out into the soft Italian evening.

"I thought you always used Hertz or one of the bigger car rental agencies," I said, as I trailed Oliver to the Mercedes that was waiting for him.

"Not Hertz, Intercontinental," he said, fitting the key into the car. "Equally big, of course. But not reliable. You'd better get in."

I glanced up at his face. Oliver had the kind of dark coloring that held up better under strain and fatigue than the blonde, fair-skinned variety. So the deepening black shadows under his eyes and the lines around his mouth were an indication of considerable stress and lost sleep.

"Do you want me to drive?" I asked.

"No. I'll do it."

"You look like you could fall asleep at the wheel."

"I wish I could. Although not necessarily at the wheel. No, I'll be all right." And he slammed the door on the passenger side, narrowly missing my fingers.

We didn't talk much on the way up, and I was just as glad for it to be that way. We'd had sandwiches on the plane, so there was no need to stop. The *autostrada* ahead of us was baked in a tawny gold light slightly filtered with gray. Far away, in silhouette, was the dome of St. Peter's, rising above the other roofs of Rome. And here and there, in single file, marched tall cypresses, a little like slender ostrich fans turned on end. The castle was about one hundred and thirty miles north of Rome, which would not make that much difference climatically, but it was on a slight hill and was both higher and cooler. All the castles and towns in that area were on hills, slight and otherwise: Perugia, Assisi, Gubbio, Spello, Cortona. . . . My mind read off the list. I had visited all of them during the summers I was at the castle when Gianetta was alive. . . . And the fact that she was dead hit me all over again.

"How long will it take us?" I asked. Always before I had gone on the one train from Rome that went straight through to the small station within a few miles of the castle.

"About two and a half hours. If we don't hit traffic."

I looked at his face again, and at his hands, gripping the wheel. "My offer to drive part of the way still stands."

"I'm perfectly all right," he snapped.

After that, I didn't say anything. But after we'd been driving for about an hour Oliver suddenly said, "I take it Rupert let you off."

"No. He did not. He was his usual unaccommodating self. I quit."

"That was a rather grand gesture, wasn't it? Jobs like that don't fall out of trees."

I knew that, and was beginning to be a little puzzled at my own precipitous behavior. Waves of regret had come over me on the plane. I enjoyed the gallery, I liked the kind of painters Rupert was interested in, and, realistically,

26

the pay, if stingy, was not much, if any, worse than that in any other gallery. Wages, at the lower echelon of the art world were extraordinarily poor, as they were, for that matter, in all the industries or professions that provided pleasant and interesting work.

"He behaved in his usual charming fashion. When I told him I wanted to get off immediately because of Gianetta's death, he said I'd have to wait till he got back."

"Still, it's a pity. He's one of the better men around."

"I thought you wanted me to come with you."

"I wanted you to come to Civitella. It would have been all right to wait a day. When did he say he could be back?"

"A day."

"Good heavens, Julia. Why didn't you wait?"

"Because . . ." I'd had an overwhelming sense of urgency about coming to Civitella. And also, if I was being honest, because he'd had the gall to point out something that I was trying not to think about: that my sudden access of grief was not consistent with the fact that I hadn't even bothered to answer the old lady's letters. In other words, he had piled on my sense of guilt. But I didn't want to admit that to Oliver, who had always been at me for ingratitude and for paying insufficient deference towards Gianetta.

"Just because," I finally said.

"You should do something about your bellicose tendencies," he said. "You might just talk yourself into solitary confinement."

Since the same thought had occurred to me, a sense of depression was added to my guilt. "I'm going to try," I said meekly.

It was night when we turned into the road where, up on a hill, rising above a thick belt of trees, the roof of Civitella, in daylight, could first be seen. Now it was a massive black silhouette against a night sky lit by a half moon and millions of stars. During the day could be seen,

27

lying between the road and the castle, fields of wheat, punctuated here and there by the dull gray of squat olive trees and rows of twisted vines. Lights were on in the farm houses, but the castle was too thickly covered with trees for any lights to be visible there. Twenty minutes later the car, having negotiated the long curving road that led up to the castle entrance, swept through an avenue of cypresses and swung sharply to the right, going through an archway.

Ahead reared the four-square building, rising some hundred feet at the tip of the battlements, the rectangular crenelation indicating that the Monaldis of the fifteenth century were followers of the papal party, the Guelphs. The long windows of the three separate stories blazed with light. Straight ahead, just before the path forked, was a statue of Carlo Monaldi, the Conte di Monaldi who had built the castle. Garbed in armor, with a sword pointing down and a dog at his feet, he guarded the entrance. Gianetta always referred to him as The Ancestor, and from time to time would stick a bunch of roses in the stone hand holding the sword. The stone had crumbled away in the succeeding centuries, so The Ancestor, or Don Carlo, which was what Oliver called him, had a somewhat moth-eaten appearance.

In front of the castle was a large triangle of lawn, coming to a point where the statue stood and the path divided. On the other side of the paths and more grass was the outer wall of the compound, with small dwellings built into the wall, accommodating in the past grooms, stables, kennels and whatever artisans the whole community needed. The rooms were now pretty much empty, though the Monaldis had, in the past century, installed running water and then given them to retired servants. Behind the wall, the ground fell away sharply on all sides, with the slopes covered with trees. At one time a moat had circled the castle, but it had long since been filled in. The only water nearby was a reservoir that had been built immediately below the slope on one side, where Gianetta's numerous guests swam in pleasant companionship with frogs, the insects known as waterboatmen, and, sometimes, snakes.

"All the bedrooms are lit; she must have had a lot of guests," Oliver said, as the car bore right. In July, of course, she would. The path circled the castle's side, then, turning sharp left, went under another arch into a large courtyard, with the castle entrance on the left, and the chapel and the *fattore's* house on the right. Opposite was another archway and beyond that, dropping from a low wall, the gardens.

"She does," I said, eyeing the cars parked all over the courtyard. According to the various plates and licenses visible in the lights from opened shutters, the cars hailed from Great Britain, France and Switzerland; there were as well local cars which could, of course, be rented like Oliver's.

A head poked out of one of the upstairs windows. Then another looked out the kitchen.

"Maria," I said, calling up. "It's me, Julia!"

"Oh, Miss Julia . . . It's so terrible. I'm glad you've come. You should have been here . . . you should have been here." The wailing voice came clearly down from the upper window. My God! I thought, will everyone be saying that to me now?

"I'm sorry, Maria. I know I should have been," I called back. There was really nothing else to say. Her head disappeared.

"Signorina Giulietta!" It was the *fattore's* voice. His front door had opened and he was coming across. "Signore Oliver! It is a sad day for us all." He spoke, of course, in Italian, and Oliver, equally fluent in his three native tongues, was answering him in a flood of the same. Standing there, listening to him and waiting for Maria to come down the two flights of stone steps, I was struck, as I had been before, by his extraordinary facility with language and accent. With a French father, an Italian mother and an English upbringing, it was natural that he should speak all three as though each was his mother tongue. But I had once overheard one of Gianetta's guests asking him how he had acquired his unaccented German. He had smiled. "I have a good ear." Now, as I listened to him pouring forth his genuine distress in the most perfect Italian, I thought of the old saying, *Lingua Tuscana in bocca Romana,* that is, the Tuscan tongue in the Roman mouth. It meant, of course, that the most beautiful of all spoken Italian was to be heard in Tuscany, notably in its great city, Florence, one hundred miles to the north of where we were now standing.

The agent, Paolo Ruggoni, was saying, "There will be a requiem mass tomorrow in the chapel. Don Renato is coming from the village."

"Where is she . . . where is her body?"

Ruggoni made a gesture towards the chapel. "In there."

"And Marco?"

Ruggoni nodded his head towards the castle entrance. "He is in there now. He came at lunch."

My cousin Marco, Marcello's grandson from his first wife, whom I remembered as a rather heedless young student revolutionary, was Marcello's heir. His own father, Marcello's only son and my mother's younger brother had been killed in a car accident. He was now, of course, the Conte di Monaldi, and with the title had inherited the Monaldi property and what was left of the money. Remembering some of his impassioned speeches, I found myself wondering whether he would use or renounce the title. And what about Gianetta's fortune? The Monaldis had been land poor for some time. Marcello had practiced law in Perugia and done a stint in the Italian Foreign Office, serving as attaché in a variety of embassies abroad. He earned a good income and lived comfortably. But it was Gianetta's money that had made the castle livable, and she was under no obligation to leave it to the Monaldis, unless, of course, there had been a premarital agreement.

"Are you coming?" Oliver had gone towards the chapel and turned at the door to ask me.

"No," I said immediately, not entirely sure why I refused so quickly and without thinking. But I said, "I must see Maria first."

Maria's stocky form appeared in the doorway, garbed formally in a black dress and white apron, but she still wore her comfortable sabots, and clacked against the stone steps as she ran down.

"Oh, Julia, I'm so glad you're here!"

Maria, who had known me since I was sixteen, alternated between "Julia" and "Miss Julia," depending on assorted variables such as whether or not we were alone or how formal she was feeling. When the short, square, distressed woman ran towards me, I put my arms around her, and held her without speaking.

Fourteen guests, including Oliver and me, gathered around the long dinner table that night. Marco, a slender young man of twenty-two, of medium height, wearing a dark suit and with his hair shorter than I had ever seen it before, sat at the foot of the table. Gianetta's empty chair remained at the head. Someone, I did not know who, had put a small vase with her favorite roses at her place. I was at Marco's right at one end and Oliver at the right of Gianetta's chair at the other. Distributed between, six on one side, five on the other, were Dr. and Mrs. Langdon, a tall, fair English couple, who resembled one another as much as though they had been brother and sister; George Roper, one of Gianetta's numerous cousins on her American side; four teenagers, three girls and a boy, whom I hadn't as yet sorted out; two elderly ladies from Boston, and a very young American couple.

Everyone talked quietly, and there were puddles of silence. As in most of the rooms in the castle, the lighting was less than bright. Marcello's father had run the first electric wires in the castle—not an easy task when dealing with three- and six-foot walls, and Gianetta, rather than starting from scratch, had, as much as possible, used what was already installed. Gianetta might have had a large fortune, based originally on whaling ships, molasses, rum, and other New England industries and since invested in rock-reliable securities with great business acumen, but she also inherited a large dollop of thrift from her New England mother's side. This thrift never left Boston's Janet MacNair, for all her marriage to an Italian journalist while residing in London, and she passed that on to her half-Italian daughter, Gianetta. "We have plenty of candles," Gianetta was given to saying. "Besides, the electricity always goes out during a storm," which indeed it did, sometimes not coming back on for hours after the storm was over.

It was a sad meal, and for me, a strange one. Between moments of saying something, or listening to something that someone else was saying, I would find myself glancing towards the head of the table, wondering where Gianetta was and how long before she would come through the hall leading into the dining room and sit down. Then I would remember: She was dead; her body was lying in the chapel, which I would have to visit later on tonight. She would never again sweep in to dinner in an elegant trailing dress, looking like one of John Singer Sargent's ladies. But I couldn't seem to hold the present in my head. A few moments later I would find myself glancing to the head of the table again. The third time I felt the odd pull to look towards the empty chair, I forced my gaze to remain straight ahead, my glance passing over the shoulders and between the heads of Dr. Langdon and a young teenage boy with thick straight blond hair and a handsome face. To keep my eyes from straying, I thought about the boy. He looked about fifteen, and, if his hands were any indication, would probably be a tall man. His eyes on the table, he kept trying to pick up crumbs of the rather thin local bread with the balls of his fingers. He looked up once, caught me looking at his hands, and plunged them down into his lap. I smiled at him, but he didn't smile back. So I transferred my gaze to the huge stone mantelpiece behind his back. Rising six and a half feet and jutting out over a cavernous hearth, it bore the Monaldi coat of arms and a brace of hideous gargoyles, one at each side. Still trying not to think about the empty chair at the head of the table, I called on my art history courses to aid in placing a date on the chimney piece. It was put there undoubtedly later than the building of the castle, because the original banqueting rooms, which were enormous affairs with towering ceilings, were all on the floor below. This floor, which was the main residential floor of the castle, had been created sometime at the end of the last century. So the chimney piece was probably only a century old, unless, of course, it had been moved from somewhere else.

Suddenly, I found my eyes back on Gianetta's chair, and she was sitting there, looking at me, wearing the long, garnet-colored silk dress that she was particularly fond of. She didn't look dead. She looked angry.

I must have cried out, because I was aware of the silence around me and of something wet on my hand. I glanced down. I thought it was wine until I saw it flowing out of a cut. Then I saw the broken glass, and the rest of the shattered goblet on the table.

"Are you all right, Cousin Julia?" Marco's voice, coming from my left, penetrated. I glanced at him. He was staring, his square young face anxious.

"Marco—" I started. "She—" Then something made me look again to my right, to the end of the table where Gianetta had been sitting. The chair was empty.

"What's the matter, Julia?" Oliver got up and came to where I was sitting, putting a hand on my shoulder.

"Let's just make sure there's no glass splinter in the cut." That was an English voice. "I think I know where there's a magnifying glass. I'll just get my case." Vaguely,

I recognized Dr. Langdon's professional voice. He scraped his chair back.

All this time I couldn't seem to get my voice going. Everything in my mind was chaotic. I didn't remember the glass breaking. Most of all I didn't know how much time had passed since that had happened. Had I had some kind of awful seizure? Yet I didn't want to admit that I didn't know.

Lamely, I fell back on my cut hand. "It'll be all right," I muttered, getting up. "I'd better go get this washed." I glanced down at the light colored suit I was wearing, and the dark green blouse. Fortunately, nothing—no blood—had spilled on that.

"Just step along here to the sitting room," Dr. Langdon said, poking his head back in. "There's a table, and I've brought a bright torch."

"It's really all right—"

"Go on, Cousin Julia. Please."

It was Marco. He didn't, I thought, need any more irritation or trouble. "All right," I said meekly, though I had always had a profound suspicion of the medical fraternity and a preference for almost any home remedy over professional help.

I went along with Dr. Langdon to the sitting room that looked out over the Tiber Valley. The tall windows and blinds were open, showing the night sky and, in the village below, clusters of lights.

"Just put your arm along here," the doctor said.

I had to grant he was both gentle and thorough, staring through a large magnifying glass at the open cut just below my wrist.

"I don't think you've got any splinters or fragments in there, but it was a near thing. An inch higher and we could have had a problem." He looked at me with a smile that didn't quite reach his eyes. "You must have stronger fingers than you realize. What are you? A demon typist?"

I toyed with the thought of replying, "A concert pianist," but knew that he would learn different within half an hour after dinner. And would also see that I had been poking fun at him. This was hardly the moment for that. "I assist in an art gallery," I said, overlooking the fact that I had just walked out on the job.

"I see."

"It happened so fast, breaking the glass, I mean, that I hardly realized I had broken it." I wanted to find out whatever it was that happened that I couldn't remember. It was a fishing expedition, and I waited to see if his reply would prove enlightening.

"The glass may have been damaged to begin with. I happened to be looking at you." His blue eyes bored into me. "You did go extremely white, enough to notice even in that rather dim lighting. But I thought, I'm almost certain, that it was *before* you crushed the glass rather than afterwards. Did you feel faint?"

"Yes," I said, grateful for an excuse that hadn't occurred to me.

"Yes, well, it's been a fearful shock. And you had to get here from England."

I looked across at him and asked a question that seemed to fall out of my mouth without my thinking of it. "Did you see her? When she was found?"

"Of course, my dear. Not in the garden; she'd been brought in and put on her bed by the time Sheila and I got back from our walk. But I saw her then. Why?"

Since I didn't know why I had asked it, I couldn't really answer his question. I said instead. "It must have been a terrible fall." Again, the words came without awareness or planning.

"It must have been indeed. The cut was deep and hit a vital spot. And then there was her age and her heart, which was not in the best condition, as we all knew."

"I didn't know."

"You didn't? Well, you hadn't been here in the last year or two, I believe. I remember Gianetta mentioning it." He extracted a piece of adhesive bandage from his case. "Yes, she'd had chest pains last winter, and gone to a doctor in London who found she had a mild heart condition, not unusual in a woman of her age. A fall such as she must have had could just have done the trick."

"You mean it was her heart, not the blow, that killed."

"No, no. I didn't mean to imply that. It was the blow. But, who knows? A younger, stronger person might have survived." He was pulling the paper off the bandage.

"You didn't give the death certificate, did you?"

"Of course not. I don't have a license to practice here. It was Dr. Nedi from the village."

I remembered the kind elderly man who had once come to give me an antidote when a snake had bitten me. "I see."

"Early bed for you, I should say," Dr. Langdon said, placing a Band-Aid on my hand. "Pity you weren't here."

There it was again. "Yes," I said. "I'm sorry about that."

He got up. "I can give you a sleeping draught if you like."

How old-fashioned he was, I thought. What would he do, shake a small amount of powder onto a piece of paper and then fold it up as doctors used to do? Or hand out a pill in the modern fashion?

I got up, too. "No thanks. I don't use them. Thank you for the bandage."

"Do you often get these attacks?" The question was asked casually just as I got to the door.

Attacks, I thought. Was he politely suggesting that I had had some kind of seizure? "What do you mean by 'attacks'? Some kind of a fit?"

There was just enough of a pause for me to realize that that was exactly what he thought. Then he said, "Hardly that. Sometimes a seizure is no more than a momentary pause, a sort of very brief unconsciousness."

36

"Did I seem unconscious?"

"Well, what is your own memory?"

I didn't much like Dr. Langdon, finding him something of a cold fish. On the other hand, there wasn't anyone other than Oliver that I'd want to discuss the matter with. I decided to tell a partial truth. "I sort of went blank for a minute."

"Yes, that's more or less what I meant. You don't have any recollection of crushing the glass?"

"You saw me do that?"

"Yes, indeed. As must others."

What was preferable: to let him think I was suffering from a sort of petit mal, or that I had gone mad and thought I'd seen Gianetta?

"How awful," I said lightly. "I had no idea I had such strength. Thank you again for the bandage." And I went out of the study, leaving the doctor there.

"You all right?" Oliver said, as I sat down.

"Fine." I smiled at him. "Just didn't know my own strength."

I kept quiet the rest of the meal. My arm wasn't particularly sore, but it seemed better to use my right hand as sparingly as possible. The wine had been wiped up, of course, and a fresh mat put down at my place. The rest of the company had moved onto fruit and cheese, while I ate the remains of my main dish. Luckily, I had cut up the small portion of meat I had taken, and the rest was a casserole of vegetables. Marco and Oliver seemed to be discussing the tidal wave of relatives and friends that would be arriving from Castiglione and Perugia in the morning for the funeral mass. After that there would be a general exodus of guests. The meal dragged on. Once or twice one or other of the guests would make a determined effort to recall some anecdote about Gianetta, as a tribute of memory or affection, and one of the others would try to pick it up. But it was too soon. Eyes would fill with tears, voices would choke up. A year from now, I thought, if we should have a reunion, here or elsewhere, then we could tell the stories of Gianetta's kindnesses, eccentricities, her passion for long trailing dresses, for Renaissance and pre-Renaissance paintings, especially those of local painters, her tin ear when it came to music, her dislike of being thanked, her fondness for young people, her irritation with people who waffled. . . .

It was then I became aware of my own eyes filling. Curious, I thought, the pain of loss was harder when I remembered her at her irascible worst, than when I recalled the several occasions when she had either bailed me out financially, or been generous in some other way. I looked across the room at Oliver, who was dry-eyed, but whose face showed fearful strain. Of all of us in here, I thought, he is the one who is feeling it most. He and Maria out in the kitchen. Vaguely, I wondered where Ludovico was. How old would he be now?

"And the awful thing," George Roper was saying, "is that there are more guests arriving tomorrow. Since nobody knows where they are, there's no way to tell them."

"Wasn't it in any of the local papers?" Oliver asked.

"Too late for the morning papers, and I don't know whether there's any afternoon local paper or not."

Neither, apparently, did anyone else.

After dinner, I went downstairs, crossed the courtyard and went into the chapel.

I knew that Gianetta had always hated the chapel, and I could see why instantly. The sugary images and dusty tinsel; the gold candlesticks that looked fake, but weren't; the hideous painting, executed in the full flower of Victorian sentimentality by a third-rate artist, on the left side just above the bank of candles; the dreadful and tortured depiction of the crucifixion on the opposite wall; and behind the altar . . . But my eyes stopped there.

I was astonished to see the Madonna, the lost Madonna of Paolo Mantori, known by the sobriquet of Paolo di

Monte Santa Maria Tiberini in honor of the tiny hamlet sitting on a hill above the Tiber where he had been born. There it was, behind the altar, above the crucifix that rested on the altar itself. Famous for a certain intensity of his blues and golds, as well as for the features of a mistress that he placed on the painted faces of madonnas, angels, Roman soldiers, and even, once, on Judas, this young painter of the hill town, who died early, leaving few paintings, had in recent years become almost as noted as his great contemporary, Piero della Francesca. And it was Oliver Landau who discovered him, sought out his paintings, wrote about him and, with Gianetta's money, made him the jewel of the small museum in Castiglione. After that Paolo's reputation was taken up and enhanced by some of the greatest living art connoisseurs, bringing Oliver's own reputation with it.

I was astonished to see the Madonna here, because it had, of course, been in the museum in Castiglione with the other Mantori paintings: one of the crucifixion, one of Christ driving the moneychangers from the temple, and one of the woman taken in adultery. This Madonna was the last to be added to the collection and was called the "Lost Madonna" because while there were records of its existence, no one, before Oliver, had been able to track it down.

But he had found it, after endless research through documents, files and letters, in another nearly abandoned chapel within a palazzo outside Venice. The family had almost died out, and the great crumbling Palladian building had fallen into decay. But a stray letter from an art connoisseur of the eighteenth century, found among archives in Rome, led Oliver to the north, where an eighty-five-year-old cousin of the ancient family lived in a modest apartment over one of the smellier tributaries of the Grand Canal. She was almost blind by then, but Oliver, gentle, persuasive, infinitely patient, had elicited from her an account of a blue-and-gold madonna, almost a child, in the palazzo chapel where she had received her first communion. She had not been back since. It was the longest of long shots. But Oliver managed to get a caretaker to let him into the chapel, and there she was, her lovely face, with its gold frame of hair, glancing down to the baby in her lap, a baby that, surprisingly, was not as hideous as most of the great Renaissance masters felt compelled to paint.

Yes, there she was now, her eyes cast down; her blue dress stretched over a thin, child's body; her face the face of Paolo's famous mistress, yet by some magic of the painter's genius transformed into something beyond a pretty model with the dark gold hair and slate blue eyes of her native Tuscany. In the transformation she had become an earthy, yet radiant symbol of the young eternal mother. I stared, moved as always by a depth in the face that went beyond color and line. Oddly, the angle of her head and something about her expression made me think of a picture I had once seen of the youthful Gianetta.

But I hadn't come into the chapel to see the Madonna, lovely and noted as she was. I had come in to pay my last respect to Gianetta, lying in the open coffin, surrounded by a blaze of flowers, which were also banked all over the rest of the chapel.

I had never seen a dead body before. From where I stood, she was foreshortened, and looked merely asleep, her hands folded on her breast, a crucifix clasped between her fingers. How untypical, I thought! Gianetta was many things, but religious was not among them. She should have been clasping roses.

I walked forward and then got a shock. Because my eyes were on her face, I hadn't noticed her dress. But she had been garbed in the same garnet silk chiffon that I had seen her in while sitting at the table. Somehow, between then and now, I had managed to persuade myself that my seeing her had simply been a projection of my own grief and fatigue. Staring at her as she lay in her coffin, I couldn't believe that quite as easily. Her features had been composed, but she still looked angry, and very real.

I slipped into one of the high pews reserved for the family and tried to say a prayer. I had, of course, been baptized a Catholic. But my father, like Gianetta, was indifferent to religion, if not actively atheistic. What with one thing and another, except for two years as a child in a convent, I probably hadn't been to mass more than a dozen times in my life. But those two years had had their effect. What was it the Jesuits were reputed to have said? Give me a child until he is seven, and you can have him after that.

Slipping to my knees on the dry, splintery kneeler, I composed my mind to pray. Nothing would come. Nothing. Instead, I was overwhelmed with the sense that Gianetta was there, beside me, very much alive, and trying to communicate with me.

"That's nonsense," I said aloud and in English.

Three or four heads in other pews that I had vaguely noticed when I came in, turned. I saw Maria's face framed in a black shawl. The others must have come from the farms. Maria looked at me, without smiling, then turned back and bent over her hands. Determinedly, I launched into an "Our Father" and then an "Ave." But the words were just words, spoken in defiance of something else that was going on. Finally I said wearily, "Rest in peace, Gianetta. Rest. God bless you," and got up and left the chapel.

The stars were blazing like lamps above the courtyard. There seemed to be more cars there than there had been before. I wondered if the guests due to arrive tomorrow had come early.

Walking slowly upstairs, I realized how tired I was. It had been a long day, beginning with my getting the telephone call from Oliver, my fight with Rupert and my quitting my job. I wonder if I'm a bloody fool, I thought, and felt depression settle down over me.

When I got to the top floor I heard a babble of voices

41

in the sitting room and decided to go in and say my goodnights before departing for bed.

All the guests seemed to be there, some of them sitting, but many standing, and there was a curious, taut atmosphere in the room. Then somebody moved and I saw that there were, indeed, three men I hadn't seen before, standing together in the middle of the room, talking to Marco, Oliver and Dr. Langdon. When I came in Oliver turned. If he had looked strained before, he seemed even worse now. "There you are," he said. "Julia, something awful. This is . . . this is Signor Birazzi . . . he is, he's the local chief of police." He paused and cleared his throat. "He's . . . they're going to take Gianetta away. There'll be no funeral mass tomorrow."

I couldn't really take it in at first. And then, it was as though I had known all along—back there in the chapel— that this would happen. Nevertheless, I said, "Why?"

Oliver blurted out, "They say they think . . . they think she may have been murdered."

TWO

The word fell like a hammer. Yet, again, I was not shocked or even surprised. My first thought was, so that's why she felt so angry. And then I pushed such absurdity away.

Finally, I said, "Why do you think that?" I addressed the police chief, a man of about forty, thickset, with the same dark blond hair and slate blue eyes seen so much in Tuscany and Umbria.

He said in surprisingly good English, "Because we had a telephone call from someone saying that it was murder."

"Do you know who?"

"No. Not even whether it was a man or a woman. The voice was . . . there must have been something—a cloth —over the telephone, the speaking part . . . what do you call it?"

"The receiver," I said "And you don't know where the call came from?"

"No. But I have been questioning the doctor here, and Dr. Nedi. We must, of course, examine her. You are her granddaughter?"

"Stepgranddaughter," I said.

"Please?"

Oliver translated rapidly.

"I see. But you are the granddaughter of the late Conte di Monaldi?"

"Yes."

"Ah."

Marco suddenly walked forward. "Where are you taking her to?"

The detective turned, "To the morgue, where she will be examined by a police surgeon."

That much was in Italian, but I was able to follow it. Marco dug his fists into his jacket pocket. "Do you have to have my permission?"

From revolutionary to nobleman in one short step, I thought.

The police chief shook his head. "No. Why?"

Marco didn't answer immediately. Then, "I just wanted to know."

"Were you going to refuse?" I asked.

Marco shrugged.

There was a silence.

"We'll let you know what we find—if anything," the police chief said. He nodded to the two men who had accompanied him, and they walked towards the door. Then he turned, addressing Marco. "I would like to have a list of all people here. You will all be here tomorrow?"

There was a silence while we looked at one another. Then Oliver said, "Everyone was going to be here for the funeral mass, but most of the guests were going to leave afterwards, and there are friends and relatives arriving from Perugia and Castiglione tomorrow for the mass, plus at least four houseguests—if not more—who were due to turn up."

The chief looked around the room. How many of you are there here now?"

"Fourteen," I said, remembering the distribution around the dining table. "Not counting the servants."

"And how many servants are there?"

Oliver answered that. "Four. Maria, Elena, Sylvia and Baptisto."

44

"How many of you were here this morning?"

There was another silence while we looked at one another again.

"Well," I said, "Oliver and I only arrived just before dinner."

"Where did you come from?" the chief asked.

"London."

"And I came from Florence before dinner." Marco said.

"And we came this afternoon, too."

It was the wife of the young American couple, sitting with her husband at a small table where they were working a jigsaw puzzle. "And we arrived in Rome this morning from New York."

"All right, thank you. Any other later arrivals?"

Silence. Then, "Weren't there some young people at the table?" Oliver said. "They don't seem to be here."

"Young people? The policeman said.

"Teen-agers," I explained. "Gianetta always has a lot of young people, particularly in July and August. They're usually cousins of godchildren or the children or grandchildren of cousins and/or godchildren, plus friends."

The chief looked around. "There must be a greater number of rooms than I thought."

"Not really," Oliver said. "Gianetta always put the boys in a sort of dormitory up in the battlements. It's a bit crude up there, only one toilet and one basin, but they can bathe in the bathrooms on this floor and they all like it."

"They're off by themselves," I added. "So if they want to make a racket, they won't disturb the others. And the girls are put into the girls' dormitory on the first floor. It used to be one of the big banqueting rooms, but there are cots in there."

The chief smiled a little. "And they would be in their various dormitories now?"

"I think," one of the Boston ladies said cautiously,

"They might be in the music room downstairs. It's the one straight ahead as you come up the stairs. They often go in there after dinner."

"And did any of them arrive this afternoon?"

"No," the other Boston lady spoke. They were both sitting on a sofa in front of an oval table, and seemed to be playing a quiet game of double patience with very small cards. "They've all been here, like my sister and me, for at least two weeks."

"And I've been here for a week," George Roper said. "I am a cousin on the contessa's American side, and I live in New York. I'm a lawyer. " And, I thought, he looked every inch the role. Tall, pepper-and-salt hair, glasses; I would have gambled a fair sum that he would be a partner in one of the prestigious law firms of Wall Street.

"Number One Wall Street," I murmured under my breath.

His hearing must have been acute, because he turned with a smile. "No. We've moved. We're in Rockefeller Plaza now."

I grinned. "Sorry."

"Overlooking the skating rink?" the police chief asked politely, surprising all of us.

"Ah, you've been there," George said.

"Yes. My family has relatives in New Jersey." He turned to Marco. "As soon as the autopsy is finished I will be in touch with you. In the meantime, I do not wish to inconvenience anyone, but it would be helpful if no one left until then." And he walked out.

When the police chief left there was total silence for a moment. Then, "My God! Murdered!" burst from Marco.

"He didn't say it was definite," Oliver said. "He simply said someone had telephoned and claimed it was that." Certainly that latest development explained why he looked so devastated.

"Some mischief-maker, I'm sure," one of the Boston

46

ladies said. "There are always people who do that kind of thing. Not that there's any truth in it, but just to create excitement. I think it's wicked. Don't you, Charlotte?" And she turned to the other lady on the sofa.

"I certainly do," the other lady said.

For a minute I wondered if they were twins. But then I saw that one was definitely older than the other, the younger one's face was rounder, and the older one looked thinner. But even with those differences noted, the resemblance was extraordinary.

"You're not twins, are you?" I blurted out, with my talent for making trivial comments at serious times.

"No. Sarah is two years older than I," said the thinner, older-looking one with some pride.

"So you don't think there could be the slightest truth in it?" Oliver said gratefully.

"Of course not," the younger Boston lady said.

"But they have to go through the motions," George Roper put in. "It's a pity, because of all the people who're supposed to be coming to the funeral mass. Is there any way to put them off?"

"I'll try and phone," Marco said, and left the room.

Pockets of conversation started up around the room. "The whole thing's incredible," George said to Oliver.

"I simply can't believe it," Oliver said. "And I won't believe that anyone on earth would want to harm Gianetta. She was generous to the point of insanity."

"We live in a strange and frightening world," the younger-looking, older Boston lady said.

I walked over. "I know we were introduced, but I don't actually think I caught your names. Could you tell me? I'm Julia Winthrop."

"Yes, dear, we know. We knew your father." The younger, elder-looking lady spoke. "I'm Charlotte Truesdale, and this is my sister Sarah Kessler. Mrs. Isaac Kessler. She is now a widow."

47

"Thank you," I said. I glanced down at their double game of patience. "Those are beautiful little cards. Where did you get them?"

"In Boston. We always travel with them, and we usually bring a pair here when we come." Miss Charlotte Truesdale's eyes, already red-rimmed, filled with tears. "It's all quite dreadful. We come every two years and stay a month. They're such wonderful vacations. Gianetta was so *good*. So gentle."

I squelched an impulse to say that gentleness was not among Gianetta's many admirable qualities. But I was not alone in the thought.

"No, Charlotte, that's not true. I loved her dearly, but she was a strong and dominant woman. Isaac always said she was one of the strongest women he'd ever known."

"Your husband?" I said, knowing perfectly well that it was, but gripped with curiosity about the late Mr. Kessler.

"Yes. That's how we knew Gianetta. Isaac was curator of a museum in Boston, and Gianetta got to know the art world very well. He said she knew more about painting than most people posing as experts."

"That's true, God knows," Oliver said, coming up behind me. "She had a practically infallible eye." He stopped talking abruptly. "I think I'll turn in. I haven't unpacked yet."

"Where has Maria put us?" I asked.

"I think you're in the room off the dining room, and I'm in that one there, the one between hers and the sitting room." He pointed to the bedroom that was next to the sitting room.

But I was not in my favorite room off the dining room. George Roper was in that room. So Baptisto had taken my suitcase downstairs to a small high-ceilinged room off one of the smaller banqueting rooms and opening onto the courtyard. It was shaped like a well because it had obviously been hacked from the bigger room, and its high

48

ceiling was totally out of proportion to its small area. There was a basin in the room and a toilet off of it. But a bathroom could only be reached by a narrow winding stair up to the next floor, cut into the stone wall. My reason for disliking the room had nothing, as far as I knew, to do with its size and shape, although the latter certainly kept it from being restful. I hated it because, when in it at night, I had never been able to sleep.

There were three factions among guests at Civitella: One faction thought that the castle was haunted, the other said the whole thing was a lot of nonsense. A third, the largest group, said nothing. One of the officially uncommitted did once comment cautiously in my hearing "I always have bad dreams when I'm here. . . ."

I had not committed myself either, not even to myself. But the fact remained that night after night, in the small room, I would lie and turn and twist until the cock in the barnyard beneath the castle wall started crowing immediately before dawn. The moment I heard that homely sound and knew that morning was about to start, I would go to sleep.

On one famous occasion, when I had had three nights in a row like that, I picked up my pillow and blanket in disgust and went upstairs to the silent sitting room. There, wrapping the blanket around me, I had lain down on the sofa and gone to sleep almost instantly.

"Pure imagination, dear," Gianetta had said, when Maria found me the next morning. But after that she tried always to put me in a room on the upper floor. I found out later that I was not the only one to take to the couch in the sitting room: A boy of about nineteen had been asleep in one of the smaller rooms up in the battlements. Once, after a night of banging that could not be attributed to a loose blind, or any other material agency, followed by footsteps that came and went in one of the attics, he, too, had taken to the sitting-room sofa, and been mercilessly teased afterwards. I remained, nevertheless, stubbornly uncommitted. If asked if I thought the castle was haunted, I always said that I found it hard to sleep and had bad dreams, and let people make of it what they wanted. I never knew what Gianetta really thought. Oliver considered the whole thing ludicrous, and never hesitated to say so.

Perhaps, I thought that night as, exhausted, I climbed into bed, I was so tired that this time I would sleep. I did, *mirabile dictu*, drift off. But I woke up abruptly some time later, my heart pounding. Then I sat up, and cursed the fact that I had been so worn out when I went to bed that I had not taken my traveling clock out of my suitcase, and furthermore had not set it. Even if I got it out now, it would not reflect the time. Well, there was always my watch. Lighting the candle beside my bed, I looked at the watchface beside the candlestick. Ten minutes past ten. I picked up the watch and held it to my ear. There was no sound. I had forgotten to wind it. It must have stopped a few minutes after I turned off the light. I had no idea what time it was. Getting out of bed, I went over to the great open window staring blackly into the courtyard, and stepped up on the slight dais that was immediately beneath the window. No light shone anywhere in the courtyard, which meant that it must be well past midnight, probably near one in the morning. Above, the stars were brilliant, and a slight breeze moved the trees through the archway to my left. Curious, I thought, staring out. I had the most overwhelming feeling of being absolutely alone. Well, I thought reasonably, I might well be the only person who was awake. Yet that did not account for my feeling of isolation. After a minute I stepped off the dais, went over to the bed, got in and blew out the candle. I had been asleep before, thus breaking the jinx that for me existed in this room. I would go to sleep again.

But I didn't. Now the memories of Gianetta crowded forward: Tall, aquiline-nosed, aristocratic, seeming far more so than her gentle, amused husband. Yet it was he who had the seven-hundred-year-old name, the heraldic quarterings, and forbears who were related to half the noble houses of Europe. Except for her dark coloring, Gianetta was every inch a MacNair of Boston, and the MacNairs, though certainly patrician as America counted such things, were simply canny traders who had made money in the previous century and hung onto it with great skill. Marcello, the Count, was easy to get on with, especially if you were young and a girl. But Gianetta—she was indeed generous and kind, but in some way she put me on my mettle and ruffled my feathers. She said to me once, "My dear, you must stop coddling your feelings." Which, of course, made me so furious, I coddled them even more.

Restlessly, I turned in the bed. Another form of coddling, physical this time, of which Gianetta did not approve, was the matter of mattresses. "I see no reason to change the Civitella mattresses. After all, we're here only four months out of the year. Any improvements should be made on the farms." Which of course was quite right. But at God knew what hour of the morning, with one's back sinking into the trough of a too-soft mattress, it was hard to remember that.

I turned again, staring this time out of the big window. And then I drifted off, thinking with considerable satisfaction that the jinx was indeed broken. But I had congratulated myself too soon. Suddenly Gianetta was there, standing by my bed, wearing the same dark red dress she had worn when I thought I saw her before, and the one she had been dressed in for lying in state. But she was standing now, her hands clutching the ends of a black shawl in a way that she had. "You must get up with me now and go to the rose garden," she said. "There's something there you will see."

"But," I protested in my dream, "it's dark outside, it's night. I don't want to step a foot out of this castle."

"But you must."

"I'm afraid." And in my dream, I knew not only that I was dreaming, but that it was true. I *was* afraid.

"I know. You've always been afraid. You have to stop."

"How?"

But then she'd gone. "Gianetta," I said, and woke up. My heart was pounding. I could hear it. And my face was wet with perspiration. I was more than afraid. I was terrified. But I couldn't think what I was terrified of, which made it worse. I lay there, trying to quiet the pounding, trying to think of soothing, positive things to say to myself. After a while it dawned on me that the pounding I heard came from somewhere other my own chest. Apart from the kerthump, kerthump of the pump inside me, there was something somewhere, outside, beating, hammering. Suddenly I remembered the young man, whoever he was, who had come down from the battlements because of the beating, and sat up. The noise had stopped. I could feel the rapid hammering in my own chest, but I could hear nothing. Then, abruptly, it started again, and it seemed to me that it appeared to be coming from somewhere in the courtyard below.

"Don't be such a chicken!" I told myself, and swung my legs out of bed. With a somewhat unsteady hand, I groped for the box of matches, and promptly knocked it to the tile floor, where it struck with a rattle. Finally I managed to get hold of it, and to strike a match, which I applied to the wick of the candle. I slipped on the robe that lay across the room's one chair, cautiously pushed my feet into my slippers (mice, spiders and scorpions sometimes found their way into the castle) and went over to the window, stepping up on the dais. Then I held the candle high and looked down into the courtyard. Because even though I was on the lowest main floor, I was still up a full flight of steps.

"I say," a voice suddenly sounded. "I'm terribly sorry,

but can you let me in. I didn't mean to get here so late."

The voice was male and English. That was all I could tell at the moment.

"Just a minute," I said.

Going back across the room I put on the light overhead. It was not a vast improvement, since the bulb was both weak and high, and those who wanted to read were better off using the candles. But it lit the area better. Then I returned to the window. "Can you step below where I can see you," I said.

Staring down from the dimly lighted window into the dark well was not much better.

"Here," the voice said. "Is this better?"

Suddenly a flashlight went on, illuminating the face below me. He was holding it, and shining it up at himself. "Do I look respectable enough?"

"Entirely," I said, a little annoyed at the amused tone in his voice. "But I still don't know you, or why you're here."

"I'm Andrea Smith. The contessa invited me when she was in Florence on her way here in May."

It certainly had the ring of truth. Gianetta had a way of scattering invitations to people she met and liked along the way, and when Maria worried and fussed as to whether or not there would be available beds, Gianetta had a way of saying, "Oh it will work out." And it always did, irritatingly so, given the amount of worrying that others, especially Maria, did. And then the name struck me again. Andrea Smith . . . That was the painter that Rupert had taken up.

"Do you know Rupert Carmichael?" I called down in a loud stage whisper.

"Of course. He handles my stuff in London. Who are you?"

"His ex-assistant, Julia Winthrop."

"Oh yes. He was steaming on about you over the telephone this afternoon—yesterday afternoon I suppose it is now—when I talked to him. He is deeply aggrieved that you walked out on him."

"Considering that my grandmother, the contessa, had just died, I thought his attitude was incredible. Of course I had to come here. You did know, didn't you, that she'd died."

"No," Andrea said drily. "He forgot to mention that. Just that you had gone haring off to Italy with some man and left him in a lurch at a particularly awkward time. I wouldn't come barging in like this if I'd known that . . . I'm sorry. How did it happen?"

"She . . . she fell."

"I see. When and where is the funeral, and is one allowed to go, or is it just private and for the family?"

"Well . . . I'd better come down and let you in," I finally said. "I can't shout explanations even in a loud stage whisper."

Turning on lights as I went, I passed into the next, much larger room, from which mine had been chopped, and stared at the door on the other side. There was a much handsomer room on that side, complete with bath in the tower. But it seemed to me that Maria had told me I was the only person on this floor, a thought that hadn't added to my comfort. The Boston ladies were in one of the rooms off the dining room, and the young couple was in another. Apparently some couple that had just left had occupied the downstairs double room and it had not yet been made up for a new contingent.

Opening another door, I entered an enormous hall with a ceiling that went up to the battlements and a balcony, the level of the floor above, which consisted of nothing but bookshelves. The conte had been a rabid collector of books, and his father and grandfather before him had added to an already distinguished library. The

54

tile floor stretched for what looked like a football field, with small Persian rugs scattered here and there, and another carpet, actually sizable, but lost on the immense floor, occupying a small portion of the middle of the chamber. Sliding my mules, I got across that, and found myself facing the billiard room, a companion to the room back of me from which my own bedroom had been taken. To the left of the billiard room was the girl's dormitory, another of the rooms in which weird happenings had been reputed to have taken place.

But strangely, with an extremely corporeal young man waiting for me downstairs, the idea of manifestations seemed absurd, which was one reason I remained among the uncommitted as far as belief in ghosts was concerned. It all seemed to depend on whom I was near or what hour of the night it was . . . I went into the hall, turned on the lights and started down the stairs to the big front door.

Andrea Smith turned out to be a tall young man with wild red hair and beard and piercing green eyes. This disturbed me a little, because I had envisioned him looking somewhat like Rupert.

"You don't look the way I imagined you," I said.

"Sorry about that. How did you imagine me?"

"Pin-striped."

"Good God! Why?"

"Because I think of your paintings as pin-striped. Very precise, very realistic."

"Thanks a lot. You could say the same for Vermeer."

"That was two hundred years ago."

"Rupert was right about you."

"What did he say, other than that I left him in the lurch?"

"That your mind was in your tongue, which was always wagging, and that you were born saying 'no.' "

"I feel the same way about him."

We glared at each other, standing there in the dim

lobby, with Andrea's backpack spread on the floor. Then I started to laugh. After a minute, he grinned.

"Do you always start off on the offensive?" he asked.

"No," I said indignantly. "I'm an extremely amenable, easy-to-get-along-with, civil, pleasant person."

"And you also lead a vigorous fantasy life."

"You'd better come upstairs."

Leading the way, I went up the first flight and then stopped. I really didn't know how the rest of the guests were distributed around, so had no idea where to put the prickly Mr. Smith. It would serve him right to put him up in the battlements, I thought grimly. But to get up there at this hour of the night meant finding a flashlight, leaving it with him, and then struggling down on my own. All during which I might wake up half the guests.

"You can come through here," I said, going into the banquet room. "I'll see if the room opposite mine is occupied."

He followed me as I went through into the smaller banquet room and then turned right instead of left.

"You better wait here. I don't think anyone is in there, but just in case, I want not to wake them." Tiptoeing to the door I knocked softly. Then I put my ear to the door. There was no reply. After a minute or so I was surprised to discover myself becoming absolutely convinced the room was empty. Why I was so certain I didn't know. Certainly there was no sound on the other side. But it was more than that. After a minute or so I knocked again, this time a little more sharply. Then, when there was still no reply, I pushed the door open and turned on the light. The room had not only not been made up, the used bed linen had been bunched in the middle of each of the twin beds. The towels from the bathroom through the far door into the tower were on the tile floor. Plainly Maria and the others had not got around to cleaning it. It was a much bigger room than the one I was occupying, and the enormously long windows faced the front. It was a handsome room, but a curious depression came down over me as I stood there in the door. Perhaps it was the glare from the white walls—because even though the bulb was as weak here as in any other room, it seemed to produce a hard, whitish light—or perhaps it was the chilly mustiness produced by stone walls and closed windows, but all I could remember was the night I had spent here when I was sixteen. That was the first time I didn't sleep until the rooster serenaded the coming dawn. But one incident marked the passage of that night. I was sitting up in bed, unable to relax, trying not to be afraid, when a mouse ran out from some hole, stopped in the middle of the room, and proceeded to clean its whiskers. Never had I been so glad to see anything in my life. It was a warm, living being, and I cherished its company and was terrified that if I made a move or a sound it would run away. How long I sat crouched, hardly breathing, I couldn't remember. Eventually, I moved or sighed or it heard some other noise and scuttled back to the baseboard and I spent an hour or two wishing it were still there.

"Well?" I heard Andrea's voice behind me. He came up beside me. "I can lie down on one of those beds quite easily."

"There are no clean sheets down here."

"I don't have to have them for one night. And the blankets are still there on the beds."

"All right."

He walked in, put his pack down on one of the beds, looked around and then said, "You didn't tell me about the funeral."

I hesitated, oddly unwilling to talk about the visit of the policeman.

"There is going to be one, isn't there? Or has it already taken place?"

"No," I said. "There's a . . . a slight delay. There's . . . there's some detail to be cleared away."

"What slight delay? Why? I mean, isn't that pretty unusual?"

"Yes." Again I paused, strangely reluctant to tell this young man something he'd find out within five minutes at the breakfast table the next morning. "It seems that there was phone call . . . somebody called the police and said, that . . . that Gianetta may not have . . . that it may not have been an accident." Ye gods, I thought, I stumbled over that as though I were the guilty party.

"You mean he thinks the contessa has been murdered?"

"Yes."

"My God!" He paced around the room for a minute. "When was this supposed to have happened?"

"In the rose garden, early yesterday morning. She nearly always went out to the garden before breakfast. She loved it and worked in it and would go to pick flowers while most of the guests were still asleep. Well, she was found there by Maria in the middle of the morning. Everybody thought she was somewhere else when she didn't show up for breakfast, so nobody got around to looking till she'd been dead for several hours."

"What made them think she was murdered?"

"As I told you, they didn't. But then somebody called the police and said that was what had happened. So the police came earlier this evening and took her away. She'd been lying in state in the chapel on the other side of the courtyard."

He made a sound and put his hands in his jeans pockets. "What a thing to have happened. Who on earth would want to hurt the old girl?"

"Nobody that anybody can think of."

"Who stood to profit by her death? *Cui bono?*"

I shrugged. "Nobody really. She probably left something to Marco, but he was her stepgrandson, not actually related to her, and he's far from poverty stricken in his own right. Besides, he liked her."

58

"Any other relatives?"

"What time is it?" I said suddenly.

He checked his wristwatch. "One-thirty. Why?"

"Well I think one-thirty A.M. is not the hour to have this conversation. Everybody within miles is asleep. And I'm not sure I know the answers to your questions anyway." I turned back towards the door. "Breakfast has always been at eight, and I don't suppose it will be any different. You can usually get coffee as late as nine-thirty, but after that the staff disperses. You want me to wake you?"

"No thanks. I'm a compulsive early riser. I'll wake up around six anyway."

"Even after getting to bed at two."

"Even then."

"All right. I'm sorry I can't offer you any sheets or towels, but you can get these in the morning."

"It's all right. I'm used to travelling without those. By the way—"

I had been on the point of going out. I turned. "Yes?"

"Nothing."

I frowned, "What were you going to say?"

"It can wait."

I shrugged. "As you wish. Well, sleep well. If disaster in some form should strike you in the middle of the night, my room is right across the way there." And I waved my arm.

"Cosy."

"No. Not cosy. Good night."

Perhaps it was the knowledge that another human being was only across the hall. Whatever the reason, I went immediately to sleep.

Breakfast the next morning was a glum meal. Andrea's presence brought the complement to fifteen, and nearly everyone was in the dining room when Maria brought the first big pot of coffee in at eight.

59

Finally George Roper said, putting down his empty cup, "I don't suppose anyone has heard from the police."

We all looked at one another. Marco looked up. "No. I'll telephone them in a few minutes." He spoke English with an Italian accent, but he spoke fluently. "Didn't Maria say there were more guests arriving today?"

"Four," I think, "and one of them's arrived. Mr. Smith." I nodded over towards the painter who somehow looked less artistically disheveled this morning than he had the night before. He had been sitting at the breakfast table when I arrived, so I had no idea what time he came to breakfast.

"Yes, of course," Marco said, and looked annoyed. "I forgot for a moment. Sorry." There was something young and appealing about Marco this morning. There was a time when he'd seemed to me to be an arrogant show-off, rather overgiven to needling Gianetta's American guests. This had been during his revolutionary phase. He never did it when Gianetta was around, and he rarely made the mistake of taking on people well able to beat him at his own game. But perhaps time and sudden death—to say nothing of inheritance—had brought a sea change.

"Who else is due to come?" This was from Oliver. He looked, if anything, even worse than he had the day before, which probably meant he hadn't slept. He glanced up at that moment to find my gaze on him, and the tight lines around his mouth relaxed a little. I smiled at him and he gave a slight smile in return.

"Would you like to take a short walk? Oliver?" I asked. "Just up the cypress grove and back?"

"Should we leave the premises? Mightn't that policeman call at any time?"

"He might. But we'd find out what he had to say the minute we got back." I paused. "There's really nothing else we can do," I said.

"No. You're right. Anything's better than sitting still."

"I'll stick around until we find out about the funeral," Andrea said. "If it's not to be private, I'd like to attend."

"How did you come to know her?" Marco asked. "I don't think you've been here before, have you?"

He *is* taking his responsibilities with a vengeance, I thought.

"Yes," George Roper put in. "I was wondering the same. As a matter of fact, I don't even remember Gianetta mentioning you. And I know she mentioned the other guests that were to come."

"I don't know why she didn't mention me, although there's no particular reason why she should. I met her at a party in Florence last May. She'd seen some of my paintings in a gallery there, and when she heard I was at the party, asked to meet me. We talked, and she suggested I come here sometime later in the summer when my work in Florence was over. So—here I am. I'm sorry she's dead, and I know it will be a great loss to the arts. She was a tremendous patron. But I can't pretend great grief because I only met her twice: in Florence, and then later we stopped off here for lunch on our way down to Rome."

"We?" George asked.

"A friend and I."

"Gianetta was like that," Miss Truesdale said dolefully. She always invited people who took her fancy, even if she'd hardly exchanged a word with them."

"Well that was one of the nice things about her," Mrs. Kessler said. "She was almost biblical in her hospitality."

"That's how she invited us," the young American wife said. "We met her at Heathrow airport when we were all sitting around waiting for a delayed flight. Of course, she was in the first-class section, but we sat at the same table when we finally had to have sandwiches at the buffet, and she invited us here."

"What are you doing in Italy? Having a vacation?" George meant to sound casual, but he was sounding much more like a lawyer trying to sort out desirable from undesirable guests.

"I'm here to study medicine," the young husband said belligerently.

"Oh. Bologna?" Marco asked, handing his cup to Maria for more coffee. For the first time since I had arrived his voice reflected the trace of sneer that had been there all the time when he was in university.

"No. Rome."

"Do you speak Italian?"

The young man blushed. "I'm taking a cram course at the university in Perugia, beginning next Monday. So's Harriet here."

I glanced at Harriet. She looked all of eighteen, with straight long brown hair, bangs and attractive gray eyes. "And what will you be doing while your husband is going to medical school?" I asked.

"I have a job with U.S. Industries, Inc. They have an office in Rome."

"She's an executive secretary," her husband said with some pride. He had dark curly hair, dark eyes and a bristling black mustache. The mustache, I decided, had a purpose. Without it, he would have looked about twelve.

I hazarded a guess. "Does your family come from Italy?" I asked him.

He grinned, showing beautiful white teeth. "Yes. My grandfather did. My father knew some Italian, but none of us did."

"Where do you come from in the States? New York? George asked.

"No. California. The Napa Valley."

I could almost see George rearranging his thinking. The wine growers of California were successful, extremely prosperous Americans. They were not exactly up from New York's Little Italy.

"I'm surprised you didn't prefer to go to an American

medical school," Miss Truesdale said disapprovingly.

The young husband hesitated.

His wife said "There are a lot more applicants than there are places in medical school."

He husband chipped in, "I applied to six, but didn't make any of them."

Marco was wearing something very like a smirk. "That's too bad," I said. "They ought to open up the medical schools more."

"Tut tut," Andrea said. "The fewer the doctors the higher the fees."

"And there's a thing called affirmative action," the future medical student said.

Marco poured some cream in his coffee. "Quite right, too. Considering how you've exploited the blacks."

"Compared to the state of a great number of Ethiopians after your enlightened annexation," Andrea said, "the American blacks are moving right along."

It was amazing, I thought, how the disparity among Gianetta's guests came stunningly to light when she was not there to serve as an amalgamating force. I'd noticed it before. There were occasions when Gianetta would have to take off a day or two for family or business reasons, leaving a houseful of guests to amuse themselves, and the factions would separate like uncongenial chemical elements.

Marco scowled. The young couple smiled. Oliver said, "Let's get going on our walk, Julia." And he got up.

"I can't stand this bickering," he said, as we strode up the bumpy narrow dirt road between two avenues of stately cypresses. "It's happened before, when Gianetta wasn't around."

"I know. If she was present she'd stand it for just so long, then she'd make some mild but unanswerable comment on one side or the other and bring the whole thing to a close. But not immediately. I think it amused her to a certain point."

"Do you? She didn't like people who coddled their feelings. One time one woman guest burst into tears and left the room. Gianetta was far more cross with her than with whoever had done the injury. And I don't blame her."

"No. But she also didn't like dissension. Last night I thought Marco had grown up. This morning I'm not so sure."

"You can't expect him to change overnight. If, since you were eighteen, you've been trying to overthrow the current social order and the establishment, it must be bewildering to find yourself part of that same establishment from one day to the next."

"Come on, now, Oliver. It's not as though inheriting the estate and the title has come as a total shock. He's always known he was going to have it."

"I suppose so. Who's this Andrea Smith? I gather he's an English painter, but Gianetta never mentioned him to me."

"Considering you're in that field, I'm surprised you don't know."

"My dear, you should know better than that. I lose all interest after the seventeenth century."

I laughed. "I suppose so. Well, to be honest, I've only just heard of him myself. The unspeakable Rupert has just discovered his work and is busy promoting it."

"Is he good?"

"Much as I hate to admit Rupert is right about anything, yes. Very."

"How you can tell with nonobjective stuff I'll be damned if I know."

"What a philistine attitude! But Andrea is not that. He's realistic to the nth degree. Those who like Andrew Wyeth will love him. Although he's not at all like him."

"What does he paint?"

"Everything. People, landscapes, boats, animals, seascapes. And yet they're not a bit like the nineteenth-century paintings. It's hard to describe."

"Umm. Well, since he didn't know Gianetta, I wish he'd pick up his paintbox and leave."

"Why?"

"I don't know. It's just something about him. Given her wealth, it was inevitable that Gianetta would attract hangers-on, people who exploited her and the place here to a marked degree. Something tells me he could be one of those."

"I'm not wild about him myself. But he's doing well. He's not some second-rate artist looking for a rich patron."

"Perhaps not. I just wish he'd go."

I looked at Oliver as, head down, he strode up the dried clods of earth that marked the path. This morning he had on gray flannels and a light tweed jacket. But, in respect to the circumstances, had put on a white shirt and sober tie. "You sound like you've taken some kind of dislike of him."

"I have. So would you if you knew what I know about him. No, I'm not going to talk about it now, so don't ask me."

The strange little chill I'd felt the evening before went down my spine. I shivered a little.

"Cold?" Oliver said, and put his arm through mine.

"No. What's the old saying? A goose just walked over my grave."

"Speaking of geese . . ."

It was almost spooky. There, waddling slowly forward into the path from an abandoned farm to the left, came six geese, marching single file. I took another step forward, and there was a loud quacking and honking. One of the big birds, wings apart, honking angrily, came at me.

"Watch out. They bite!" Oliver said.

I stood still. The goose, flapping his wings, hissed at me.

"He reminds me of Rupert," I said.

"I never knew you hated him so much. Why did you

continue working for him?"

"A little thing called salary, not that it amounted to a living wage. Also experience. He runs a good gallery."

"Yes. I'm bound to admit you're right. He does. But's he's a surly, difficult so-and-so."

"You can say that again." We walked for a while.

"One wonders why," Oliver said after a minute.

"One wonders why what?" Sometimes Oliver's delicate English locution produced in me an American bluntness.

"One wonders why he's so difficult."

"Some people just are. They were born on the wrong side of the bed and have been there ever since."

"That's a singularly un-Freudian thing to say."

"I'm tired of Freud explaining why I should feel sympathetic to people who are rude and hostile."

"Is that what he is?" Oliver asked drily.

We reached the top of the grove and looked over the beautiful, tawny countryside. At the bottom of the hill on which we were standing was a road; beyond that the ground rose again to a much higher hill, with a white farmhouse half way up, and the crenellated top of a ruined castle on the summit. Invisible to the eye from where we stood, a tiny road led beyond the castle to an even tinier church.

"Do you want to go any farther?" I said.

"No. I think we should get back."

"Oliver, the police of all nations take forever to come to a conclusion."

"Nevertheless, I think we should be there." He looked down on me from his six feet. "Why are you so anxious not to be there?"

Until that moment it had not occurred to me how much I wanted not to be in the castle. But I knew then I would give a lot to pack my bag and leave. "I don't know," I said slowly.

"It's interesting," he said, as we turned and started back down the path. "You've never come here as often as you could, or as much as Gianetta wanted you to come. You could have been a great help to her."

If he had just not added that sentence, I might have pursued in a gingerly fashion the thought that was beginning to emerge from the question of why I had avoided the castle as much as I had. I had assumed it was my difficulties with Gianettá. Now I was not so sure. Gianetta was dead, but my sense of urgency about leaving was just as great, if not greater. But Oliver's last sentence had put me on the defensive about Gianetta as all his statements were inclined to. "Gianetta didn't need any help," I said sharply. "Till the day she died she was one of the strongest, most competent people I've ever known."

"That's not what I meant. But let's not quarrel." Again he took my arm, and we walked back to the castle.

"Any word?" I asked, as I came into the sitting room where, untypically in the middle of any morning, all the guests were gathered.

"None," Dr. Langdon said. "By the way. How's your hand?"

I had forgotten all about it. "It must be fine. I'd forgotten about it."

"I'll take a look at it again after lunch if you like. Though if you'd forgotten about it, it sounds as though it were getting along very well indeed."

As to be expected, now that he had mentioned it, the hand started to throb slightly.

The next two guests arrived just after lunch. I was in the kitchen talking to Maria when I heard a car drive into the courtyard. Moving towards the window I glanced out. It was an English car, a fact that was obvious even from that height, because of the clearly inscribed sign on the bumper—black lettering on white: GB. Great Britain. Now who? I thought.

"Who is it, Miss Julia?" Maria said from where she

stood beside the sink, finishing the washing up.

"My God!" I said, as I saw a man emerge from the right-side driver's seat. "It can't be. I mean—it just simply can't . . ." my voice trailed off. It was. David Brownson, my former lover, was busy opening up the trunk of the car, while a female was getting out of the passenger's door.

I whirled around to Maria. "Did you know David Brownson was coming?"

"Well, the contessa did say something about his coming. But I wasn't sure when."

"But she always talks—talked—over with you what rooms the guests would have. She must have told you before . . . before yesterday that David was coming."

Maria looked at me levelly. She was so Italian-looking that it was still a surprise to hear the tones of Pimlico come from her mouth. "Perhaps she did, Miss Julia. But with . . . with everything that happened things like that went out of my mind."

There was no question that Maria must have known about the relationship that had existed for four years between David and me. Maria was far more than a servant to Gianetta. She was probably her closest friend, though the relationship stayed formally in the traditional place that both found comfortable. Certainly Gianetta must have discussed David's and my off-and-on affair with her, because she discussed everything with her. Nevertheless I said, "You knew about David and me." It was a statement, not a question.

"Oh yes. But with everything that happened it didn't seem very important."

It was not meant to be a put down, and I didn't take it as such. But it was an overwhelming reminder of reality. In the great scale of first things, my narcissistic preoccupation with my romantic life did not count.

"You're right," I said, turning back to the window. "But it's a humbling thought. I wonder what on earth brings

68

him here. In all the years he and I were together he never met Gianetta."

"I'm sure I don't know Miss." I looked back quickly at Maria. Her pensive gaze was back on the dishes she was rinsing. But her retreat to an uncharacteristic servant's defense made me think just the opposite. I'm sure she knew something about David's coming here that I didn't know. I looked back out the window. David's tall blond head was coming across the courtyard with a blond female head reaching to about his shoulder.

"Who is coming with him?" I said.

"He mentioned he'd be bringing somebody, but I don't remember who."

The truth? I didn't know and couldn't guess.

A curious agitation seized me. Until this moment I had not realized how passionately I did not want to see David Brownson ever again. Evidently I had managed to push down and out of sight my sense of humiliation and betrayal not only at his leaving me, but at the way he left. To overcome this I had given him a private nickname to soothe my lacerating sense of injury: "the Gutless Wonder," a man who did not have the courage to face me and tell me that for one reason or another he felt impelled to return to his wife.

So what was he doing here? And, speaking of his wife, who was that with him? Phyllis Brownson, I knew, had dark brown hair.

I could hear their feet coming up the last flight of steps leading to the second floor. Involuntarily, my whole body made a motion forward, to get out of the kitchen and into the dining room before they could see me. From there I could slip down the narrow winding stair outside one of the guest's rooms, leading to a sort of passage outside my own room. But then I stopped. I decided I wanted to see David's face when he first saw me and before he had time to learn from anyone that I was here. Feeling a little sick

69

at the stomach, I marched into the dining room and then towards the big staircase. David and his blond companion appeared just as I seemed to be going into the living room. He stopped, his face going absolutely still, and the color draining out. Then it flooded back. "Hello, Julia," he said. Either, I thought, he was a superb actor, or he really was caught short. In that way I had a small advantage; I'd had about ten minutes in which to absorb the knowledge that I was about to meet him.

"Hello, David," I replied, cool as a duck pond in December. I turned then towards the girl and received a slight shock. She was only about fifteen, which meant she must be Anastasia, his daughter, whom I'd never before met.

"Hello, Stacey," I said, using the nickname by which her father always called her when speaking about her.

The blue eyes stared back at me. "Hello," she said finally. Her coloring was David's but her features showed a resemblance to her mother. Not a happy child, my mind registered automatically. I turned back to David. "And what brings you here?"

"The contessa invited us," he said, seeming almost to fumble at his words. "We met in May in Florence, where she was staying before she came on here, and she suggested we stop off on our way to Rome."

"She certainly was busy as a bee in Florence. You're the second contingent from there she invited."

There was an awkward pause. "Well," he said. "I suppose we'd better go and pay our respects. Is she in there?"

It had only been a day, yet it seemed astonishing that anyone would not know what had happened. "You mean you haven't seen the papers?"

"Papers? Newspapers? What do you mean?" David had a fine, craggy face, with straight brows and a hawk-like nose. With his brows drawn down over his nose he looked more than ever like an irritated falcon.

"Gianetta's dead," I said baldly.

It was the girl who gasped. I looked at her. She opened her mouth, then looked at David.

"How? When?" he said.

"She . . . she had some kind of accident in the rose garden. We're not quite sure how, but she . . . she struck her head."

After another long pause, David said, "Or?"

You cannot live with a person for four years without knowing him well. David was a journalist, but he had had legal training, and there was more than a touch of the probing, investigative reporter about him. He knew I was holding something back.

"We don't know. The police have taken her body. There seems to be some possibility of . . ."

"Foul play?" Curiously, coming from his mouth, the words did not sound melodramatic.

"That is *weird!*" The words burst from Stacey's mouth.

I looked at her. "It's tragic and horrible, but why weird?"

David put his hand through his daughter's arm. "Come on Stacey. It's a coincidence, a long coincidence, maybe, but still a coincidence. You know that's all nonsense anyway."

"What's nonsense? What are you all talking about?"

David made an impatient gesture. "It's a lot of rubbish, but there was some kind of party in Florence given by an English couple. We were there and so was the contessa. The wife rather fancied herself as a fortuneteller and needed no persuading to whip out her cards. When she got around to telling the contessa's fortune, she produced a card that seemed to throw her into some kind of trauma. One of the guests, stupider than the rest, asked what it meant. The fortuneteller blurted out, 'violent death.' There was one of those ghastly silences, then the contessa, obviously trying to pass it off as a joke, said lightly, 'Perhaps somebody will murder me, then.'"

THREE

At his words suddenly, once again, I saw Gianetta in her garnet-colored dress, holding the ends of the shawls. It was clear and vivid and she was standing there beside David.

"What's the matter?" David asked.

"Nothing," I said, between almost paralyzed lips.

"Then why are you looking like that?"

"Isn't the possibility that my grandmother was murdered enough to stun anyone?"

"As you were always the first to remind people, she was your stepgrandmother. Which doesn't necessarily mean you would care for her the less. But I don't remember your being that close to her." Two or three biting replies sprang to my ready tongue. But the presence of Stacey held me back. I didn't know how much—if anything—she knew of our association.

"I'm sure you're right," I said, giving a standard soft answer that carried its own teeth.

"Are you?" David asked. "You must indeed have mellowed. Come Stacey," he said, as I gathered myself for a fight.

They turned toward the sitting room. David and I had spent our four years alternating passionate love scenes with equally passionate fights. Watching his tall figure disappear through the door, I found myself admitting to myself for the first time in months that I missed those skirmishes. But there was always Rupert, with whom I enjoyed equally spirited battle. Only there wasn't . . . I had quit. Feeling hollow and depressed, I followed David and Stacey.

The police chief telephoned Marco that afternoon after lunch and asked that the guests be assembled in the sitting room before dinner where he could talk to us.

"Did he say why?" I asked Marco. The phone had rung in the middle of the long fallow period following lunch, when some of the guests gave up whatever struggle against the afternoon nap they had been waging and repaired to their rooms. Others lay in deck chairs on the terrace at the side of the castle, reading, doing double acrostics, or snoozing. It was not a time to visit museums, galleries, monuments or churches, except, of course, those churches that remained open all the time for prayer and meditation. At four o'clock, when the worst of the heat had passed, all the public places opened up again. The fact that the police chief had telephoned in the middle of this sacroscant siesta time impressed me with both his seriousness and the seriousness of what he was doing. Until that moment, I realized, I had confidently expected the police department to release Gianetta's body with some kind of shame-faced explanation for having taken and held it.

"He didn't say anything about whether he was returning Gianetta to her family for burial?" I continued.

"I asked him that, naturally," Marco said. "He refused to answer. He just said he'd see us this evening. I'm going to go around and tell everyone. Would you tell anybody you meet, too, Cousin Julia?"

"Yes. Of course." I glanced at Marco's face. All of a sudden he seemed stiff with youthful pride. How quickly the burden—as well as the rank—of being head of a great family had descended on him, I thought. And there was little I could do to help. He and I had never liked each

73

other very much. He had needled me and I had needled him right back, so it was to be expected that he would be on his dignity with me at a time like this.

Suddenly the phone started to ring. Marco went out into the hall to answer it. In a minute or so he was back. "Do you know anything about any correspondence Gianetta had with some woman in Venice?"

"Good heavens, Marco! Gianetta had correspondence with hundreds of people."

"I know that."

"What's her name?"

"I couldn't quite catch it. Signorina Gertrude something. She seems old and has a thick German accent."

"What does she want?"

"I'm not sure. Something about a letter she wrote."

"You told her about Gianetta's death." It was a statement, not a question. I was therefore astonished when Marco, a little flushed, said, "I tried to, but I couldn't get a word in edgewise. She kept on shouting. I think she must be deaf."

"Would you like me to talk to her?"

It was a mistake. "Of course not. There's no reason why you should bother yourself with that."

"How did you leave it, then?"

"Really, Julia, I may not be American, but I am reasonably efficient. You answered my only question, so there's no need to trouble you further." He disappeared back into the hall.

I went into the sitting room, thinking about a story told by one of my teachers: if you think one person you've talked to is mad, there's a good chance you're right. If you think two people you encounter are mad, it's still within the realm of possibility. But if you decide that three or four are mad, then you'd better check with a doctor immediately. The odds are, you're the one who's mad.

I had fought with Rupert, David and now Marco—

hardly a good sign. "All the world is mad except thee and me, and sometimes I think thee is mad," I said aloud.

"You're probably right," a voice said.

I looked up. Andrea strolled in. "I keep having the feeling that everyone would like me to leave, but I'm determined to stay and pay my last respects. I didn't know the contessa well, but I liked her."

"You are in a large majority," I said, beginning to lay out the little cards for a game of patience.

"But you didn't?"

"Yes. I liked her a lot. I sometimes had trouble maintaining my own independence, but that was my problem, not hers."

Andrea ambled over and stared down at the seven cards I'd put down. "Powerful and dominant people sometimes have that effect. Can I kibbitz?"

"Sure. Pull up a chair. We can play a double game if you want."

"No. I'd just like to see how you do it. I must be one of the few people who's never played cards."

"How did you escape?"

"Easily. I just refused all invitations."

I glanced at him out of the corner of my eye, remembering our conversation in the small hours of the morning. With his rather wild red hair and stained jeans he might look like your average sloppy artist, but he had a pin-striped mind, which argued a great deal of self confidence.

"You must have a great deal of what the psychologists call ego-strength," I said.

"What in God's name is that?"

It means you know your own mind and see no reason to go around acting like a chameleon and/or being a people-pleaser."

"Well then why don't they say so instead of all that repulsive jargon?"

"You sound just like Rupert. No wonder you get along so well."

There was silence for a moment, though I was aware that he was eyeing me thoughtfully. Then he said, "Is there any news of any kind? I mean, have the police let you know what they've found—if anything?"

"The chief of police called a while ago and said he wanted to talk to the assembled guests tonight before dinner. That sounds to me like he's found something we all would wish he hadn't."

"And how do you feel about it?"

I stared at the cards on the table. "I think I'll know that when the police chief comes and says what he has to say. I suppose even now, knowing that his coming doesn't bode any good, I still won't accept that anyone . . . that anyone would want to kill Gianetta. There's always a slight chance—I'll admit a very slight one—the policeman will say something else."

Andrea, who had been staring at my hand, which I had carelessly laid down face up, said, "Following the logic of what you've already done, I assume you put the numbers in sequence, but in alternating colors. In that case, why haven't you put that red seven on the black eight there, and the black queen here, the queen of spades, on the red king there."

I stared at the queen of spades and realized I'd been staring at her for a while. "Do you know what just happened?" I said. "Stacey Brownson, who arrived a few minutes ago with her father, David, said that in Florence in May, some fortuneteller, telling Gianetta's fortune, turned up a card that meant violent death, and Gianetta, as a sort of joke, said 'Well perhaps somebody will murder me then,' or some such words."

"Yes," Andrea said. "I was at that party. I remember it."

I looked up. "What on earth were you doing at the party?"

76

"I told you. I was in Florence with . . . with a friend and was going the rounds of the English-American art group there."

"Well don't you think it's strange?"

He stared at me for a moment, then put the queen onto the red king. "No stranger than the fact that I was sure someone was in my room last night, but when I turned on the light there was no one there. You didn't tell me about any family ghosts."

"Are you psychic?" I asked.

"Yes. Why?" Then before I could answer. "Are you?"

"I've never thought so. But I've never been able to sleep on that floor. I've always thought it was because when I was down there, usually no one else was on that floor."

"Being isolated and alone has never bothered me. But there is something there. Here—you can put this two on that three." He placed the card, and then straightened. "And just for the record, before I decided that my visitor was—er—immaterial, I examined every square inch of the room there and the bathroom. There is no other door, entry or exit. And the windows, as everyone knows, are barred."

"But you're sure someone was there."

"Quite sure."

I looked up at him. "How can you be sure? I mean, what happens?"

"It's difficult to describe. You just know. Haven't you ever had the experience?"

I was pondering telling him about Gianetta's highly visible appearances to me, which I attributed entirely to my imagination, when Oliver walked in.

"Marco woke me up with the cheering news that our cop friend is coming here to talk to us tonight. What's going on?"

"I don't know any more than you do. We were just discussing it."

"We?" Oliver said sharply. Then, as he caught sight of Andrea, "Oh."

"Come on, Oliver," I said. "It's not as though Andrea were puny. He's even taller than you, and wider." It was true, I thought. Andrea was by no means fat, but he seemed broader than Oliver's rapier thinness.

"I was looking into the light," Oliver said. "Julia tells me you're a good painter," he commented to Andrea, who had moved from his stance in front of the folded back blind.

Andrea made a slight acknowledging gesture towards me with his hand. "Julia is right."

Oliver gave him the ghost of his old satirical glance. "No false modesty there."

"None whatsoever." Andrea looked down at my game. "You haven't finished," he said.

After a while, Oliver, who had been staring broodingly out the window, said, "There's another guest coming, isn't there?"

"I'd forgotten about that." I gathered up one completed suit and put it to the side. "There is, yes."

"I wonder who."

"With Gianetta, it could be anybody. Did you know, by the way, that David Brownson arrived this afternoon?"

Oliver turned. "David Brownson? Your—" He didn't finish the sentence.

"That's right," I said drily. "My . . ."

"Your what?" Andrea asked.

"Her former lover," Oliver said after a pause.

"Thank you for the public relations," I said.

"Well, I shouldn't have asked, I suppose," Andrea conceded, "although, with all those pregnant silences, it fairly leapt to the eye."

"If it fairly leapt to the eye, then why did you ask?" Oliver said.

"And why are you so hostile?" Andrea's slightly tilted

78

green eyes seemed to blaze coldly at the older man.

I watched this encounter with a certain inner satisfaction. Oliver had a waspish tongue and could get the better of most people. With Andrea—as indeed with Rupert—he had met his match.

"Sorry," Oliver said lightly, not sounding as though he meant it. "One could say I was upset."

"One could say it, but one wouldn't necessarily believe it," Andrea said.

Oliver flushed a little. "Since, according to what you said at breakfast, you did not know the contessa well, I wonder why you're staying. The funeral services will most likely be for family and close friends."

"Because until I learn that is indeed the case, I would like to remain long enough to pay my respects."

Dr. Langdon walked into the room. "I take it," he said, going over to where the daily newspaper had been thrown and picking it up, "that the policeman wants to talk to us about his findings after the autopsy." He glanced over the columns. "Nothing seems to be in here about the contessa's death."

"Has anyone from here sent a notice?" Oliver asked.

"Wouldn't Marco be the one to do that?" I said.

"Yes. Has he?"

"You'd better ask him. Not to my knowledge."

"They'd hear, eventually, wouldn't they?" Andrea said.

"I suppose. Especially if—" Oliver stopped abruptly.

"Especially if there were a juicy murder to report," Andrea said drily.

At five-thirty all the guests were in the sitting room, Mrs. Kessler and her sister, Miss Truesdale, on the sofa; Dr. and Mrs. Langdon on another small love seat across the room; the young couple, whose surname I still didn't know, sitting opposite each other at a card table; the teenagers grouped in an alcove beside one window; and Oliver,

Marco, Andrea, David Brownson, Stacey and I sitting around in a variety of armchairs and straight chairs. I had placed myself behind a jigsaw puzzle which seemed to consist mostly of vast acres of sky, and was trying to put one piece of delft blue into a whole series of others, all indistinguishable from one another. I could, I thought, look on the front of the box to see what the picture was to cheer myself on. But Gianetta always considered that cheating. She was a passionate putter together of puzzles and there was always one in the process of being assembled, usually on a card table not far from the central window. As soon as that was done, it would be left there for a day or two to be admired, and another puzzle tossed from its box—all its pieces separate—on a second card table. Fortunately, the room was large enough to accommodate the two puzzle tables, another card table used for playing the small cards, and a larger table in front of the big sofa. There was yet another table—a low coffee table—in front of the love seat that was big enough for a card game, a Scrabble contest or even a small jigsaw puzzle, although Gianetta did not favor that table for puzzles. It was low, and pieces were often lost from it. The loss of a piece of . jigsaw puzzle upset Gianetta far more than the loss or theft of a piece of jewelry, china or silver. Because after a completed puzzle had been admired for a day or two, it was broken up and put into its box, which was then placed at the bottom of the pile of puzzle boxes on a shelf near one of the doors. When its turn came to be assembled again, a missing piece could drive Gianetta into one of her rare displays of temper. Despite this plethora of tables, there was still a fair amount of space in the middle of the room, occupied at the moment by Cassandra, the castle cat, who lay stretched in all her gray and white splendor.

As I gingerly tried to fit my blue piece into another blue piece I heard the distant sound of a car coming into the courtyard. Since the sitting room looked out over the side of the castle and into the Tiber Valley, and not over the courtyard, I couldn't be sure. But it was enough to make me alert. I waited to hear footsteps coming up the stone staircase, but, as none sounded, I finally relaxed. After all, I thought, cars that pulled into the courtyard were not always guests of the castle: they could be friends, guests or business associates of the agent's, or one of the farmers, or a priest, come to marry, or confirm or bury . . . which brought me back to thoughts of Gianetta. But at that point, I was aware of steps coming slowly up the staircase. I looked up and towards the door. So did everyone else. Conversation slowed and then stopped. There was a tight silence. Then a man appeared in the doorway. Expecting to see the fair-haired, square featured countenance of the police chief, I was stunned to see the dark-haired, thin-faced visage of my former employer, Rupert Carmichael.

"Hello, Rupert," Andrea said pleasantly. "What a surprise. We were all expecting the local policeman."

"I think he may be in the courtyard on the way up," Rupert said in his somewhat drawling voice. "He drove in just in front of me, and seems to be talking to the man who lives opposite."

"The agent," Oliver said. "What brings you here?"

"Gianetta invited me. Yes, I know she's dead. I learned that from Julia. Since I had been expected, I decided to come anyway."

"A bit unusual, isn't it?" That was George Roper. "I mean, perhaps a phone call might have been more helpful."

"Why?" Rupert said. "If there's to be a funeral I'd like to pay my respects."

"You didn't say anything about coming here," I said, overcoming my sense of shock.

"You didn't stay long enough for me to say anything," Rupert commented, strolling into the room. "You seemed so determined to leave in a fury that it appeared almost unkind to prevent you."

Andrea grinned.

"What utter rubbish!" Oliver almost exploded. "You tried as hard as you could to prevent Julia from coming with me yesterday morning. You showed about as much concern for Gianetta as—"

But at that moment, the long-awaited police chief's figure emerged into the doorway. After Rupert's entry, his was almost anticlimactic.

"Good evening, sir," George· said loudly. Vaguely I wondered if he was trying to take command away from Marco.

"I am glad you are here," Marco said, walking forward, his hand outstretched, as though to repudiate George's assertiveness. "What news do you have for us?"

But the police chief was not about to be hurried. He shook hands with Marco, looked around the room and walked slowly forward. Except for his watchfulness, there was something about his action that reminded me of an actor taking center stage. Although it was far too warm for a fire, he went to the empty fireplace and took up his stance there. "Good evening," he said in his stilted, if excellent English. "Since most of you here are English-speaking, I shall try and talk as much as possible in English. If it is necessary for me to speak in Italian, I'm sure the conte will translate for me."

"Or I could," Oliver said. The policeman bowed slightly in his direction. Then he straightened. "I am sorry to have to report, that after the doctor's examination, there is no doubt. The contessa was killed, murdered."

The words fell like missiles into the room. For what seemed a long time no one spoke. Then the young husband said, "Murdered."

The police chief turned towards him. "Ah, Mr . . ." he took a list out of his pocket. "Mr. Robert Orvietta."

"Yes."

"And Mrs.?" He looked at the young wife.

"That's right."

"You already have a list?" Marco spoke. "I made one up for you."

"That is kind of you. I want to have yours too. These were just notes I picked up from Signor Ruggoni." He turned back to the young couple. "And you are from?"

"California. North California." Robert Orvietta said.

"Both of you?"

"No." Mrs. Orvietta said. "I'm from Connecticut originally. I was studying at Berkeley when we met. That's part of the University of California."

"Ah yes. The free speech movement. It all started there, didn't it."

"That was more than seventeen years ago," Mrs. Orvietta said almost reproachfully.

The policeman smiled. "And therefore passé."

The girl blushed. "Well, I was only five."

"And your maiden name?"

"Harriet Hunt."

He made a note on the sheet he'd pulled out of his pocket. Then he looked at the two sisters on the sofa. "And you are Mrs. Kessler and Miss Truesdale?"

"Yes," they chorused.

The plump one spoke. "I'm Mrs. Kessler and my sister here is Miss Truesdale. We're from Boston."

Slowly the policeman went around the room, checking on who everyone was, where they lived, what time and by what means they arrived.

"I arrived two days before . . . three days ago," George Roper said. "I came down from Milan and arrived at Terontola. Gianetta met me."

"She drove herself?"

"Oh yes. She drives . . . drove all the time."

"That is a winding road and over the mountains."

"I'm well aware of it, but she drove it two or three times a week to pick up guests."

"Conte?" The policeman faced Marco.

"I arrived only after Cousin Gianetta's death. I came from my flat in Florence."

"You also have a flat in Rome?"

Marco shrugged. "It is really more of a room. I go there when I wish to see friends."

"You went to the university there?"

"No. To the one in Milan."

"I see." The police chief turned his attention to the teen-agers, most of whom seemed to have been there several weeks. Others had arrived more than a week before. The policeman listened to each, made more notes and turned to the Langdons.

"And you and your wife, Doctor?"

"We arrived four days ago. We drove ourselves from England. What—how did the contessa die?"

"By a blow on the head. We have examined the garden very carefully. Rocks there were used as part of the walks and along the top of the wall. But, given where she lay—or where you say she lay—and some of the grass and dirt showing the imprint of a body, there is no way she could have struck her head by a fall. It had to be a blow. Naturally," he said somewhat emphatically, "we wish that the contessa's body had not been removed. But, of course, you couldn't know that there would be any suspicion. And —" he addressed the doctor directly—"she was dead when you had her carried in?"

"And had been dead for more than two hours, I would guess. Surely your own medical expert would know that she had not been moved before she died."

"We are just checking," the policeman said.

"What was . . . what do you think struck her?" Oliver asked.

"Probably one of those rocks. They have sharp edges and are heavy. We have taken them to our headquarters for further examination."

And once again, as though in the flash of a tongue of lightning, I saw Gianetta falling, the blood spurting from her white hair, something in the corner of the picture that again I missed. But I did not miss the glittering edge of the rock, now crashing down. . . .

". . . all right?" The voice was behind me, probably belonging to whoever's hand was on my shoulder. I glanced up at Oliver's face.

"Fine," I said quickly, although I felt somewhat queasy. Then I glanced around. I did not want anyone—especially Dr. Langdon—thinking I was coming down with some kind of seizures. But the police chief was talking to Rupert and everyone's attention seemed fixed on him.

"And you arrived just now?" The policeman was saying to Rupert.

"I pulled up just behind you, and came upstairs while you were talking to the *fattore*."

"And what was your relationship to the contessa?"

I waited somewhat dourly for his answer. Rupert had not been, in his own phrase, one of the adorers at the shrine, one of his more derisive descriptions of many of Gianetta's visitors. Which perhaps accounted for the fact that Gianetta's opinion of Rupert was inclined to be mixed. "Arrogant" was a word she frequently used concerning him. On the other hand she respected his opinion, and sometimes needled Oliver by quoting some statement of Rupert's about a piece of art, especially when it ran counter to Oliver's own. Since Oliver was one of Europe's most respected critics and authenticators, especially in his particular period, this could be depended upon to enrage Oliver almost to the point of speechlessness.

"Why do you do it?" I once asked Gianetta.

"Oliver takes himself so seriously," she said, helping herself to another wedge of the local cheese and some more salad. We were at one of the rare lunches when we were alone. I always enjoyed these occasions, although I had the feeling that both of us were relieved when guests showed up to increase the party. It was on those infrequent occasions when we were alone that I became aware of the tension between us. It lent our relationship a certain bite and sparkle. Gianetta was not dull, and I don't think she thought I was. But then, I reflected, trying to be just, neither of us could be thought restful people.

"What's wrong in taking oneself seriously?" I asked on that occasion, knowing perfectly well that to Gianetta it was a sin out-ranking, in her estimation, other frailties such as lust, avarice and anger. "After all," I went on, "Oliver's become what he is by talent, hard work and some kind of God-given intuition. He's one of the top men in the world in his field. Arab moguls send for him to authenticate some canvas they've bought as a hedge against inflation."

"How very American you are," Gianetta commented. "This worship of the work ethic!"

"A work ethic that has supplied many European collectors with enough money to fulfill their aristocratic tastes."

"Yes," Gianetta said, in no way discomposed, "the Monaldi Museum has much to thank the MacNairs for. But it didn't make my cousin Abner MacNair any the less a pompous, pietistic old goat, just because he rose from the ranks by hard work. It just made him smugger."

"And I suppose all your titled friends, with their quarterings and lineage are strangers to smugness?"

"Are you talking about Marcello, your grandfather?" Gianetta asked pointedly, knowing perfectly well I wasn't.

"I'm not, and you know it."

"Then what are we quarreling over?"

That, too, was typical of Gianetta. I was a poor fencer. I'd still be sticking doggedly to defending some point, while she had shifted ground at least twice and managed to put me thoroughly in the wrong. "Have some more cheese, dear. It's local and particularly good."

86

"I know that. I've been here before. But no thank you."
And I knew, of course, I sounded like a sulky child.

I dragged my mind back, wondering how much of the conversation between the police chief and Rupert I had missed. It turned out, nothing. A servant had come and was whispering something to the policeman. But I had been totally distracted for a period of time. How long—a minute? Two or three seconds? More? A terrible fear gnawed at me. Was I truly developing something like petit mal? Had I started thinking about Gianetta in such detail because I had seen, so vividly in my mind a few moments before, the rock come crashing down on her skull?

I looked up again, forcing myself to pay attention. Rupert, I noted, standing across the room from me, waiting for the policeman to finish so he could answer his question, was scowling at me, his brows drawn down over his bony nose.

"What's the matter with you?" he asked rudely.

"Nothing."

"You look like you've seen a ghost."

"More to the point, she saw you come in," Oliver said.
Rupert ignored him. "You're pale as milk."

I was furious with him. Now everyone's eyes—including the policeman's, was on me.

"Thank you so much," I said. "Why don't you stop making personal remarks?"

Rupert shrugged. "Your tongue seems to be in its usual vigor. Obviously nothing much can be wrong."

"Miss Winthrop had one of these spells yesterday," Miss Truesdale said. "It's probably shock over the dreadful news about dear Gianetta. One can hardly blame her."

"Julia can hear of whole communities being wiped out without losing an eyelash," Rupert said. "I've seen her do it."

"Just because I was curious as to what had happened to the art treasures in that town whatever it was—"

"—where half the inhabitants had been killed by earthquake," Rupert finished with a grin.

"—doesn't mean I didn't care about the people." A small part of my mind knew perfectly well he was being poisonous just for the sheer joy of it. But I bit. I always bit. That was my idiocy.

"It just meant you put first things first," Rupert said genially. "What's this about your having some kind of fit yesterday?"

Dr. Langdon cleared his throat. "Tests would have to be made, of course. . . ."

The policeman's eyes visibly lit up. "You have been having these seizures before?" he said.

Envisioning the headline, *"American girl kills grandmother in seizure,"* I stood up and said slowly and loudly, "I have never been subject to seizures. I am sorry my momentary blankness seems to cause such public discussion. There are no seizures in my family—"

"The genetic influence, while strong, is not exclusive," Dr. Langdon put in, sounding as though he were delivering a medical paper. "A blow on the head—"

"Which I have not had," I said. "There is nothing whatsoever wrong with me. Nothing." I sat down. It was a lame defense because I was not about to tell the truth: that while I was convinced—despite all my worries—that I had not had a seizure, I was indeed having powerfully vivid hallucinations featuring my stepgrandmother. I felt sure that in the policeman's mind I could wield a rock just as easily in a hallucination as in a seizure. It was a depressing thought, even with the comforting reflection that Oliver and I were in London the morning Gianetta was killed.

The doctor cleared his throat again and gazed out the window. The policeman looked disappointed and turned back to his audience. Rupert glared at me and I glared back. If having hallucinations about his instant removal to another continent—or even another planet—might get rid of him, I would conjure one up as fast as possible.

The police chief, finishing his round of inquiries, said, "But there are two more, are there not?" And looked around the room.

"David Brownson," I burst out. "And Stacey."

"I knocked on the door and told them," Marco said.

"Brownson!" Rupert snapped. "Good heavens! the faithful do indeed gather."

"What faithful?" the police chief said.

I closed my mind and concentrated on a particularly pleasant hallucination: Rupert being torn to pieces by lions.

"A private joke," Rupert said. "Nothing to do with anything."

At that apt moment David and Stacey appeared. Halted on the threshold by what was obviously some kind of interrogation. They stopped.

"Have we missed something?" David asked.

"Come in and be grilled along with the rest of us," Oliver said. "This is the police chief, who just brought us the happy news that Gianetta was killed by a blow to the head."

David glanced around, then spoke to the policeman. "Is it now absolutely certain?"

"Completely. You are—" he consulted a list, "David Brownson and his daughter?" He pronounced the name Brown-son.

"Bronson," David said, giving the correct phonetic pronunciation. "Yes, and this is my daughter, Anastasia."

Stacey, I thought, looked rather peaked. It could have been, of course, the news the policeman just gave out. Since I was not looking at her when she and her father walked in, I could not be sure. But it seemed to me that a certain tense, almost frightened expression was on her face when she arrived.

"Please come in," the policeman said. He looked around the room, almost visibly on the verge of offering them chairs. But there were none. All seating space was occupied. Before he could speak David asked, "Do you have the remotest idea who did it?"

"That is what we are trying to discover. Where were you yesterday morning?"

"At what time?" There was a slight edge to David's answer. Like many journalists he viewed the police of any nation with a jaundiced eye.

The police chief consulted his notes. "At any time between, perhaps, six and nine or nine-thirty in the morning."

"Then Stacey and I were in our beds in Rome. We had arrived late the night before from Naples and were sleeping in."

"Please . . . sleeping in?"

David smiled a little. "An English expression. We were sleeping late to make up for lost hours in bed."

"Ah. And at what hotel were you staying?"

"The Flora. On the via Veneto. Do you know it?"

"Who does not? A first-class hotel."

He didn't say *and not cheap,* but somehow the words seemed implicit in the silence. Which evidently explained why David added, "This is partly a working vacation. I'm on a roving assignment for my paper at the moment."

I looked at his finely drawn face—the face that had had such an electrifying effect on me the first time I'd seen it—and knew that his words were meant to say, *and am traveling on an expense account.* And because it was such a typically David thing to say, I smiled. David could have stayed at the Hotel Flora or the even grander hostelry down the via Veneto for a month and paid the tab easily. His excellent royalties from his highly successful books had made him a rich man in his own right—quite apart from his wife's wealth. But like all fastidiously leftish intellectuals, he disdained the trappings of money, even as he loved being surrounded by them, as long as the money was old enough and understated enough and had passed through enough well-bred hands.

David, seeing me smile, smiled back. The old magic was there, betrayal and all. "And where is Phyllis these days?" I asked. It was tactless, inappropriate and uncalled for. Yet just asking after David's wife served to remind me that he had returned to her—and to all that she represented: money, family, power—of his own volition.

"She is, I believe, well. We haven't seen one another for a while." His words were delivered with a curious emphasis. Then he turned to the police chief, "Phyllis is my wife. We are, however, separated and awaiting a divorce."

"What? Again?" Rupert said. "Your lawyers must have a hard time keeping count."

Rupert, who was neither tall nor wide, had been standing half hidden by one or two other people. But his voice, perhaps his best feature, was unmistakable.

David's head swung around, trying to locate the source of the voice. "Ah, Rupert," he said, when he had found him. "I thought it was you. What on earth are you doing here? You were hardly one of the late contessa's greatest admirers."

"Perhaps not. But we were friends. I didn't know you knew her."

"No. But then why should you?"

At this further display of bickering among the late contessa's guests, a look of satisfaction spread over the police chief's rather impassive countenance. The more the squabbling, the more information he would pick up.

"But somebody really killed her?" The words burst from Stacey.

"Yes, Signorina, I'm afraid so." His voice was unusually gentle. That Stacey was upset was obvious. She looked wretched. "You were fond of the contessa?"

"I only met her once. In Florence."

"But you speak of her as though her loss gives you pain!"

"No, it's not that. I mean, of course I liked her, even though . . . but that's not what I mean, that's not the reason I'm upset. It's . . ." Her voice faded and she stared at the ground.

"Yes?" the policeman said helpfully.

She shook her head, still not looking up. "Nothing."

David put his arm lightly around her shoulder. "My daughter reads too many gothic novels and has too much imagination, don't you darling?"

"Daddy, please . . ." The tortured cry of the embarrassed teen-ager gave me a curious pang. I used to watch other girls at my posh boarding school squirm in real or affected fluster when suffering the affectionate attentions of the male parent. That was one problem I never had. My sire was never around to subject me to such tender discomfort, and if he was he would be about as liable to give me a hug in public as to take off his clothes.

"And what is the young lady imagining?" the police chief said in a hearty tone that did not match his piercing look at her.

"Nothing! Absolutely nothing!"

"You're the journalist, aren't you?" Andrea said to David. "I think you've worked with a cousin of mine, Toby Smith."

David turned. "Good heavens yes. Toby and I were in the Middle East together. As a matter of fact we had a conversation only two days ago about my assignment here . . . ." Removing his arm from around his daughter, David strolled over towards Andrea, and some of the intensity left Stacey's face. Quickly and gratefully she glanced at Andrea. Suddenly I found myself wondering if Andrea had deliberately produced his cousin to get public attention off the wretched girl. If so, it had been an act of unusual sensitivity. As Stacey slipped back into the room and more or less merged with the others, I heard the policeman say to

David, "And what is your assignment here, if one may ask?"

David turned. "I suppose there's no reason why I shouldn't mention it, though I usually don't talk about work in progress, except, of course, when I'm trying to encourage information. I'm doing a series of pieces on the growing terrorism and its new link with art forgery and art theft. . . ."

"Art forgery?" Rupert said sharply.

David turned to him. "Yes," he said coldly. "Why?"

"And art theft?" Andrea said.

"Well it looks as though there might be a connection," David said. "It's a bit hazy right now, but there seem to be indications that something links all three." He was answering Andrea far more graciously than he was Rupert. Rupert, I thought at that moment, would, hands down, win any competition for the most unpopular man for miles around.

"You know you really don't have to work hard to be universally hated. . . ." I murmured to him.

He grinned. "No arguing with natural talent."

"Mr. Carmichael here is an expert in art forgery," Oliver said to the policeman.

"Indeed. Interesting."

"I would have thought that was more your line." Rupert flung the line back to Oliver.

"Yes," Chief Birazzi said. "You are the . . . the *Directore*, of the Monaldi Museum in Castiglione?"

"Yes. I'm its curator. But that doesn't mean I am an expert on art forgeries."

"But you did authenticate one or two canvases for the contessa, didn't you?" Rupert said.

"Yes, although most of my work has been in locating paintings by local masters that had been lost or mislaid. Their authentication was often done by others."

"Who?" Rupert said brusquely.

Oliver turned to Birazzi. "If you want the names of the

paintings and of those who authenticated them, I'll be happy to supply them. But I would like first to refer to my papers and notes."

"Squashed," I said *sotto voce*, to Rupert.

Oliver smiled at me. Rupert looked as though he would like to kill me.

"I will now, if I may, talk to the servants. This way, Conte?"

"I'll show you," Marco said. And then—"The body?"

"We will keep it a while longer. There is another I would like to have examine it. One must be sure. And the contessa was a person of some note."

"Of course."

Just as he got to the door the police chief turned around. "I hope very much this will not inconvenience you, but I would be grateful if you would all remain for the next day, at least. After that, I hope to be able to allow most of you to leave."

It was while we were having drinks before dinner that something made me say to Oliver, "I was surprised to see the Madonna in the chapel. I thought it had pride of place in the museum."

"It did. But something must have stirred up Gianetta, because a year or so ago she announced that she wanted it in the chapel."

"That's pretty funny. It's the kind of thing Marcello would have wanted, but then he was a devoted Catholic. I don't think Gianetta cared a thing for any religion."

"At seventy-eight, she was beginning to think about what used to be called 'last things,' although she would have denied it as craven rubbish. Perhaps this was her way of acknowledging it. All I know is that she wrote to me and said she wanted the Paolo Madonna in the chapel and would I arrange it? So of course I went to Castiglione and brought it here and put it up."

94

"I'm surprised that you didn't install some kind of security. It's just sitting there, one of the world's masterpieces, worth God knows how much, and I don't think the chapel has more than that rusty old lock on the door."

"Can you think of a better way to advertise to the world at large that she has a valuable painting in unguarded possession, than to have bells and locks and heaven knows what else installed? The news would be over the countryside in nothing flat. Come one come all—take a valuable art work. What with the terrorists kidnapping industrialists and judges . . . it was far safer just to let everyone think she'd found it in some second-hand store—I mean all the peasants around here. They wouldn't know the difference. No—if she wanted to have the Madonna handy, she did it the right way."

"What about David's statement about the link between the terrorists and art theft and/or forgery?"

"You'd better ask him. Candidly—but I'd better remember to be charitable."

"Come on, Oliver."

He gave me an enigmatic look. "Julia, as far as I'm concerned, the only really intelligent move David Brownson made in his whole life was to fall in love with you. More fool he for going back to that high-nosed idiot of a wife."

"Apparently it's bust up again. You heard him talk to the cop."

"Oh yes. It was said, I feel reasonably certain, for your benefit. However, if he's sincere this time, I'll recant and eat crow."

I smiled. "I don't believe that. Such a sight would outrage the imagination."

He put his hand lightly on my shoulder. "I know you're not even related by blood, yet there's something about you that reminds me of Gianetta, always has." He smiled. "That's why I like you so much." His fingers closed on my shoulder. "Remember that wonderful summer when

I taught you about art, and all because you'd dropped that awful brick about the Raphael in front of Gianetta?"

"Yes," I said. "I remember." And it all came sweeping back.

Gianetta had been as scathing as only she could be about my gauche obliviousness of Italian painting. "Yes, dear," she said witheringly, as we came out of the Uffizi in Florence, "it was an original Raphael—good heavens, what did they teach you in that country of yours? Cheerleading? What on earth was your father thinking of?" We started down the sunbaked steps. Everything not in dark shadow seemed bleached pink and gold.

"Not Italian painting, Stepgrandmother," I said, addressing her by the title I knew she loathed. "Behavioral psychology was his line." That, too, she despised.

"How your mother could have fallen in love with a trainer of tame rats—" I should, of course, have been terribly offended. Offending me was what Gianetta had set out to do. But since I had my own problems with my father's preference for laboratory animals to people (except, of course, pretty young girls) I was not in the least offended.

"Astonishing, isn't it," I said. "But then when it comes to people Italians have extraordinary taste. Haven't you found that?"

Since my jibe was meant for Marcello's choice in wives, I waited for some kind of axe to fall. To be dismissed from Civitella for impertinance had a certain charm of its own, although I knew perfectly well that the moment I had actually left I'd bitterly regret it. And I would regret also being rude to Gianetta. But not enough to take her insults. There was silence for a moment, then Gianetta said, "You know it is one thing for a nineteen-year-old girl to be rude and another altogether for an old woman like me. My age entitles me to it. I've been looking forward to it for decades. When you reach my age you can be rude too, but not until then."

"That's not fair," I said.

"As one of your American presidents said, life *is* unfair. Such a wise statement for such a young man—no wonder he was murdered!"

"Just because John Kennedy said it, it doesn't make it holy writ!" I muttered.

"Oliver!" Gianetta said, as Oliver came up the steps to meet us. "I want you to teach this illiterate child something about Italian painting."

"Oliver doesn't have to teach me anything," I said. "I can find my own teacher."

Oliver hadn't said anything in reply. He just looked at Gianetta and said, "What you need to do is go up to Renata's and put your feet up. There's something about your expression that leads me to believe that your feet or your back is hurting. Perhaps both."

"There are never any taxis around here," Gianetta said crossly.

"I just came in one and he's there, waiting."

"Oh very well. You can bring Julia later. Goodbye, my dear," she said to me. "You really should not pay any attention to me. Oliver was right you know, about my feet!"

"You don't have to—"

"Let's go get an ice or a drink," Oliver said. "I've just been haggling with a dealer. It's the most exhausting work on earth—pleasant, but exhausting."

Once we were seated in the big piazza with our Campari ordered, Oliver said, "Gianetta's right. You mustn't pay any attention to her when she gets like that. All it means is, she's tired. She's very fond of you."

"I may know nothing about art," I said grumpily, "in fact I know I don't, but even I know that that plaster David in the other piazza is a copy. But when I ask her if a Raphael is, she practically pretended she didn't know me."

"It'll be great fun to teach you."

"There's no reason why you should bother."

97

"Please?" He smiled at me. I'd seen his expression be witty and acerbic or dry and worldly. I'd never seen it rather straightforward and kind.

"Why should you want to?"

"Because I spent many years teaching before I started in museum work. I love it. And because I'd far rather start with a *tabula rasa* and imbue you with some of my own ideas than have to unteach a lot of things I didn't like. It'll be wonderful. We're both going to be here for a few weeks this summer, and we can leave Gianetta to be with her other guests. She needs a change from worrying about her museum. Do say you will?"

And that was when I fell in love with him.

I'll never forget that summer. Oliver rented a car from somewhere and we'd leave after breakfast each morning. We went to Perugia, where, in the museum, we saw paintings by the local master—named for his city—Perugina, and others by Pinturicchio, Bonfigli, Piero della Francesca and Fra Angelico. In a nearby church in Perugia we saw an early Raphael. Another morning we went to Assisi to the basilica to see the panels—many times restored, as Oliver acidly pointed out—reputedly by Cimabue and Giotto and/or their students. We drove to Cortona to the little museum there, with its radiant Annunciation by Fra Angelico, to Spello with its chapel frescoes by Pinturicchio, to Castel Rigone where, in a church, was hung a sixteenth-century madonna by an unknown artist before whom even the most worldly and cynical burned candles for special causes. "Even Gianetta," Oliver said.

"Gianetta? She'd never!"

"She did."

"And did the Virgin come through?"

"As a matter of fact, she did. There was a particular painting that Gianetta wanted for the museum ('the museum' always meant the Monaldi Museum). We'd all given up. Then on the day I was going to place something else in that particular niche, the owner called and said he'd changed his mind and he'd sell it."

"And she thinks that made him do it?"

"Who knows what she thinks!"

"Is that the only example of the Virgin's—er—cooperation?"

He grinned. "Isn't that enough?" Then he got up. "We have to go, Julia. If we don't get out of here now we'll never make it to the museum in San Sepolcro."

So we got into his small Fiat and raced to Borgo San Sepolcro where Piero della Francesca's vigorous "Resurrection" drove everything else out of my mind. Then we went to a plain chapel in Monterchi to view Piero's Madonna del Parto, showing two angels holding back the flaps of a fur-lined tent where an extremely pregnant Virgin, in a dress let out at the seams, rested her hand on her enormous stomach. It was painted for the church at Monterchi, according to Oliver, because the artist's mother originated there and he had wanted to honor her. On the way back I drove while Oliver read to me from the words and wisdom of Bernard Berenson.

We spent a week in Rome and another in Florence, three days in Milan and two in Siena. We drove to Arezzo, where we saw more Piero della Francescas and ceramics by della Robbia; to Ravenna for the fourth-, fifth-, and sixth-century mosaics; to Urbino to the ducal palace containing more Pinturicchios; and to Gubbio where dwelt a curiously oriental-looking madonna by Ottaviano Nelli.

By the end of the summer my head was a hodgepodge of Byzantine influence, mediaeval elongation, Renaissance flesh tones, Christ fully clothed on twelfth-century crucifixes, and the near-naked suffering human being by the beginning of the Renaissance.

Finally, of course, we went to the Monaldi Museum in

Castiglione, a small town twenty minutes from Civitella and an hour away from Perugia.

Once a mediaeval village with its bridge, its trickle of river and its palazzo, Castiglione was now a bustling modern community with its own industry, mostly relating to farming equipment. Branches of the Monaldi family had come from the country around Castiglione and the family palazzo of one of the branches, now the town hall, had been their residence.

The museum was housed in a small square house set in a garden not far from the center of the little town. Gianetta had bought the house on Oliver's recommendation. Built around an inner court, its modest size seemed right for a memorial to Marcello. And, slowly, Oliver started filling it with paintings, pieces of sculpture, manuscript fragments and other treasures, as many as possible by local artists.

The pride of the museum was, of course, the Mantori collection. Assembled in the main room were seven paintings, including the Madonna: the crucifixion, the Sermon on the Mount, two of the Holy Family, Mary Magdalene, and the Transfiguration. Mantori lacked Piero's vigor, but he had a lyric quality of his own. His faces of Christ did not need the conventional halo; they radiated a powerful Grace hard to describe. Mary Magdalene and the two Virgins in the paintings of the Holy Family were obviously versions of the same model as the one he used for his famous Madonna. And there was no question about it: She bore an odd resemblance, elusive but visible, to Gianetta.

"They're wonderful, Oliver," I said, knowing how much Mantori was his discovery. "You should be very proud of them."

"They're nice, aren't they, well worth all the *Sturm und Drang* in getting them."

In the other rooms there were, inevitably, given the country and the period, many other madonnas, one by La Spagna, one attributed to Fiorenzo di Lorenzo and a Virgin and Child with Angels by Perugino and his assistants. There was a predella panel by Bartolomeo Caporali, and some Sienese pictures, including a madonna by Taddeo di Bartolo, Pinnacles and Prophets by a student of Duccio and a Madonna and Child by Guido Pelmerucci. One of the best pieces in the collection was a piece of sculpture attributed to Donatello.

"Can't you be sure?" I asked Oliver.

"Back that far it's sometimes a bit iffy. Great artists, both painters and sculptors, often had workshops full of students, and more than once battle lines have been drawn in the art world as to whether one particular piece of sculpture or painting is by the master himself or by his students under his supervision."

"Doesn't that make things a bit difficult when you're trying to say which is by whom?"

"To put it mildly, yes. Hence the battles."

"Are there any here that there are doubts about?"

"No, or they wouldn't be here. Come along, or we'll be late for dinner." He strode so fast along the corridor leading to the front door that I could hardly keep up with him.

"How on earth do you tell whether something's real or not?" I asked, as we spun along the road back to Civitella.

"By intuition, voodoo and the laying on of hands."

"No, Oliver, seriously. I mean, with one of those paintings, how would you know whether it's by the painter in question or by his students—or by somebody trying to fake an old masterpiece?"

"Style, subject matter, color, and, if things really got down to the nitty gritty, chemical analyses of the paint, the canvas, the wood and everything else. And then half the experts would disagree with the other half, each calling the other a fraud."

"I'll ask Gianetta—" I started.

"You'll do nothing of the sort." Suddenly he sounded

angry. "I won't have her bothered by nonsense like that. She's had enough—" He didn't finish the sentence.

I had never seen Oliver cross before, and—such was my state of abject devotion by that time—I was stricken that I had displeased him. After waiting for a minute for him to go on, I finally said timidly, "Are you angry with me, Oliver? Did I say something wrong?"

He glanced at me quickly. Then his equally sudden smile turned the landscape into sunshine for me. "No. Of course not. You couldn't." And he picked up my hand and kissed it.

I adored him.

It was the winter after that that I started studying art in school, putting some order into the chaos of visual images that filled my mind. But Oliver remained not only my first but my greatest teacher, and I continued to love him long after I knew, somehow, that I was no longer in love with him, and that there were avenues of his life about which I could only guess.

"Do you think Oliver is a homosexual?" I asked Gianetta once.

"I really don't know. Perhaps you'd better ask him." It was the kind of rebuff at which Gianetta excelled.

"It's not the sort of thing you ask a person, straight out," I said.

"No. I didn't think it was, either."

And the subject remained there. As I started moving in art circles first in New York and later in London, I met people who took it for granted that Oliver was, indeed, homosexual. But I met an equal number who scoffed at the idea, and pointed to any number of girls whom he had not only escorted everywhere—plenty of well-known homosexuals did that—but had been obviously in love with. But never, of course, with me. I would have spurts of seeing a great deal of him. Then I wouldn't see him again until we found ourselves together in Civitella. Then, a few years later, I met David Brownson.

Evidently Signor Birazzi had decided that the four teen-agers could be allowed to continue their journey. It turned out that they, plus the doctor and his wife, had, on the day of Gianetta's death, arisen at three in the morning, in the pitch dark, and had driven in two cars to the foot of Monte Accouto, a cone-shaped mountain visible from the main road, and had climbed to the top in time to watch the dawn come up. And the party did not return till nine-thirty.

"But why did you not say so?" Marco asked the Langdons, when the police chief appeared after dinner with the news.

"It never particularly occurred to us to mention it," Dr. Langdon said, managing to convey the impression that only excitable non-Britains would think it worth commenting on. "We do it every year, it's sort of a summer ritual. And I don't think we're the only ones. But we certainly go up at least once when we're here, and the young are always game."

"Well," the police chief said somewhat drily, "it seems you're not the only ones to consider it a summer outing. A whole group of hikers from Germany went up, too."

"Yes, I know. They were most annoyed when they saw we were up a good half-hour ahead of them." This was the fair-haired boy.

"So," Signor Birazzi said, "you are all free to leave when you wish."

Three of the teen-agers, consulting among one another, decided to go. The fair-haired boy, Terry MacNaughton, would stay. He was due to meet a relative in Milan in two days and had nowhere to go in the meantime. The Langdons elected to stay until the funeral.

Rupert had been offered either the second bed in Andrea's room or the single room up in the battlements, on the side opposite from the boys' dormitory.

"You'll have to use the bathrooms on the second floor," Marco said.

"So it's a choice between sharing quarters and a private bath with Andrea, or having a room to myself and a bath on the lower floor."

"I'm sorry we don't have anything better for you," Marco said huffily. "I realize you're probably used to much better."

"Calm yourself," Rupert said. "The most primitive conditions in the West are luxury compared to the ruin I inherited. No modern conveniences there. They've all collapsed."

"Do you mean to say that your ancestral manor doesn't even have running water?" I asked.

"My dear, Blenheim didn't have running water at one time."

"That hardly counts, when running water was unknown. But it's not unknown now, at least outside England."

"A little hardship just keeps us tough," Rupert said, staring down at the cards I'd laid out. "Which patience are you playing?"

"The simplest one. If you want to make it a double game, there's another pack over there."

"All right," he said, retrieved the other cards and sat himself down opposite me.

"You're good," I said grudgingly, a quarter of an hour later.

"My grandmother used to be a demon at this. She made me play with her."

"Have you decided yet whether you're going to be alone and unwashed or with Andrea and bathed?"

"I think with Andrea and bathed. I wonder if that means the first definite onset of middle age."

104

"I don't think it's middle-aged to want to be clean. How disgusting! You've won!"

"It comes from being able to do two things at once."

I yawned. "Last night was not the most restful I've ever spent. I'm going to bed."

I left the rest of the party upstairs, and made my way to the floor below, opening one great door after another, and turning on the lights. Economy and some of Gianetta's thrift should have indicated that I turn off the lights when I had got to the other side of the big halls. But I told myself that the others coming down—Andrea, Stacey and Rupert —would need them.

Fifteen minutes later, dressed in my robe, and carrying my various bath articles, I came back up and made for the nearest empty bathroom. Then after a long hot bath, I went down again, read for a while, blew out my candle, opened the shutters and snuggled down in bed, praying that after an almost sleepness night, I would go to sleep. My prayers were answered. Ten minutes later I was sound asleep.

I became aware that there was a noise, an unhappy noise of some kind, but it was part of the strange dream I was having. Gianetta, her voice making a most uncharacteristic sound, a sort of keening, was sitting in her dining chair, rocking back and forth. I kept asking her, in my dream, what she had lost. All she could say was "It's there, I know it's there. I keep asking you to look."

"What's there?"

But somehow, she never told me, or the words never got spoken, or I didn't hear them. I knew there was something fearfully important that I was supposed to do, but I didn't know what it was, and even less could I function with Gianetta making that dreadful noise. The trouble was it kept getting louder and louder, so that it was coming towards my room. . . . The door crashed open.

I woke up, my heart pounding.

"Daddy, Daddy, where are you? There's somebody in my room. I know there's somebody there."

I could see the figure dimly in the faint grayness that came from the window. It was standing by the door. Somehow, with shaking fingers, I lit a candle. I don't know what I expected. But I certainly didn't expect to see Stacey, her face contorted with fear, clinging to the doorknob. When I lit the candle, she shrieked.

"Stacey!" I said. "Hush! You'll wake the house. What's the matter?"

I got out of bed, holding the candle, and went over to the terrified girl.

"There's somebody in my room, I know it. I can't stay in there. I won't."

"Who? Who's in your room?"

"I can't see them. I thought this was Daddy's room. Where is he?"

"He's in the room directly above. If you want we can go up the stairs and wake him up. But let's talk first."

I turned on the light, sat her down on the side of the bed, put a robe on and sat down beside her. "Now," I said. "What happened?"

"I'd been asleep and then woke up. I don't *like* the room in there. It's cold and creepy. And I'm the only one for miles around. But then tonight, I woke up, and was lying there, when I heard these steps coming across the room towards me. They *weren't* my imagination. I don't care what Daddy says. They were loud and hard and sounded like a man's. And they were coming to the bed. I sat up and yelled, 'Don't come here, go away. Get away from me.' The footsteps stopped. And then started going in the other direction. That's when I got out of bed and came to look for Daddy. I thought he was in here." She paused, sniffing, and seemed to be groping in her robe for a

106

handkerchief. "I suppose you think I'm a coward. Or crazy."

I got up, pulled a couple of tissues from a box and sat down. "Here. No. I don't think you're either. Or if you are, so am I. I don't like this room. Never have."

"You don't? Have you heard steps?"

"No. I really haven't heard anything. But I do find it creepy, and somehow disturbing. But, since I feel less so when I know people are in that double room across the billiard hall, I've always felt it was something that came from my own sense of isolation. And the girls' dormitory is even more remote."

"But would that make me hear steps? Because I *did* hear them."

"I'm not disputing that for a moment. But it's possible, isn't it, that with all these guests in the castle, let alone whatever servants are coming and going, someone could have simply mistaken their way?"

"But how? I mean he—it—didn't come through the regular door."

"But there's another door, isn't there? On the other wall."

"Yes."

"Well, it's possible he could have come from there. It leads to Gianetta's old master bedroom and bath upstairs."

"Oh!" It was not a reassuring sound. I remembered the anecdote of the fortuneteller. David could have been somewhat on target when he said his daughter read too many gothics. But this was not the time to repeat that. More to the immediate point—where was I going to put Stacey now? I certainly could not suggest that she go back to that room. I glanced at the bed. It was, at best, a three-quarters bed. "Well, you could stay here. It would be a pretty tight squeeze."

"I'd stay here like a shot if there was no other place,

and if you didn't mind. But I'm a frightfully restless sleeper. Isn't there anywhere else? It's such a huge place."

I remembered then a tiny room upstairs, not much more than an alcove, that had been partitioned off the sitting room, and lay between it and a small anteroom where flowers were arranged.

"If you don't mind a room not much bigger than this bed and the most puritanically small of single cots, then I think I know of a free space."

Stacey giggled. "I don't mind." Then she said anxiously, "It's not down here, is it?"

"No. Upstairs. Come, we'll go up the winding stair here and I'll show you. Let me go first and I'll turn on the lights, such as they are."

At the top of the stairs on one side was the door to David's room, on the other, the entrance to the dining room. The steps, in the best mediaeval fashion, were narrow and winding.

"Your father is in there," I whispered, indicating his closed door. "We're going here through the dining room."

We tiptoed across the wide tile floor. The long table had been set for breakfast, and someone had put a fresh flower at Gianetta's place mat.

"Where is it?" Stacey whispered, as we left the dining room.

"Down here."

I led the way down the wide corridor, turned right at the main stone stairs, and then left, going through the little flower room with its sink, a variety of vases on a table, and two pairs of large garden scissors hanging on nails on the wall. The door had been recently put into what had been a doorless alcove. Groping around to the right of the door, I found the light switch. Since this room was of relatively recent renovation, the light was much brighter. The tiny chamber did indeed have a slightly well-like effect, since it had been cut from a much bigger space. But it was still far less daunting than any of the rooms downstairs.

"Here. Yes, it's empty, but the bed has been made up. I can't guarantee those are unslept-in sheets. Do you care?"

"Not a bit. It's much nicer than the room downstairs. Thanks awfully, Miss Winthrop. It's fearfully nice of you. I'm sorry I woke you up."

"That's perfectly all right. And you'd better call me Julia. The other sounds too formal. If you need me, I would suggest you go down the main stairs and through the main reception hall downstairs—the way you came last time. You're welcome to use the winding stair we just came up, but it's trickier, and you might find it hard to locate the lights. I'll show you where the hall lights are, and the ones that control the stairway lights."

"Good night," I whispered when I'd done this. "I think I'll take my own advice and go down the lit stairs here. Sleep well."

When I got to the bottom I turned off the main lights and went into the great hall, turning on the lights as I did so. Then I hesitated. I felt I should go, now, into the girls' dormitory to see if I could find any evidence whatsoever that anyone had, as she said, come into her room. Like Stacey, I found the idea totally unpalatable. But it wasn't much more palatable to return to my own room and lie there thinking about it.

Making a decision, I moved to the right, went into a small billiard room with its table in the middle, and then through that to the girls' dormitory. Evidently Stacey, in her flight, had either not found the light or hadn't waited to put it on. My hand groped on the walls on both sides of the door inside the room. But there was no light switch. Neither was there one on the billiard room side. That was not entirely unusual. Many of the rooms did not boast wall switches. Frequently, the rooms were lit by separate lamps with the switches on the lamps themselves. Or, of course, the switch could be on the wall next to the other door across the room. In either case it meant going into the room and finding it. Why don't I wait until tomorrow, my mind temporized? Coward, I told myself, and took a step in. If I just stand here a moment, I thought, until my eyes get used to it, I'll see where the lamps are. Or I'll see the light switch on the wall opposite. It was a perfectly sensible argument. The trouble was, it didn't work. I stood there, as the moments dragged past, waiting for the oddly thick black to thin into gray, for the weak light from the billiard room to penetrate the dark. But none of that happened. The only light of any kind to show came from a few forks of lightning making brilliant jagged scars against the night sky. Perhaps it was because it was the middle of the night and I had been up so long; perhaps the night had grown chill as it sometimes did up in the Umbrian hills. Maybe it was my overready imagination, sparked and fed by what Stacey had blurted out, but it seemed to me that along with the impenetrable black, there was a creeping chill. My cotton robe was not warm. I stood there, hugging my arms around me, shivering, forcing myself not to do what I wanted to do: turn and go out immediately.

"Don't be an idiot," I told myself. Then, because anything was better than just standing there, I slid my foot in its mule forward and forced my other foot to follow it.

"This is ridiculous," I said aloud.

And then I felt it: the hair on the back of my neck stirring as though a wind had brushed it. I had read about such things. I didn't believe they existed. Now I knew they were true. "Go away!" I suddenly cried.

A light shone then, powerful and probing, a shaft of white blazing past me from behind.

"What the hell are you doing here?" A voice I knew very well said.

I swung around, released from whatever held me. I

could see nothing, of course, because of the brilliant light shining from the flashlight.

"Oh Rupert," I said weakly. "You'll never know how glad I am to see you." I took a step then, and fell flat on my face.

FOUR

"**D**id you hurt yourself?" Rupert's voice was gentle, oddly un-Rupert-like.

I got myself up and in a sitting position on the floor. "I don't think so. What did I fall over?"

"This." And he shone the light on a rather moth-eaten tapestried footstool.

I felt him kneel beside me and put his arm around my back, his hand cupping my head. "All right?"

"Yes. Just my dignity is sore."

We were still in the dark. I found I was a little dizzy and shaken and I wanted to rest a minute before I pushed up onto my feet. Rupert had switched off the flashlight, and we were in the dark.

"Rupert," I said suddenly. "Stacey . . . she came plunging out of this room because she said she heard steps coming toward the bed. She was terrified. I calmed her down and took her to the little room off the flower room. Then I thought I'd just see for myself what was here. I was convinced her father was right; she'd just read too many romantic novels. But something was here. I can't tell you how I know. But I know. I didn't hear anything. But I couldn't find the light switch and was waiting for the dark . . . for my eyes to get used to the dark so I could either switch on the bedside lamp or find the wall switch over there. It was cold. And the dark didn't get any lighter. And then . . . well, I knew something was there, and I couldn't move. That was why I was so glad to hear your voice." And somewhat to my surprise, I reached out a hand and took his. His fingers closed around mine. There was a queer little silence. Then Rupert said, "Let's try to find some light."

The flashlight went on again, and swung over the walls and furniture, revealing lamps on either side of a bureau, two beds at right angles against walls, and another bed, with bedclothes thrust back. Rupert released my hand, went over to the lamps and put them on.

The light looked the brighter for our having been in the dark, and it revealed not one other door, but two, the second opening in a narrow strip of wall beside the bureau. Both doors were open.

"I wonder where these lead to," he said.

I rubbed my shin. "Well that one there, leading to the stair, goes up to the master bedroom, Gianetta's old room. I think Marco's there now. I didn't know there was another, so I don't know where it goes."

Rupert, who had a navy blue robe over his blue pajamas, turned the light into the second door. "This seems to lead to a staircase, too, but one going down. And it smells like hell," he finished off.

"Ugh! Why don't you close it. And the other one."

"It might be interesting to see where it leads."

"Tonight?"

"Why not?" He turned around and looked at me. Suddenly I realized he had on glasses. "I've never seen you in glasses before. You look different."

"How different?" He was still flashing his light down the steps going from the second door, but he turned and looked at me as I hesitated.

"More reassuring," I said finally. "I think your naked eyes must be intimidating."

He snorted. "That's a lot of nonsense."

"No it isn't. I would have found you much easier to

113

confront if you'd been wearing the glasses you have on now, rather than the contact lenses I suppose you wear during the day."

"Rubbish."

"I don't know why you don't say 'balderdash!' It would be completely in character."

"Like Colonel Blimp. A much-misunderstood man. I thought I was descended from Ebenezer Scrooge."

"You are."

"Another maligned man. I'm going down. Why don't you go on back to your room." And Rupert disappeared.

Feeling refreshed and reassured by our wrangling, I came to the head of the steps and saw his light disappearing. "Wait for me," I said, and started after him. He was right. An unpleasant smell emanated from below.

He turned the flashlight back up and waited till I joined him, limping a little.

"Did you hurt your foot?"

"Barked my shin."

"Umm. Okay, can you see ahead now?"

"Yes."

"Well, don't rush."

His own mules slapped on the steps; we went down for what felt a long time.

"This seems much longer than the winding stair leading up from my room." My words had a queer, hollow echo, tunneled by the narrow space.

"Yes."

We kept on going down. The smell was stronger.

"Something smells," I said, trying not to breathe through my nose.

We rounded another curve and the smell was unmistakable. Rupert stopped. "I want you to go back upstairs," he said.

I found a tissue and held it to my nose. "What are you going to do?"

114

"I'm going to see what's causing this smell." He looked back at me, his face impassive in the dim light reflected back from his flashlight.

"Rupert—do you think it's a body?" Stupid question. It had to be. Only dead meat could smell that way.

"Of course. But it could be the body of a recently deceased rat. On the other hand, it could be something else."

"Or someone else."

"That's why I want you to go back upstairs."

"I'll wait for you here." I backed up a few steps and then sat down, my tissue held to my nose.

"You'll be in the dark, because I'm taking this torch with me."

I didn't want that. "Then I'm coming with you."

He shrugged. "All right. But keep right behind me."

To make sure that I didn't lose him, I put a hand on his shoulder, and he and I started down again, with me following his feet step by step. We didn't have far to go. Rounding another curve. I saw the sharp cone of the light sweeping in front of Rupert. The smell got more sickly. Then the light poured across clothes, legs, a head with blood on it, staring eyes. "Stop!" I whispered. Rupert put his hand up on mine.

"Steady," he said in an even voice. Then, a moment or so later. "All right?"

"Okay."

"Then stay here. As you can see, I'll only be a foot or two away."

"No. It's all right. I'll go with you."

We went down the last two steps. Rupert walked to the body, which was a bare few feet away, and stared down at it.

"Julia, are you able to look?"

"Yes."

"Do you recognize him?"

I forced myself to look at the horrible face. Whoever

he was—and he seemed to be a slight youth in his early twenties—he had died in fear and anger. It was hard to judge, with the features contorted like that. Yet there was something very familiar about him.

"Well?"

"Rupert, I can't be sure; I'm certain I've seen him but I can't remember where or when, or who he is."

"I'd say, from the look of him, that he's Italian, which is logical enough, considering we're in Italy. But in this place you never know. I think I ought to just take a look around, if you can bear to stand there a minute."

"All right. But—just don't leave me here in the dark very long with . . . with that."

"I won't. I promise."

I saw his light go along the floor which, unlike all the other floors of castle, was rough stone. Then the light seemed to retreat and go through a passage of some kind. After that, it disappeared altogether. I took a deep breath and held it, and tried to think of something else. It must have worked, because though I was standing in the dark a few feet from the body of someone who had obviously died a dreadful and violent death, I didn't experience that eerie fear that, whatever it was, had made the hair on my neck stand up. Nevertheless, I waited with considerable eagerness for Rupert's return, and was powerfully relieved when I could see the light from his flashlight coming before him like a gold carpet.

"Where did the passage lead to?" I said, as he came towards me, skirting the body.

"I'm not sure. I didn't go all the way to the end. Come along. We're going back upstairs. I'll hold the light so that you can see it."

The way back up seemed even longer than the way down.

"These stairs seem longer than any of the other stairs," I said.

116

"They are. I'm almost certain that room we've just left is below ground level. Probably a dungeon, originally."

"What an appealing thought!"

"But wherever the passage leads, our unlucky chap lying there came from its other end, because he bled the whole way. "Good, we can see the light now."

We reached the top of the steps and went into the bedroom from which Stacey had fled.

"The steps that scared Stacey . . ." I began, "they couldn't have been . . . they couldn't have been that boy, could they? I mean he's been dead a while, hasn't he?"

"I'm no coroner or expert, but I'd say a couple of days. Did you say that Marco is in the bedroom leading up from that door?"

"I think so. It *is* the master bedroom, and he is, now, the master."

"Are you guessing? I mean, is that an assumption, or do you *know*?"

"I can't remember that he or anyone *told* me that he is occupying that room. But I seem to know it."

Rupert gave one of his snort-like sounds. "You should take up dowsing or divining."

"I could have just overheard it in the ordinary way, without Marco having told me. Where are you going?"

"Upstairs to see if your information is right—however acquired."

"But you'll wake him up."

"I have to do that anyway, Julia. These are his premises, have you forgotten? And you and I have discovered a corpse on them. Don't you think he should be informed? I mean, it's not the kind of thing you drop casually at breakfast . . . I say, old chap . . . I meant to mention it to you earlier . . . but there's a body in your dungeon."

"I suppose you're right," I said grudgingly.

But Rupert was half way up the stairs.

In a few minutes he was down again. "Either you've

been misinformed, or he's spending the night somewhere else."

"You mean he's not there?"

"Yes, Julia, that's exactly what I mean. He's not there. Neither bed has been slept in. However, I think you're right about it being nominally his room. His suitcase, I'm pretty sure it's his, is open on one of the beds, and the closet contains an extra suit and raincoat."

"I suppose they could belong to anybody; any male I mean."

"But I don't think they do. They look like Marco's, and they're the right size."

"Well, where on earth would he be?"

"He might simply be out for a night on the tiles. Maybe he has a girlfriend around here?"

"Around *here*?"

"Why is that so unthinkable? I can think of half a dozen country houses or obviously occupied castles that I saw on the way here, all within half an hour's drive. Castiglione's only a quarter of an hour away. Perugia—a major city—is less than an hour. If you drive like hell you can get to Florence in an hour and a half and Rome in two."

"But with Gianetta dead and as yet unburied?"

"What's that got to do with it? Were they that close?"

"I don't know. I suppose not." I paused. "I guess you're right. They didn't have that much to do with each other."

"Gianetta wasn't even here eight months of the year. By the end of September she'd hotfoot it to England and her nice London flat. Her guests were mostly English and Americans, and those that weren't came largely from Northern Europe."

"But she and Marcello lived in Perugia during the winter for years."

"She may still have friends there but whenever you've talked about her summer guests, they've mostly been English or American, haven't they?"

"Yes. What's this got to do with Marco having a girl-friend?"

"It's got to do with the fact that he would hardly be so smitten with grief that he'd restrain himself from visiting a girlfriend if she were around. Or anyone else."

I stood there in the middle of the girls' dormitory and thought about it. The great mediaeval fortress around us was silent. In the long narrow window I could see the fork of lightning again—this time closer. The chill I had felt before—yet strangely enough not in the basement-dungeon —returned. I shivered a little. The tongue of lightning flickered again through the window. "Is it just me—" I started to say, when the room lights blinked once and then went out. "Rupert!" I said anxiously.

"I'm here. I'll put on my torch again." There was a moment's pause and then there was the same carpet of white-gold light on the floor.

"How clever of you to bring that," I was determined not to let my teeth chatter.

"I've been here before, you know. And the lights here are as temperamental as the water supply. It's probably that mild storm that's put them out."

"I keep forgetting that you've been here. Since you always disliked Gianetta—"

"I did not, repeat *not*, dislike Gianetta. On the contrary. We were friends. Which didn't mean that I bought all her enthusiasms or thought highly of all her friends."

"Like Oliver," I said crossly, concentrating on not letting my teeth chatter.

"Why are you so belligerent, now, at this moment, standing in the dark. Why on earth should you care whether I like Oliver or not?"

"I don't know," I said finally. "I think it's because I'm afraid."

"Afraid of what?"

"There's something wrong with this room, Rupert. You probably think I'm raving or hysterical or both, but there is."

"Do you always promote a fight when you're afraid?"

"I don't know. Yes, I think so." This time, to my humiliation, I could hear my teeth knocking together.

And then suddenly two arms were around me. Without even thinking I put my arms around his neck. I could feel his stubble against my face, and the silky stuff of his robe under my hands. It was indescribably comforting.

"Better?" he said.

"Yes." It was amazing, I thought, what a warm, close body could do.

And then the lights came on. He stepped away from me. "Come along," he said, "I'm seeing you back to your room."

After closing both the passage doors, he pushed me ahead of him, and went through the door leading into the billiard room. Turning out the lights as we went, he led the way back across the main hall to the other former billiard room that stretched between the double room he shared with Andrea and my room.

"I'm coming into your room and have a look around," he said.

When we got to my room he examined the lock on the door. "Where's the key?"

"I don't know. It's never had one so far as I remember."

He grunted, went through the door leading to the stairway going up, and then, while I waited for him, went up the stairs and came down again. "There's no lock here, either." Then he looked out the window. "Well," he said, "at least that's a twenty foot drop. Now," he said, coming back into the middle of the room, "I'm going to take you across the way. I want you to sleep in my bed for the rest of the night, and I'll sleep in here."

"With Andrea?"

He grinned. "I don't think he'll wake up and be so

120

overcome that he'll ravish you in the morning."

"I didn't say he would. But won't he think it peculiar?"

"You can explain it all to him."

"Don't you think this room is safe?" Half of me wanted to be reassured about the room, which I would have to sleep in again, and the other half of me wanted to have my unpleasant impressions of it confirmed.

"That's not the point. Gianetta is dead and we have a dead young man of unknown origin downstairs. Given all those circumstances, I'd sooner you'd be in a room with a hefty type like Andrea to protect you. If anyone is planning a nocturnal visit here, they'll find me. What a pleasant surprise for them! Come on."

Rupert didn't turn on the light when he opened Andrea's door, just beamed his flashlight onto the other bed, where Andrea lay, wrapped cocoon-like in his sheet, his wild red hair spread out all over the pillow. "Hop in the bed here. I don't want to wake him up." Once I was in the bed, with the sheet pulled up, he simply said, "Good night," and left.

I had a great deal to think about, lying there, with my eyes getting used to the gray shimmering in from the window: Stacey's visit, the footsteps she heard, the body downstairs, Marco's unslept-in bed, Rupert . . . . But I must have been worn out, or felt safe for the first time that night, or something. Because I was asleep before I thought of any of them.

Andrea's bed was empty and made when I awoke the next morning. The sun was pouring through the long windows, and everything that had happened the night before seemed unreal. Flying across to my own room I found the bed there made, too. According to Andrea's bedside clock, it was ten past nine. I brushed my teeth and flung on a blouse and skirt and within about ten minutes was up in the dining room. Obviously I was the last to arrive: there was only one place setting there. In front of the place on a trivet was a coffee pot under an English tea cosy, and surrounding the setting were cereal, bread, butter, honey, and a glass of orange juice.

I poured myself some coffee and was relieved to find it at least medium warm. Then, carrying the cup, I glanced into the kitchen. Dishes were piled in the sink and on the big table in the middle, but there was no one there, which was unusual at this time of day. Pausing long enough to drink some orange juice, I walked towards the sitting room, still carrying my coffee cup, and heard then the hum of voices behind a closed door, which was also unusual. The sitting-room door was closed only when we were trying to induce the over-friendly bats that flew in at night to leave through the window and not fly into the hall. Opening the sitting-room door, I looked in.

Signor Birazzi was there, in his favorite place in front of the fireplace. So were Rupert, Marco, Maria and the cook. Maria was sitting on one of the chairs, her hands in front of her face, crying. The others looked up when I came in.

"Maria," I said, going over. "What on earth's the matter?"

She looked up then, her dark face streaked with tears, her eyes full of pain. "Oh Miss Julia, it's Ricardo, Ludovico's son. His body was found last night in the basement. My grandchild!"

I opened my mouth and glanced at Rupert. He frowned, and shook his head a little. Somehow I knew he was trying to tell me that Maria didn't know that I was present when her grandson was found.

"I'm sorry, Maria," I said. "Terribly sorry." I patted her back, and when she groped out with a hand, I took it and held it. I didn't want to ask her any of the questions that were crowding through my mind. So I just sat there, holding and occasionally patting her hand. After a minute the cook stood up. "Come," she said in Italian, "I will take you to your room." She glared at the police chief, as though daring him to prevent her. But he merely nodded.

When they had left I said, "What happened?"

"Signor Carmichael would not let us wake you," the policeman said accusingly. "But you were with him when he found the body, yes?"

"Yes," I said.

"And you heard, or," he consulted his note, "Miss Stacey heard, footsteps?"

"Yes. But I don't know what, or whose . . . or . . ." my voice trailed off.

"Or?"

"Or anything." I was not about to explain that I was not sure they were even human or natural.

"Where are Miss Stacey and her father?"

"I just got up. I don't know."

"They went off to Perugia immediately after an early breakfast this morning," Marco said. Seeing Signor Birazzi's eyebrows climb, he said, "There is nothing unusual about that. That's what guests always do—go off to see museums, art galleries, churches. In her own way the contessa ran one of the great guided and unguided tour centers of Umbria."

"At a time like this? With the discovery of a second body?"

Marco looked mildly uncomfortable. "I had not told them. They went before . . . before I arrived for breakfast."

"Then how did you know where they had gone?"

"They left word with Maria."

"With Maria—when she had just heard about her grandson?"

Marco was looking increasingly distressed. I glanced at Rupert, who was wearing his sardonic look. Putting those two facts together, I deduced that Marco had not told the police chief of his own absence during the night.

The police chief looked at Rupert. "And you did not tell them what you had found?"

"I felt it was Marco's place to do that, as the present owner."

"You did not wake him up and tell him of this when you made the discovery?"

Rupert looked at Marco. Marco said reluctantly, "I did not spend the night here. I spent it in Perugia."

The police chief bent a long look on him. Marco stuck out his chin. "You did not ask us not to leave the premises, Signor Birazzi. You simply wanted us to stay in the vicinity, which I did, and returned this morning."

"Well," the police chief said finally, after an uncomfortable silence, "from first examination the doctor seems to think that Ricardo Natale died at about the same time as the contessa. The doctor will have to perform an autopsy, of course, and will tell us then whether or not this is accurate." He examined his notes again. Then he looked up at Marco. "Now tell me about this Ricardo Natale. It is understandable, perhaps, but I could not get this information from his grandmother at this time."

Marco shrugged. "I know almost nothing. I have never seen this Ricardo before. He lives in Milan with his father, Ludovico. His father is a professor at the university there. He has not lived with Maria since I was born, so I have seen him perhaps once or twice when I was a child. His grandfather was Giuseppe Natale, who owned the farm there, the one beyond the gates. It is now owned by his great-uncle."

"Ludovico's uncle?"

"Yes." Marco shrugged. "Half-uncle I suppose. Maria married Giuseppe when his wife had been dead some years. He already had three sons. Then little Ludovico came along. When Giuseppe died, his oldest half brother got the farm and Maria and Ludovico moved back with Gianetta and my grandfather."

"I see." The police chief looked at Rupert and me. "You did not know him."

"No," I said.

"Nor me," Rupert said.

"Do you know his father?" Birazzi asked, looking at me.

I shook my head. "I've only been coming here for the last twelve years, and from everything Gianetta—the contessa—told me, he'd been long gone before that."

"Did she speak of him much?"

"Not particularly. Why?"

The chief didn't answer that. He closed his notebook. "I am going back to the station. I will be in touch with you later. Arrividerci."

As soon as the policeman had gone, I went first to the kitchen. Finding only Baptisto there, rather sullenly washing the dishes by himself, I went back down the main staircase through what was known as the music room, up some more stairs, and into the first of the two rooms that were actually not in the castle proper but in the archway between the castle and the agent's house, forming one side of the patio.

The door was not quite latched, so, after knocking as quietly as I could, I poked my head in. Maria was sitting in an armchair staring out the window. The cook was opposite, in a straight chair. The quickness with which she rose indicated to me that she was more than ready to yield her post to me.

"I must see to lunch," she said in Italian. "Perhaps the signorina will sit with Maria."

Maria looked around. "There you are, Miss Julia," she said. And even at a moment like this and after all the years I'd known her, it was still a slight shock to hear Pimlico come out of such an Italian-looking face. As I sat down I said, "Did your people come from around here, Maria?" It seemed a frivolous question to ask at a time like this. And yet, it might serve as a slight relief to distract her from Ricardo, even for a moment.

"No, Miss Julia. My people were all from south of Naples. Whenever we fought, Giuseppe would fling that at me. You know, there is a lot of feeling between the Italians of the north and those of the south. My mother used to tell me that, but I never believed her." She sighed. "I will send her up an apology. She was right."

"You can light a candle for her."

"Not me. I'm low church—Church of England."

I couldn't have been more astonished if she'd said she was a Hindu. "Good heavens, Maria. Wasn't your mother a Catholic?"

"Oh yes. I mean she was born RC." (Maria used the initials like any Protestant Londoner.) "But she wasn't very religious. She always said one church was as good as another. It was my dad who was the churchgoer. I used to go with him." We were silent for a minute. Maria continued to stare out the window, facing, ironically, I thought, the chapel, though I wasn't at all sure she was focusing on it. Then she said. "That used to be a big cause of fuss between Giuseppe and me. He wanted Ludo brought up Catholic, and I gave in, finally. No use to be wrangling about it all the time. And it wasn't as though a good C of E church was around the corner. But after his father died, I didn't worry with taking Ludo anywhere much. And the contessa wasn't religious. But the count used to get after me. Told me to send him off for confirmation and first communion. Perhaps he was right. Perhaps God is punishing me." And she started to cry.

"I don't think God is Protestant or Catholic. And He certainly isn't punishing you. After all, as you say, Gianetta wasn't religious. . . ." My voice trailed off. I couldn't have chosen a worse comparison if I'd tried.

126

Maria's large black eyes were filled with tears. "No? And what about her being murdered, too?"

"Maria, that's nonsense, as your vicar at home in London would be the first to tell you, and so would the priest here, I'm sure." I spoke without the faintest idea of whether or not the priest would agree or would pronounce the papal anathema on her, if priests did that.

"Ah Miss Julia, there's times when you sound so much like the contessa you'd think it was her talking, so you would. You're more like her than you know."

This was not a new statement. And I wasn't beyond being pleased by it. Nevertheless, I couldn't prevent my eyes from flying to the mirror behind the bureau. There I saw my blond hair falling almost straight to my shoulders, my eyes a narrow blue-gray. Whatever genes my Italian mother had passed on to me were thoroughly hidden. I looked as New England as a covered bridge.

Maria must have seen the direction of my gaze, because her own met mine in the mirror. "Oh, you'll not see it at first glance. But once or twice lately, I've had quite a turn looking at you. Maybe it's the angle. But it's like she was standing in your body."

Flattering resemblances were one thing. That sounded a little too reminiscent of those flashes of hallucination I'd had since I arrived.

"We're not even related you know, Maria. She wasn't my grandmother. Just my stepgrandmother. So there couldn't be any resemblance except accidental."

There was a silence. "That's right. You're not. It's funny, isn't it, that I should be forgetting that."

"You loved her and you've been fond of me, and I probably imitated her without thinking of it. Something like that."

"I had a dream about her last night," Maria said. "I dreamed she was standing by my bed and trying to tell me something. But I couldn't hear her. Something about a letter."

I debated telling Maria of my experiences with Gianetta since she'd died. Then I decided against it. With Ricardo lying there (except, I thought suddenly, the police had probably removed his body), she didn't need any more anecdotes of that rather ghostly kind to focus on.

"Perhaps she was trying to warn me," Maria went on.

"Perhaps," I said skeptically. Then I reached out and took her hand, which was on the arm of the chair, and we sat like that for a while. I'd never before been in the position of comforting someone after a death, and I had no idea of what to do or say. Was it better to talk, or not to talk? To mention the deceased or not? Usually the motto of my life had always been, when in doubt do something. Now, I decided, when in doubt, it would be better to do nothing. Perhaps she would drift off to sleep.

But she didn't. I sat with her stubby, workworn hand in mine, sometimes staring down at the calloused fingers, and the wide, clean square nails, sometimes looking out at the chapel. It was a strange sort of communication: no words, no looks, just hand-to-hand between two women of vastly different ages and background. Yet a communication it was, and I became slowly convinced that more than just grief for her grandson was treading round and round in her mind like giant footsteps. It was a very strange feeling indeed, all the more so because it made me remember something I had forgotten: this particular experience had happened to me once before, when I was a child.

It was one of the times Gianetta and Marcello were visiting New York. I was in the hospital, recovering from having my appendix removed. Marcello came to see me, bringing flowers. Then he sat beside the bed and just held my hand for a while. I was feeling embarrassed at first to have this elderly Italian gentleman sitting there, holding my hand—I must have been about eleven—when, long after the embarrassment had faded and I was totally relaxed and rather sad, he said suddenly to me, "What is making your heart sad, Julietta?"

And I said, "Daddy sent Samson to the ASPCA and they euthanized him." And I started to cry.

"But you will see him when you go to heaven," Marcello said, "sitting beside the throne of God, purring and waiting for you."

Afterwards, when I thought about the words, they seemed in the worst tradition of rococo religious cards. Yet they sounded to me then as ordinary as if he had said, "But you will find Samson sitting on your father's lap when you get home." Except that no animal that had any sense would dream of sitting on my father's lap.

"Are you sure?" I had asked him.

"Of course. I am more than sure. I know."

After a while I had said to him, "How did you know I was sad?"

"Your hand told me."

There was an even stranger question that I didn't think to ask until after they'd gone back to Italy: how did he know about Samson at all? That he was a cat? My mother had long since been dead. My father was rarely around when they were, and he had been in California that trip. And Samson's demise had happened the year before, when I was in boarding school and my father decided he had an allergy to cats. Years afterwards, I realized he hadn't meant to be cruel. He just didn't think about my feelings at all, or, of course, Samson's. To him animals were no more and no less than inanimate objects, including the rats who supplied his scientific information.

When I was up and out of the hospital, I received a postcard from Italy. On it, in beautiful white, gold and blue colors, were God on His Throne and, beside Him, sitting up like an Egyptian deity, a white cat with green eyes. On the back of the postcard, in my grandfather's handwriting, were the words: "You see?" I never did find out who the artist was or where Marcello had found the card. But it gave me great comfort.

Now, the same communication through the hand seemed to be happening again. "What's bothering you, Maria?" I asked. "I mean, it's more than just Ricardo's death, isn't it?"

There was a silence. Then, "You always were sharp, Miss Julia." She sighed. "That wasn't like the contessa, but it was like your grandfather, the Conte Marcello."

"Why are you troubled? I'm not just being nosey. I think you need to talk about it."

"Miss Julia, if I could talk about it to anyone, I could talk to you. But I can't talk to anyone. It would—I just can't."

"All right," I said. "But remember, I stand ready to listen."

"I'll remember." And she squeezed my hand.

After a while I said, "I suppose the police have told Ludovico."

"Yes. He'll be here this afternoon. Poor Ludo, poor Ludo."

"Does he have other children?"

"No. Just the one boy."

"What about Ricardo's mother?"

"She died a year or so ago, but she and Ludovico had been separated for years before her death."

I tried to picture Ludovico, but I kept coming up with an image of an older version of the boy I had seen in the basement. Of course, that might be entirely accurate. Boys often did resemble their fathers. "How old is Ludo now?"

"Forty-four."

We sat there in silence. Perhaps because I had revealed the fact that I was aware something was troubling her, Maria, although leaving her hand in mine, seemed to withdraw. But whatever it was that was bothering her did not go away. It was there, almost, I thought, like another presence in the room.

David, Stacey and Oliver returned from Perugia just before lunch. "It seemed like a good idea to get away for a while," was David's brief explanation, when they came into the sitting room. Stacey was heavy-eyed, and the delicate skin under her eyes seemed bruised. Oliver looked bad, too. His face had lost none of the strain it had shown since I had met him at the airport. My heart went out to him. Of all the people here, with their various preoccupations, he was—with the exception of Maria—the one who most genuinely grieved. I went over and put my arm through his. "Did you have a restful time in Perugia?" I asked, simply to be saying something. And I wondered if, on their way upstairs, anyone had told them about Ricardo.

He put his arm around me briefly. "I wouldn't exactly call it restful. We went to the city museum to look at the Pinturicchios and the Peruginas, mostly to show David and Stacey. She's a nice child, but she seems to have had some kind of bad experience in the night."

"She's not the only one. Has anyone told you about Ricardo Natale?"

I could feel a jolt go through him. "What about him?" he asked.

"My God!" David Brownson said. He'd been talking to Marco, but had now turned towards Oliver. "Did you hear? The body of one of the servants' grandchildren has been found."

It was curious, I thought, to hear Maria described simply as "one of the servants." Yet to someone who was a stranger, that was essentially what she was.

"I was just telling him," I said.

"Where?" Oliver asked.

"Apparently in one of the subbasements, an exdungeon, or something," David said. He looked at me. "I hear you found him. Bad luck!"

"It was even worse luck on Ricardo," I said.

"How did you happen to find him?" Oliver asked.

Briefly I told him, starting off with Stacey's arrival in my room in the middle of the night. There was a short silence. Oliver was staring down at the drink in his hand. We were standing around in the sitting room before lunch was announced, and Baptisto had brought the drink tray, something that normally appeared only before dinner.

"Did the police say how he died?" Oliver asked finally.

"No. They took him away and no doubt will visit us again with the news."

"Poor kid," Oliver said. "And poor Maria."

"And poor Ludovico," I said. "Did you ever know him? Or did you come too late into Gianetta's life ever to see him."

"I did know him, actually," Oliver said. "He came to Oxford on some kind of a summer course many years ago, and we encountered one another there. One of those 'isn't it a small world' coincidences."

"Oxford?"

"You knew he was some kind of professor at Milan University, didn't you?"

"Yes. But I can't seem to keep that fact in my head. It keeps sliding out."

"Tut! Just because he's Maria's son?"

"No, of course not," I said crossly. And then I knew that that was indeed part of the reason. "I wonder what the boy was doing here, anyway."

"Visiting his grandmother, I suppose."

"But then why—?"

"If you're asking, then why should he be murdered when he is harmlessly visiting his grandmother, the answer is, I don't know."

132

The lunch bell sounded at that point, bringing back Gianetta's presence. She had acquired the bell on a trip to the Far East and had installed it as a fixture in the Monaldi household. Somehow its highly idiosyncratic chime made it seem incredible that Gianetta wasn't there to lead us in, and an outrage that her tall elegant body was lying somewhere on some coroner's slab. Abruptly, my appetite went.

Lunch was silent. It appeared heartless to discuss ordinary topics. Talking about Ricardo's death would have been tactless, with Maria, red-eyed but durable, passing some of the dishes. And I didn't think anyone wanted to talk about Gianetta's murder.

After lunch I went to my room downstairs. Two nights with little or no sleep were having their effect. I could hardly keep my eyes open. After closing the blind and taking off my blouse and skirt I lay down in my slip and was asleep before I knew it. When I woke up and looked at my watch I realized I had slept more than three hours. It was now almost five. I was lying there, drowsy and unwilling to get up, when I heard a car drive up and, in a moment or two, the slamming of a car door and the agent's voice. Ruggoni, I decided, almost asleep again, must have been visiting somewhere. Then I heard another male voice responding. Or perhaps, I thought, it was the police chief back again amongst us. That thought served better than an alarm clock. This time I sat up and realized that if I hoped to get any sleep during the coming night, I had better get on my feet and stay on them.

After another bath, I put on a linen dress and went upstairs to the sitting room. When I pushed open the door I saw Oliver standing in the middle of the room talking to a tall, light-haired man of about his own age. Both turned when I opened the door. For a second all three of us stood there, as though everything had stopped. I had the curious feeling that something was trying to push itself from my unconscious to the surface of my mind. But before it could succeed Oliver said, "Come in, Julia. You've met Ludovico Natale, haven't you? Ricardo's father."

It is a terrible shock when people don't look the way you've imagined them. Oliver's somewhat barbed insinuation that I couldn't associate a professorship with Maria's son was on target. Ludovico Natale did not look like a peasant. He had the kind of face or expression or something that bespoke intellectual pursuits, and his body seemed perfectly at home in the same sort of well-worn, well-tailored clothes that Oliver, Rupert and most of the other men I knew wore.

"How do you do," I said, hoping devoutly that my surprise did not show in my face.

"How do you do?" he replied, shaking hands. His voice was another shock. He spoke almost unaccented English, and it was not the English of Pimlico, either. It was certainly not Eton or Harrow, but something in between.

"This is Julia Winthrop," Oliver said. "Marcello's granddaughter." Not "the conte's granddaughter," I thought, but "Marcello's." And then reproached myself for being a classic snob.

"I'm so sorry about Ricardo," I said, ducking addressing the man by name or title.

He made a gesture with his hand. We stood there, saying nothing. Oliver strolled over to the window and stared out at the valley.

"Have you, did you talk to . . . to Maria?" I said.

"Yes. I went to her room. She is resting," Ludovico said.

Why was everything so difficult? I wondered. "Is there anything I can do?" I said.

"No. It is kind of you to ask. There is nothing." A slight accent showed up in that string of words. One would know that he was neither English nor American, nor, for that matter, from any English-speaking country, unless, of course he had emigrated . . . I dragged my mind back. Ludovico was staring down at the jigsaw puzzle that someone had completed. "I remember these now," he said. "The contessa used to do them all the time. A pleasant time-filler for a lady." He glanced up, the slate blue eyes curiously expressionless.

"You're not very much like your mother," I said. "I would never have known you as her son." It was a rather foolish remark, but in saying anything at all I felt as though I were pushing a boulder up a hill.

"No." He lifted from another table a piece from a puzzle that had been only a third completed and fitted it into its niche. "I never saw my English grandfather. He was dead before I ever got to England, but I'm told I resemble him quite closely."

To my vast relief the door was pushed open again and Rupert came in. "Have a good nap?" he asked me.

"Yes, thanks. I slept like one . . . poleaxed," I finished lamely. I had been about to say "dead" but the maladroitness of such an analogy struck me before I got the word out.

"Well, you've had some restless nights." As he strolled into the room, Rupert's eyes were on Ludovico. Certainly as looks went, Maria's son had it far over Rupert Carmichael, rivalling Oliver Landau's handsomeness.

"This is Ricardo's father, Rupert," I said quickly, before he could put his foot in it in some way. "Ludovico Natale. Ludovico, this is Rupert Carmichael. We were together when we . . . when we found your son."

"I'm extremely sorry," Rupert said formally, holding out his hand.

Ludovico took it. "*Grazie*," he said, for the first time speaking in Italian.

Oliver spoke up from the window. "We were waiting

for the police, who are supposed to be on their way here. But would you like to see where your son was found, Ludovico?"

"Yes, I would. Thank you."

A spasm of pain flickered across Ludovico's face. And in that moment, when some kind of facade cracked, he looked like Maria's son. It was not feature, and it certainly wasn't coloring or build. Perhaps, I thought, as they walked out, it was expression.

"Strange chap," Rupert said.

"Why do you say that?"

"I dunno. Didn't seem like somebody who'd just lost a son, and he certainly didn't seem like the maid's son come back to visit."

"That's a very snobbish statement, but before you jump all over me for saying so, honesty forces me to admit that I was thinking the same."

"Well it fairly leaps to the eye. There's something else there, too, that bothers me. But I can't think what." There was silence for a moment. Then Rupert said abruptly. "I've persuaded Andrea to take your room tonight. I want you to come into his room with me. I'll sleep in the other bed."

It was so like Rupert's high-handedness that I opened my mouth to protest automatically. Then it occurred to me that I really didn't want to spend another night in my own room alone. "Thanks," I finally said. "Do you think the world at large will be shocked?"

"Does it matter?"

"Well, Gianetta always observed *les convenances* even when she knew perfectly well that some couple she had firmly placed in separate rooms had been living together for years. She always said it was because of the servants."

"A useful excuse," Rupert said.

I thought that one over. "Yes, probably. On the order of 'one mustn't frighten the horses.'"

"I hope you don't object to sharing the room with me," Rupert said stiffly.

"No," I said, thinking of the eerie fear that came over me in the room that I hated so much. "It's better than being alone."

"Do be careful about a comment like that. It might go to my head. See you later." And he walked abruptly out of the room.

"Now what on earth—" I thought, and then mentally shrugged. I had to remember what I had managed to forget: that Rupert could be difficult, capricious, tyrannical, stingy and tiresome. The mere fact that he had been both kind and supportive in the past few days shouldn't count for too much, I told myself.

Ludovico was not present at dinner. Where he went no one seemed to know, but since having him eat at the castle, either in the dining room or in the kitchen, would have been extremely awkward, everyone was relieved. Marco spent most of the dinner time fulminating against the local police chief for not releasing Gianetta's body.

"It is outrageous," he said, pouring himself a fourth glass of wine. "What they are waiting for I do not know."

"Weren't they sending for someone else?" George Roper said. "I mean another pathologist?"

"He should certainly be finished by now." Marco swallowed the last of his wine. His cheeks were beginning to be flushed.

"These things sometimes take time," Dr. Langdon murmured.

Marco suddenly snapped out something in Italian.

"Steady on," Oliver said. "It's a strain for all of us."

"Dear Gianetta," Miss Truesdale said. "How much we all miss her!" A single tear brimmed over her right eye and coursed down her cheek.

Curious, I thought. I had forgotten about the Boston

sisters. They, and even George Roper, Gianetta's cousin, seemed to be on the periphery of whatever was happening, rather like walk-on characters in a play. And then George stepped stage center.

"By the way," he said, "I called Gianetta's London lawyer today. I couldn't be too sure as to whether he had heard of her death."

Marco, who had polished off another glass of wine and sent to have the carafe refilled, said, "I could wish, Cousin George, that you had mentioned this to me first. As head of the Monaldi family—"

"Yes, yes. I thought about it, but you weren't around, and I know Sir Humphrey rather well. And, of course, I represent her American family." There was a silence. "And money," George finished. The word dropped into the silence like an iron ball.

"You Americans—" Marco started.

"I think we should all remember that Gianetta was an American," Oliver said carefully. "She could have had dual citizenship, but she chose to keep her American citizenship."

Marco, quite red now, glared, but finally dropped his eyes.

"I believe Sir Humphrey is coming over tomorrow and bringing a copy of Gianetta's will," George said.

"Her will?" Marco said. "It is not in Perugia with the family lawyer there?"

"No. It is in London with Sir Humphrey Barrett."

"I will telephone our lawyer in Perugia," Marco said. "And ask him to come if there is to be a reading of the will."

"Oh I don't think there's going to be anything as formal as that." George helped himself to a pear from the fruit dish in the middle of the table. "Just a quiet consultation with members of the family."

It was almost impossible to tell, I thought, watching

George peel the pear with a neat, even gesture, whether he was getting any satisfaction out of putting Marco in his place or not. Or even whether he was even aware of doing it, or was simply making an announcement of general interest. Few people, I reflected, watching him strip that lumpy piece of fruit, would be able to make the skin come off in one, unbroken spiral. But when it fell, it was not only in one piece, it was of a consistent width.

"Bravo!" I said.

He looked up, his lawyer's eyes penetrating behind the steel-rimmed glasses. Then he smiled slightly. "Would you like a piece of pear?"

"Thanks." I held my hand out.

He quartered the pear and handed me a piece. Abruptly Marco got up and stalked out of the dining room.

One of the guests I had lost sight of was the fair-haired boy, Terry MacNaughton. Perhaps, I thought, this was because he was so inordinately quiet. Having gone to girls' schools my entire life and with no younger (or older) brothers, I felt singularly unqualified to make any judgment about Terry's demeanor. Yet surely, I thought, this withdrawn quality was something more than shyness. After dinner, drinking some of Maria's thick black coffee in the sitting room, I watched Terry seat himself behind one of the card tables in the farthest corner of the room and apply himself to the unfinished jigsaw puzzle. But he was certainly not pursuing it with enthusiasm. Head cupped in hands, he would spend long minutes staring at the table. After a while, with a second cup of coffee, I strolled over and pulled up a straight chair. He lifted his head abruptly.

"May I?" I asked. "I've never done this one, have you?"

"No—no, I don't think so."

It was one of those puzzles half of which seemed to be sky, which meant an enormous number of blue pieces, indistinguishable from one another except by shape. All except the complete puzzle addict could go mad.

"Do you do a lot of these at home?" I asked, picking up a blue piece and comparing its concave curlicues to the convex curlicues of the completed part.

"No."

"Where is home, by the way?"

"London."

"Have you been here before?"

He shook his head. "No."

After another minute I said, "When did you say you were leaving?"

"Day after tomorrow. Only two more nights." The last sentence was blurted out.

I finally found a piece that looked as though it might fit. "You're all by yourself up there in the battlements," I said, "I think I'd find it sort of creepy."

I saw his face jerk up. "Have you ever been up there at night?"

"No. It's usually reserved for the males of all ages."

"Oh."

"The girls are put in the dormitory beyond the music room. Stacey didn't like it at all. She came to my room in the middle of the night and demanded to be let upstairs."

I had all his attention by this time. "But you didn't come up."

"Oh yes we did. We came up the winding stair that leads out of the dining room."

"You didn't come into the sitting room?"

"No, come to think of it, there was no need. We went to the little room that's on the other side of that wall, an ex-flower-room, really." I looked at his rather set face "Why?"

He touched one or two of the pieces. "I was sleeping on the sofa there. I came down."

"Was there something—did something bother you?"

"There was a perfectly horrible row—a banging that went on and on."

There was so much tension in his voice, I said carefully, "I take it it couldn't have been just a window."

"No it was *not!*"

"Well I think it's very brave of you to admit it. I wouldn't want to spend the night up there. Stacey heard steps in the girls' dormitory and came roaring out of there in the middle of the night, and I haven't slept well. You're not the only one."

The boy flushed then. I smiled at him, and he gave a relieved smile back.

"If I were you," I said, "I'd wait until the others have gone to bed, and bring your blanket and pillow down again."

"I will."

Andrea lounged over towards me at around ten. "I gather that we're to exchange beds. But we're to change in our own rooms."

"Yes." I said. I found myself wanting to explain to Andrea that this was an arrangement only for my peace of mind. I also wanted him very much not to broadcast it. "Andrea, this may sound strange, but I really don't want to have to go into explanations."

"Your secret is quite safe with me," he said, grinned and left the room.

After a while I went downstairs, got into my night clothes, took my robe and book and went and knocked on the door across the billiard room. It was opened by Andrea, also in his robe.

"Your timing is perfect. I've just had a bath. Sweet dreams." He bowed to me with mock courtliness and walked across the wide billiard room, his slippers slapping against the stone floor.

Leaving my robe on, I got into bed and adjusted the

141

rather weak reading light. When my watch said eleven, I turned it off, took off my robe, got back into bed and snuggled down. But I was still awake when Rupert knocked quietly on the door panel. At least I assumed it was Rupert. "Who is it?" I whispered.

"Rupert."

"All right. I'm in bed, you can come in."

I turned on the light switch beside the bed as he came in. "I wasn't asleep."

Rupert grunted, picked up his pajamas from his bed and disappeared into the bathroom. After about twenty minutes of splashing around he came out, turned out the light and got into bed.

"Don't you want to read some?" I asked.

"No. Not tonight."

"Because it won't bother me if you do."

"It would bother me, if it were vice-versa, so I'm sure it would bother you. Besides, I have a portable gadget with me that I can fit a book into and that lights it up if I want to."

I heard him pulling the covers up.

"Do you snore?" I asked.

"I don't know. Since I'm asleep I can't know myself, and either I don't, or my companions have been too polite to tell me."

Funny, I thought, turning on my side. I somehow didn't associate Rupert with companions. But why not? So far from his being asexual, there was a virile quality about him, although I would have been surprised if someone had told me that womanizing was one of his pursuits.

"Rupert, do you have a girlfriend?"

"Yes. Of course. Did you think I didn't?"

"I somehow figured you as some kind of grumpy perennial bachelor."

"Those went out of style a long time ago."

"What's she like?"

"Who?"

"Your girlfriend, of course."

"Extremely pretty and extremely bright. She also has a nice disposition."

"Unlike some people you could name, right?"

"Quite right."

"Well she'd need it to live with you. How will she feel when you tell her you and I spent the night in the same room?"

"I won't know until I tell her, will I?"

For some reason I was rather annoyed. "You've kept awfully quiet about her. Has she been in the gallery?"

"No. I never mix business and pleasure."

"That's exactly the kind of stuffy comment you would make." Silence. Then, after a minute, I said, "Rupert—"

"Are you going to sleep and let me sleep?"

"Sorry."

Despite my nap I was still tired, and went to sleep almost immediately. Then I started to dream, a dream filled with long corridors and winding stairs. I seemed to be looking for something that was always just out of reach. After a while my search became more urgent. I kept opening doors, feeling each time that whatever it was I had to find would be on the other side, but every time I found another hall with a turning at the end, another corridor ending in a staircase, another door that I stood in front of, afraid to open, afraid not to open. By this time it was a fully blown nightmare. I knew that I was dreaming, but I felt trapped in the dream, worried lest I couldn't get out. Then finally I came through one more door and found myself in the rose garden. This time Gianetta was picking roses and putting them in a flat basket.

"Can't I do that?" I asked in the dream. "You must be on time."

"I'll be on time," Gianetta was saying. And then added

with that slight tilt of the nose that was so characteristic of her. "One usually is for one's own death."

"Don't say it," I said in the dream.

"Why not? It's already happened. That's not important. What is important is that you find the letter."

"What letter?"

"That letter from Venice."

And then, as had happened in an earlier dream, I saw her start to fall, the blood springing from her head, and out of the corner of my eye—I started to scream. As the blood came in a flood I screamed again and again. Then something took hold of me threateningly and was shaking me.

"Be quiet!" Rupert said, shaking me. "Do you want to wake the whole castle? Wake up, Julia. Now come on! Wake up. It's only a dream."

He was sitting on the side of the bed, his robe flung around him, his hair on end, shaking me for all he was worth. The light was on, a cool air was coming from the long window. The room looked solid and real and of this world.

I let out my breath. "Oh God! Rupert," I said. "I was having the most horrible dream."

"Obviously. What about?"

I told him.

"Venice," he said. "Are you sure you dreamed that Gianetta said Venice?"

"Yes. Positive. Why?"

"Because there was a letter from Venice. That was why Gianetta invited us. And I have a feeling that what was in that letter had something to do with her being killed."

FIVE

I stared at him, then said slowly, "There was a phone call from Venice, the first day I was here."

"Why on earth didn't you say so?"

"Well how was I to know it was important? I didn't even take the call. Marco did. Some old and rather deaf woman. But there was something about a letter she wrote . . . ." My voice trailed off. "To tell you the truth, I forgot about it immediately."

Rupert made an exasperated sound.

"Well I'm sorry," I said, indignantly. "As I just said, I had no reason to think it was important. But," I added, after a minute. "I wish I could remember everything Marco said. In the dream—" For a moment the dream was back, with its urgency and the flowing blood and quality of terror. I sat with my arms wrapped around me, shivering a little. The dream was terribly vivid.

"Did Gianetta—in your dream—say what was in the letter?"

It was (in the dream) just before the blow fell, cleaving her head so that the blood came from it in a living stream. That was when she said something. But I couldn't hear it. "I can't remember," I said, feeling miserable. "I can't quite get it. I can see her talking and almost hear her, but not quite."

"Pity," Rupert said. "If we just had a hypnotist handy, he—or she—could put you under and you'd remember it in a flash."

"Is that true, or just one of your strange beliefs?"

"It's one of my strange beliefs, but it also happens to be true." He got up and walked around the room. "Have you ever had dreams like this before?"

"No. Not really. I've always had queer dreams when I've been here. So have other people. But mostly just sur-realistic-sounding nonsense. Not this kind of thing, not the kind of instruction that practically says, go to such and such a location and start to dig. You'll find a buried treasure. Do you?"

"Do I what?" His tall, narrow body, taut as a bent spring, was moving around and around in a circle covering the middle of the floor, the ends of the beds and back.

"Do you believe such dreams are trying to tell me something?"

"I haven't the faintest idea. But I don't rule out the possibility."

"I thought you were a rationalist."

"If you mean that I cling to the belief that intelligent discourse can be brought to an argument or dilemma and produce a result, then yes, I'm a rationalist. But that doesn't mean I'm such a Cartesian that I countenance only that which I can see, touch, hear, smell and taste. I do believe there are more things in heaven and earth, etc. However, since you don't seem to be able to interpret your own dreams, then back to the practical. Do you have any idea who has Gianetta's correspondence? What happened to it after her death?"

"None. I suppose the person to ask would be Marco."

"Yes-s-s," Rupert said dubiously. "Something tells me that young man is not going to be helpful."

"Are you just being your usual cantankerous, suspicious self, or do you have some reason for saying that?"

146

Rupert put his hand in his pockets, took out his spectacles, put them on and looked at me. "I'm being my usual cantankerous and suspicious self."

"Oh."

Rupert walked around the floor a while longer. I glanced at my watch, which was now ticking away merrily on the night table. One-thirty. It wasn't even yet the middle of the night. Gloom descended on me. It seemed days, rather than simply hours, till morning. I drew my knees up to my chin, and then rested my forehead on them. Why didn't I just leave tomorrow and go back to London?

Where the idea came from I didn't know. But to leave now seemed infinitely desirable, a consummation devoutly to be wished. I would throw my clothes into my bag, walk down the short cut, on the dirt road to the main road and thence into Castiglione where I would go to the station. I would take the first train that left for Terni, at which junction I would then await a train to Rome. With any luck I might make the journey in time to take an evening flight to London, if there were any. . . . Or, I might order a taxi and go over the mountains to Terontola, and take the first train to Florence, from where I would take another taxi and go to the airport outside Pisa, whence, with any luck I would be able to take an evening flight to London—

"Have you gone to sleep?" Rupert's voice cut sharply into my fantasies.

"No. I was just thinking how wonderful it would be to leave tomorrow and go back home to London."

"You can't leave before the funeral. Aside from the fact that it would look callous, I doubt if that policeman would let you."

"He wouldn't mind. I was in London when Gianetta was killed and he knows it. So was Oliver. So he has no reason to hold me."

"You needn't sound so smug about it, and it still would look bad to go."

There was another silence, while Rupert continued walking around. After a minute it seemed to me that something that I had heard, without being conscious of the fact that I was hearing it, had stopped. "Rupert, did you hear that?"

He stopped. "What?"

"There was a noise, and it stopped. The funny part is, I wasn't aware of it until it stopped."

"What kind of a noise?"

I thought for a moment. "A kind of rhythmic thud. But far away."

Rupert shrugged. "Probably some machine or electrical appliance that goes on and off."

"Such as?"

We stared at one another. Finally Rupert said, "A refrigerator."

"No refrigerator that I've ever known thuds like that. They whirr, tick tick, throb and wheeze, particularly if they're old. But they don't have that almost drumbeat cadence."

"But didn't you say it had stopped?"

"Yes."

"Well we can hardly go looking for a noise that has stopped."

"True." But my mind slid to Terry and Stacey, two highly imaginative and easily frightened youngsters.

"Perhaps if you go back to sleep again you'll dream whatever Gianetta was telling you was in the letter."

"Thank you. But I'd just as soon not have another nightmare."

"Well, suit yourself. We might as well go back to bed."

Going over to the bed, he turned off the light, then after, I assumed, taking off his robe, got into bed. The bed squeaked as he wiggled down. I was half expecting him to say something to sign off, like "Good night," "Sweet dreams," "Rest well," "Arrivederci," or something else civil. But nothing but dead silence emanated from the bed a few feet away.

After a while I said, "Rupert, is there some reason you're so difficult and grumpy most of the time?"

There was a long silence and I assumed he had ignored the question as unworthy. But he surprised me by saying, "Yes."

"What is it?"

"It's none of your business. That's what it is."

"Sucks to you," I muttered under my breath, utilizing a schoolgirl expression I had learned in England as part of our cultural exchange.

I fell asleep wondering what was responsible for Rupert's chronic sweetness and light. Unrequited love? But he said he had a girl. A wasting disease? No such luck, I thought savagely. It struck me that for someone with whom he had worked closely for several years, I knew extraordinarily little about him. "And where were you?" I whispered into the sheet, "at the time the murder/murders were committed?"

It was only a joke to amuse myself, based on the countless mystery novels I'd read and old-fashioned whodunit movies I sat up late at night in the States and watched. But suddenly I flopped over on my back and stared at the black ceiling. Where indeed had Rupert been? Had he said? Had anyone asked him? I couldn't remember. He certainly arrived after Gianetta's death, and after, I assumed, Ricardo's, although the police chief had not given us much information about that. But he could have been anywhere. No, I suddenly remembered, he was in Geneva when I called . . . but he was the one who called after I had telephoned over half of Europe leaving messages. He said he was in Geneva. But had there been any confirmation from an operator, either Swiss or English? I couldn't be sure, but I didn't think so. I seemed to remember that it was one of those direct calls that had gone straight through.

I started to sit up, but stopped myself. I didn't know whether Rupert was asleep or not, but I didn't want to attract his attention.

It was at that point, lying there, with the light from a high moon trickling in the window, that I gave thought, for the first time, to who might have committed these crimes. Why had it taken me so long? What had I been thinking about instead? The answer to that was I had been thinking of all kinds of things, mainly of the ghostly variety, preoccupations brought on by being by myself in the room across the way that had always filled me with discomfort, by Stacey's experience in the girls' dormitory, by finding Ricardo's body, and finally by my own dreams and hallucinations. So that it was only now, on the third night after the murders, that I was coming to grips with the extremely material question of who committed them. The more I considered the matter, the more I realized the suspects included almost everyone except the party who had gone up Monte Accouto and were seen by German climbers, and Oliver and me. The rest, even if they were not staying at Civitella, could certainly have been in the vicinity, could have executed the crime and then left and gone anywhere, to any one of a dozen places, including, say, Perugia, Florence—or Geneva, which was probably no more than an hour's flight from most Italian airports. If, of course, Rupert was telling the truth about his location. Which he may not have been.

And all this time, when I had not bothered to think about who the culprit might be, and after such a terrible death, to whom had I, however unconsciously, allotted the role of murderer?

The moment I put it that way to myself the answer became clear: some terrorist. Gianetta was known in this

150

whole section of Italy to be an extremely rich woman, with income deriving from vast American holdings. Wouldn't she be a natural target for an enraged Marxist revolutionary? Even with the police chief here, questioning people as to where they had been, I was able to dismiss his probing because I was sure he would come up with the same answer. Friends in London, year after year, had implored Gianetta not to travel to a country known for the savagery of its underground and the kidnapping, torture and death of its prominent citizens. Her reply had always been the same: "I have lived a rich and wonderful life. If I am to die that way, then so be it. I am an old woman and it doesn't matter. I would not consider spending the summer anywhere but Civitella."

But supposing it was not a revolutionary. Supposing it was—

I glanced over to the next bed, to the black-humped shape I could barely make out. Was I sharing quarters with a murderer? And what would be his motive? Find that mysteriously missing letter and I might find out. In the meantime, what about the possibility of a terrorist? The person who could answer that would be David Brownson. I would query him about that in the morning. As I turned over it occurred to me that with that thought my heart had started beating a little more rapidly.

The police chief arrived while we were still having breakfast and made the announcement that whoever had killed Gianetta had almost certainly killed Ricardo. The wound appeared to be from the same instrument, and after going down the passage along which poor Ricardo had lurched, they had discovered that the other end led through a door into the rose garden.

"Which must mean that the dungeon is pretty far down," I said to David Brownson, sitting opposite. "The rose garden is well below the castle."

"Mediaeval dungeons were frequently far down, nicely out of sight, sound or smell, so that those unlucky enough to displease the castle owner could be disposed of without disturbing the guests." He looked up at me. "I'd rather like to talk to you." He spoke with more hesitancy than I had ever known this self-assured journalist to show before.

Since I wanted to talk to him also, this suited me very well. "Why don't we go for a walk after breakfast. It would be a relief to get away."

We walked up the cypress grove, then down the hill and up the opposite one to the remains of the castle ruin at the top.

"Tell me about the terrorists," I said, after a few minutes of small talk. We had scuffled down from the top of the cypress grove and were starting the long, slow climb up the opposite hill.

"It's a large subject. What do you want to know about them?"

The trouble with David—rather the trouble with me— was that I kept forgetting how extremely attractive he was. It seemed such an obvious thing to keep losing sight of, but even when I was angriest at him, even when I felt reasonably sure I no longer loved him, I would see him again at a party and his potent blend of good looks, intelligence and success, stronger than any love potion, would strike me afresh. I had been by no means the first woman to have made a fool of herself over him. Yet for four years I would have sworn by all I held sacred that he loved me in return.

"Well," I said, concentrating on the subject, "what's the connection between terrorism and art forgery?"

"More art theft than art forgery. Revolutionaries need money; it's a chronic problem with them. So they rob banks and do the usual criminal things to get it. But weapons, explosives, transportation, hideouts, forged papers and so on, are, like everything else, costing more and more. So they've had to devise new ways to get funds. Let's say a rich Arab or rich South American would like to own a Canaletto, a Raphael, a Botticelli or a lesser painter and is willing to pay for it, no questions asked. Well then, for a huge sum, someone might be willing to steal it."

"But wouldn't that rather defeat its own purpose? If anything that important is missing, what collector would be able to show it, however rich? Surely to people like that to be known to own such a master is most of the kick."

"Not entirely. It's an incredible hedge against inflation. Thirty years from now wouldn't any museum be overjoyed to pay enormously to get it back again, no questions asked, if that's the only way they could get it back? For another, it could slowly become known that such and such a multi-millionaire had an art collection shown only privately to a few people, in which it was rumored there were some extraordinarily valuable paintings. These people don't live in Western Europe or North America. Who's going to turn up asking awkward questions? And if somebody does, all said millionaire has to do is blandly to deny it. He still gets the kick, the kudos."

"I suppose so."

We climbed up in the hot sunlight, passing a silent and deserted farmhouse and an orchard full of vines. The sun beat down on the roadway. A motorcycle passed us and honked chirpily. On the pastures covering the hill opposite the wheat was ripe and golden. But my mind, grappling with the castle deaths and the reason for them, barely noticed the familiar, tawny countryside. "But does forgery come into it at all, or did I imagine it?"

"Only in the sense that our terrorists, if they think they can pass a fake off as a true master to some foreign tycoon, wouldn't hesitate to do so."

"But wouldn't the deceived tycoon be furious enough to have his henchmen take revenge of some kind?"

"If he finds out. But if his collection is private, then

he may not. Also, our terrorists are not your usual thieves, slipping in and out of society where they can be got at. First, you'd have to find them. It's an occupational risk, of course, but they wouldn't be past arranging a little faked authenticating if they could get away with it." We walked on for a few minutes. "Why are you so interested? It would be flattering to think that you had taken a sudden new interest in my career, but somehow I don't feel it's that. So, what is it?"

"Did it ever occur to you," I said slowly, "that Gianetta could have been killed by a terrorist?"

"Of course. Given who she was, what she represented and the state of this country as it is today, such an answer would fairly leap to the imagination."

"But would they kill her that way?"

"There's no set way of—as they would call it—executing an enemy of the people, which includes everybody but themselves, and which would certainly to them describe anyone as rich as Gianetta. The only aspect that makes me doubt whether they are responsible, is that no one has telephoned some newspaper or radio station claiming to have done the deed. Usually that's the whole point of the thing, a show of muscle."

"But why Gianetta, who's done so much for the area around here: improving the drainage, restoring the farmhouses, putting in running water?"

"All the more reason. That would make her the worst enemy of all, one who enslaved the people by doling out bribes in the form of largesse."

"But when she helped the people—"

"Julia, don't be stupid." David spoke sharply. Like Rupert he did not suffer fools gladly. "They're not interested in people. That's just rhetoric. They're like all ideologists; they're interested in their concept of the perfect society, and are perfectly willing to keep on killing until it is achieved."

I shivered. "Yes. You're right." We walked on a few steps. Then I said, "Do you think this—the murders of Gianetta and Ricardo—could be political acts? Only this morning and for the first time it occurred to me that they might not be. And somehow, awful as the political thing is, the idea that the murderer might be one of us is far worse."

"Yes, I think it probably is a personal, not political, act, and yes, in this case it's far worse."

"I wouldn't know where to begin to think."

"Well, *cui bono?* To whose good does it redound?"

"We'll probably learn that when the English lawyer arrives this afternoon. By the way, my cousin Marco was not happy to hear that from George, was he?"

"No, what's with Marco? I gather he spent his student years eager to overthrow the establishment. Now that he *is* the establishment, he's as stuffy as an Edwardian banker."

"Well, there's always been a bit of friction between the American and the Italian branches of the family. The Italians look on the Americans as rich but crass, and the Americans look on the Italians as aristocratic but useless. I think it burns Marco, as it has burned other members of the family here, that Gianetta had all that MacNair money, and that they had no control over it whatsoever. The fact that Gianetta left her will with her English solicitor is probably the final salt in the wound." We walked on a bit. "Do you have any ideas?" I blurted out. "I mean, about who could be the culprit?"

"Absolutely none, Julia. You'd be more liable to than I. At least you know the various *dramatis personae*. I don't."

What David said made all too good sense. But it was not what I wanted to hear.

"What I'd like to talk about," David said, "is us. That's what I came to Civitella to do. It was because I wanted to do that that I was able to talk Gianetta into inviting me."

The first few words of that sentence were not out of his mouth before every muscle in my body had stiffened. My

155

defensive reaction was immediate.

"There's nothing to talk about, David. We had an affair that lasted for four years. At the end of that time you walked out on me. End of story."

"I never explained to you—I couldn't at the time—why I did walk out."

"At this point it's hardly necessary."

"I think it is. Phyllis had made a final plea that we give the relationship one more chance. I felt I couldn't refuse."

"Why couldn't you have said this to me at the time?"

"Because I didn't trust myself. If . . . if I had confronted you with that, I . . . I felt . . . I was afraid that I would never have the courage to go through with it. . . ."

The trouble with walking with David, with being with him, I thought, was that it brought back so vividly all the other times we had been together, the evenings when he would come home late from some assignment, tell me about it while I cooked something for him in my kitchen, and then after we'd made love, talk about it in bed. . . . For a moment my mind shut him out as I wondered if there was something profoundly wrong with me. I missed our love-making. What I missed even more were the long talks in bed, relaxed, laughing, at one in a sense that never existed at any other time. . . .

"I thought of a variety of possible responses," I suddenly came to to hear David saying, "but dead silence was not one of them. I must say, it doesn't do much for my ego."

"I don't think your ego needs tender loving care, David. It was always extremely healthy."

"Is this just a nice way of telling me I'm a conceited oaf?"

"What do you want of me, David?"

"I want us to get married."

"One of the great facts of our life together, whether

good or bad, I am now not sure, although once I would have said it was all bad, is that you are already married."

"Phyllis is getting a divorce."

"I see. Phyllis is getting it. You mean she is walking out on you."

Pause. "That's the way we . . . it was decided the thing would be done."

"Very gentlemanly."

He stopped and turned in the roadway. "Come on, Julia. You have a right to punish me. I deserve it. But the sarcasm is above and beyond. You know how these things are done."

"I know how it was done in my case. No courtly suggestion that I be allowed to walk out on you, so that I wouldn't lose countenance before the world at large. Your departure was very public. We knew a lot of people together, David, between your world, the world of books and journalism, and mine, the world of art. And we had been together in those worlds for a long time. When you decamped you hurt me a lot, but you did something else: you made a fool of me. That's a lot harder to swallow."

"So it was your pride that was wounded."

"Of course. Are you trying to tell me that that shouldn't matter? If that's the case, how come you're being so careful about Phyllis's?"

"Because, if you must know, that was her price for the divorce. If I wanted you I had to let it seem that she was leaving me."

By this time we had both stopped, and were facing each other on the last incline of the road. David put his hands out and grasped my arms. "I want us to be married as soon as the divorce comes through. And then we can live properly together and I can make up to you for all the wrong you've had to endure."

I had envisioned, fantasied this scene, or one like it,

157

so often. In half my fantasies I would melt into his arms. In the other half I would tell him what he could do with his abject apology, his finally expressed yearning to have me for his own. What I had not envisioned was my sense of intense irritation, even boredom, and a very strong feeling that there was something left out.

"David," I said. "There's an English saying: "Don't boil your cabbages twice. I think our cabbage has been boiled once and that's it."

"I realize your desire to punish me—."

"I don't want to punish you," I said, wondering if it was true. "I just think there's nothing to fire up again." How could I think that so strongly at the same time as I was noting the handsome charm of his high cheekbones and the hollows under them, and remembering how his mouth felt the first time he kissed me. . . . "I think it's time we turned back," I said.

I was either more convincing than I had thought, or David was a fine tactician: he abandoned the discussion of ourselves completely. Even his voice was different as he talked of the paintings he and Stacey had seen with Oliver in Perugia. "I must say, Landau may have been the contessa's tame curator, but he knows a hell of a lot."

"Yes, he does." My old loyalty surged up, and I discovered to my shock how much I resented David's rather arrogant journalistic commentator's manner applied to the older man.

"And I don't think it's fair to call him Gianetta's tame curator. He did a wonderful thing for her, it's true. Gave her an outlet for her energy and her money. But he also did a lot for the area. He collected some fine pieces of art for that little Monaldi museum. Other museums had been looking for a few of them for some time, but had failed to come up with them—like the Madonna, for example. Everyone knew Paolo had done one and left it in the church at Monte Santa Maria Tiberini. But it had disappeared a hundred or more years ago and that was that, until Oliver dug around and found it."

"I know. By the way, why didn't we see it when we were in the museum in Castiglione?"

"Because it's in the chapel. No—you didn't go in there when Gianetta was lying in state. But it's there all right. I saw it."

"But—isn't that insanity? I can see him putting some of the other works he's got in the museum there—a painting from the school of Perugina or school of Piero della Francesca and so on. But the Madonna is the pick of the museum. And anyone could walk into the chapel here and take it."

"When I pointed that out to him," I said, as we turned towards the gate of the castle, "he said that to put in alarms and locks and sirens would announce to everyone in the countryside that a valuable item was there and the safest way was to pretend it was of no great value."

"But why did the contessa want it there? From everything I've been able to gather, she wasn't particularly religious."

"According to Oliver, she took a sudden notion to have it in the chapel. Something to do with her age and approaching mortality."

"Even though she hardly ever went in?"

"I know it doesn't make much sense, but she didn't go into the Monaldi Museum more than once a year, and then she had to be dragged in by Oliver. I think she liked the *idea* of the museum more than she liked the museum, if you follow me."

"Yes. I suppose I do. The chase itself rather than the quarry. Most of us have a touch of that."

And you certainly do, I thought. How he had pursued me, and how much his attitude had altered when once I was won! I wrenched my mind away from that. At the very least, it could make me angry, and something told me that

I needed to keep my cool. "By the way," I said, to change the subject, "did Stacey tell you about her midnight adventure?"

"Yes. I gather she sleeps now in the tiny little room. You were very kind to her and I thank you for it. But I was right about one thing. She does read too many gothic fantasies, ghost stories, stories of psychic phenomena and all. I wish I could get her to stop. Forbidding her seems to do no good at all. She simply says what bothered her downstairs is nothing like what she reads."

"I'm bound to tell you that I too am not entirely happy when sleeping alone on the lower floor. And it was down the steps leading from the girls' dormitory to the basement that Ricardo's body was found."

"You're not going to tell me that you suspect evil spirits hovering round that, are you?"

"I don't know that I'm going to tell you anything. But I always have bad dreams when I'm in the castle, and I've never been able to sleep well in that little room below yours. So my sympathy is very much with Stacey."

"I'm sorry, but I'm quite sure the whole thing is sheer nerves, on your part as well as my daughter's."

"You're entitled to your opinion."

David sounded cross, which pleased me. His poise was usually uncrackable. Then I lost some of my own as he reached out and took my hand. "Thank you. I'm glad you will defend to the death my right to say something with which you totally disagree."

I used the excuse of picking a grass blade and blowing it between my thumbs to remove my hand from his. He really had a lot of *chutzpah*, I thought.

After lunch we were told that the police were releasing Gianetta's body, and that we could have the funeral mass whenever we wanted to. Marco was the one whom they called, and he said that he had set the time of the mass for one o'clock the following afternoon. "And, of course, Ricardo's body will be there, too. The mass will be said for them both. Gianetta would have wished it."

That evening, before dinner, I told Oliver about my dreams containing the reference to a letter in Venice. "Do you know anything about such a letter, Oliver?" I asked. It occurred to me that if anyone knew, he would.

"No. I don't. Have you mentioned it to Marco?"

"No. I keep having the feeling that if I did he would think it further evidence of an American plot."

"Umm. Have you mentioned it to anyone?"

"Only Rupert."

Oliver grinned. "Did he have any helpful suggestions?"

"He said we should get a hypnotist who would put me in a trance and draw from me an account of what Gianetta was saying in my dream."

"As practical and sensible as most things Carmichael has to say."

"Now now," I said. "I don't know why you and Rupert are like two dogs meeting each other. You both immediately begin to growl."

"Chemistry, I expect. Did he say anything else about the letter?"

"Only that there was one, quite apart from my lurid dreams. Apparently Gianetta had told both him and Andrea when she saw them in Florence. It came from Venice, which seems to have some special significance, a fact I wish I'd known. I might have done more to talk to whomever it was from Venice who called."

"What call?"

"Some old woman who seemed to be deaf called here the evening we arrived. Marco answered the phone and couldn't make head or tail of what she was saying except that it did have something to do with a letter."

"Did he say who called?"

"Apparently he never got that bit of information. Not only was the old woman deaf, he said she talked with a thick accent. He did say one of her names. . . ." I hunted through my mind, "but I can't remember what it was."

"Useful. If it occurs to you, you might let me know."

"All right."

"And if you suddenly remember what the letter said in your dream, or you have another dream about it, you might let me know that too."

"Ay ay, sir."

"Considering your rage at Carmichael, and the shabby way he behaved when you asked for time off to come to Italy, you seem to have got awfully friendly with him lately."

I was acutely aware of this, and unable to give myself a reason for having, apparently and temporarily, buried the hatchet. I clung to the idea of its impermanence. "It's only temporary, Oliver. Somehow here, with Gianetta dead, it seems . . . well, irrelevant . . . or do I mean irreverent . . . to keep our own particular war heated up."

Oliver's dark eyes probed into mine. "Did Gianetta like him?"

I was a little surprised at his question. Oliver had been with Gianetta more in one year than I had been with her in my whole life. "Good heavens, Oliver! You know much more about the way she felt than I ever did."

"Gianetta could be cagey. She didn't always say exactly what she thought."

"Well I certainly found that to be true. But I'm surprised you did. If anybody was the fair-haired boy you were."

"I'm not anybody's boy, Julia. I thought you, at least, knew that."

There was a short silence. Oliver and I were standing by the big open window of the sitting room. The drinks tray was on the table. Everyone else was around, chattering, pouring themselves drinks, waiting for the bell to sound.

162

It was a weird moment for some kind of declaration to be made. Yet I felt that that was exactly what Oliver was doing: making a declaration. But what kind? To what purpose? I wasn't quite sure.

"I'm sorry, Oliver. I didn't mean to imply . . . ." Imply what? I thought, scurrying around in my mind. "Anything . . . demeaning or belittling," I finally finished. It was a polite evasion. Oliver might be a fine art critic, in fact I knew him to be one of the best, and a more than adequate curator. But when Gianetta, in some of her more imperious moods said, "Jump!" he unquestionably jumped. Everybody knew this to be true. It was the price of her patronage and of the museum. Why was he trying to deny it now? I glanced up and saw a look of such intensity in his eyes that I felt a shock wave quivering through me. And then it was gone, covered by a film of amused charm.

"Sorry," he said lightly, straightening up. "I must be more upset than I thought." He moved towards the drinks tray.

"By the way," I heard Rupert say to George Roper who, drink in hand, was stolidly reading through a copy of that day's *Herald Tribune*, "where's the English lawyer, Sir Humphrey Barrett? I thought he was to be here this afternoon."

"So he was. But his plane was badly delayed, so he decided to spend the night in Rome. He'll be here tomorrow morning."

Fresh drink in hand, Oliver strolled back. "I meant to ask you, how do you find your room? You used to hate it."

"I still do," I said. I was profoundly grateful to see that neither Rupert nor Andrea had gossiped about the change of beds between Andrea and me. Considering that it was merely for my safety, to allow me to sleep, and in view of the corpse that had been found in the dungeon, there was no particular reason I should be so secretive about it; particularly in the light of the liberated sexual views of the contemporary world. With the exception of the sisters from Boston and perhaps George Roper, there was hardly anyone in the room who did not consider him- or herself liberated. Yet I most ardently did not want people to know that I was sharing a bedroom with Rupert. I especially didn't want Oliver to know. Why I felt this so strongly I was not sure, or perhaps, a nasty watchdog in the back of my mind said, I did not wish to know.

"How did you sleep last night?" Oliver asked abruptly.

Suddenly I remembered the dream, so vivid that Oliver himself seemed to fade.

"Fine," I said after a pause, "apart from the nightmare."

"It's possible Carmichael was, for once, right about getting a hypnotist or some such to find out what Gianetta was trying to tell you. You did say she was trying to tell you something, didn't you?"

Did I? I wondered. "Yes. But, since there isn't a hypnotist, the matter is academic."

"Perhaps Marco knows a hypnotist," Oliver said.

I suddenly realized he was quite serious. "Come on, Oliver, Rupert was just making one of his feeble jokes."

"By the way, when did you tell him? He left long before you came down for breakfast and only just got back."

My God, I thought. Does Oliver know that Rupert and I shared a room last night? And if he does, what does it matter? I couldn't answer my own question. I had no idea why it mattered. But I was quite sure it did. Oliver himself settled my dilemma.

"Rumor hath it that you and Rupert decided that while the cat was away, dead, the mice would play."

The degree of bitterness in his tone was astounding. It had the salutary effect of arousing my easily triggered anger.

"Why should you care?"

"In view of Gianetta's sense of propriety—"

"Come off it, Oliver. It's true that Gianetta was enough of a basic Edwardian to believe that a certain decorum before the servants was desirable. But she was well aware of the sexual liberation running rampant around her and did not concern herself too much about it. And what's more, if she did think I was doing something I shouldn't, she'd tell me double-quick, not hint around the way you've just done. Yes, I spent the night in the double room with Rupert in the other bed instead of Andrea. If you'd been waked up in the middle of the night by hysterical girls and found dead bodies you might understand better. It's not passion, it's for safety so that I can get a decent night's sleep. You make me tired. And there's the dinner bell, thank God." And I walked away from him, ignoring the "Julia" he called after me.

I managed to seat myself on the same side of the dinner table but as far from Oliver as possible, so that he could neither talk to me, nor look at me from across the table, and bent my wits as to how I could avoid him after dinner. I was more upset than I had realized I would be. The thought that my degree of upset might be in proportion to my degree of . . . affection (I carefully avoided any stronger word) sifted across my mind. But I firmly pushed it away.

By dint of sitting between people or in a card or scrabble game after dinner, I managed to keep Oliver at bay. He made a determined effort cut me away from the others, rather in the manner of a cowboy separating a steer. But he didn't succeed, although once, when I was finished with one game and hadn't started on the other, he stepped up and said "Julia—I would like to talk . . ." But he was interrupted by no other than Rupert himself who came breathing over my shoulder and looked at the gin rummy hand I had just laid down. "If you won with that," he said acidly, "then your opponent must have been retarded."

"Dear Rupert," I said, "always the one to give a girl a boost."

He sat down opposite me, swept up the cards and started dealing them out to the two of us. "How about a large wager," he said. "Something like a pound a point."

"No wonder you're always crying poor, if you gamble like that. I suppose all the wages you should have spent on your underpaid employees have gone to the horses or the football pools."

He had put his spectacles on and was staring through them as he regrouped his hand. "A man has to have an outlet," he said.

"Not so ferociously at others' expense, though," Oliver said from behind me.

Rupert raised his eyes to the tall man standing behind me. In that light his eyes were very blue and very piercing. "Not all of us can develop rich patrons," he said deliberately.

It was as insulting as, I was quite sure, it was meant to be. And it had the effect of driving me back in Oliver's corner, which I was reasonably sure was not what Rupert had in mind. I put down my cards.

"That's a thoroughly rotten comment, Rupert."

"Many truths sound like that."

I got up, pushing back my chair. "Oliver, would you like to take an after-dinner walk?"

"Yes." He answered me almost automatically because he was staring down at Rupert. "I don't know what your game is, Carmichael, though I can guess. But it won't work. The contessa kept an eye out for Julia when she was alive, and I am doing it now. Come on, Julia."

"I would like to apologize," Oliver said, as we went through the archway, "for my stupid comments earlier this evening."

"It's all right." I spoke a little curtly because I was

already a little sorry for my impulsive invitation to Oliver for a walk.

"No—it's not all right. It was unforgivable. I should have known—"

"Oliver," I said. "It's forgotten. Truly. Let's talk about something else."

We walked in silence for a while. Then Oliver said, "I don't want to risk your wrath by going on with the subject, but—it was jealousy, you know."

He certainly had my attention. "Jealousy? Of Rupert? You must be joking!"

"Perhaps, but you've seemed awfully friendly in the past few days and—now don't blow my head off—to someone who feels about you the way I do, your spending the night in the same room with Carmichael is like a red flag. You can call it irrational all you want, but that's the way it is."

"Well," I finally said lamely, "as I told you. It didn't mean anything except ease of mind to go to sleep."

We walked on for a while in silence. The moon was large and the color of butter, and poured through the cypresses and gate in front of us. I found I was terrified that Oliver would make some physical gesture that I wasn't ready to cope with. Why, I thought, am I so unlike so many women I know? From everything they said they all seemed able to handle gestures of affection they wanted, in other words, they responded to them gracefully, or that they didn't want, in which case they discouraged them, also gracefully. I am twenty-eight years old, I thought. David Brownson didn't have to coax me into bed. Why am I so different now?

Without thinking I edged a little away from Oliver.

"You don't have to be afraid I'll make a pass at you," he said. "I won't, although I'd like to. I don't know why it took Gianetta's death to make me see this. Maybe it was because when she talked about you I was reminded

167

constantly that you were almost twenty years younger. Whatever the reason, it's come to me in the past couple of days that you're the only person I've ever truly and consistently cared for." He glanced at me. "I think you know that. But I can wait."

My conversation many years previously with Gianetta as to Oliver's sexual inclinations sifted through my mind, but it seemed remote and irrelevant. Much more to the point, how much my younger self would have given to hear those words, words which now seemed to evoke only a strange guilt! Why, oh why, I wondered, did things seem always to come at the wrong time? Who was it who said, be careful what you pray for, you may get it? "I don't know why I'm not, well, more responsive," I said. "Once upon a time what you just said would have sent me into the seventh heaven."

"I know. Ironic, isn't it? But I take hope that the feeling is still there." He took my hand. "Is it?"

"I don't know," I said, unhappily.

"I think David Brownson's unspeakable behavior might have something to do with it," he said grimly.

Did it, I wondered? And then, as though to reproach me for forgetting, I felt again that terrible flash of pain that sliced through me as I stood in my own hallway, reading his note. How could I have persuaded myself that it was mostly wounded pride? Pride was the least of it. Something far worse had been damaged. I put my hand out and touched Oliver's arm. "Thank you for being so . . . so forebearing. I don't know why I'm being like this. I've never been a prude. Heaven knows I'm not a virgin, and wasn't when I started having the affair with David. But, something happened to me after that, and I haven't sorted it out, yet."

"You will, in time. And I want to be there when you do."

"Please," I said, "I can't think of anyone I would

rather have pick up the various pieces."

Just as we were about to go into the castle, Oliver gave me a soft kiss. It was unexpected and gentle.

When we were back in the sitting room we found some of the guests had gone to bed. Only the Boston sisters, Terry, Rupert and Andrea were in the sitting room. "Where is everybody?" I asked, as we went in.

"Bed," Rupert said. He was sitting at the table and had spread the cards out in one of the more classic forms of patience.

I was still angry at him, so I carefully avoided his table and went to look over Terry's at the one near the window. "What are you doing?"

"I found these in the bureau upstairs. Do you know anything about them?"

"Good heavens," I said. "They're Tarot cards, aren't they?"

"Yes. My mother won't allow them around the house."

"Why ever not?" Oliver said. He had come up behind me.

"Oh, she thinks they're wicked. All connected with evil spirits, that kind of thing."

"Then why are you playing with them?"

He shrugged unhappily. "I suppose because they're here."

"Did you say Tarot?" Mrs. Kessler said from the sofa, where she was doing needlepoint.

"Yes."

She looked over her half moon reading glasses at Terry. "Where did you say you found them?"

"In a drawer in the bureau in my room. I was looking for some more postcards to send to friends," he added hastily.

Mrs. Kessler put down her needlepoint and went over to the table. Pushed to one side was a large piece of silk cloth. "Were the cards in this?" she asked.

"Yes. Wrapped up inside a box."

Mrs. Kessler held the cards for a minute, looking down at them. "It's very strange," she said. "I've known Gianetta for many years, and have been here for at least six summers. Yet I've never seen these cards. I never knew they existed here, and I would be astonished beyond words to learn that Gianetta had any interest in them whatsoever." She ducked her head, looking over her glasses at Terry. "Where is your room?"

"Up in the battlements."

Was there an odd quaver in his voice when he said that, I wondered? No, not even a quaver, just a different sounding note, I decided, and a slight blinking of his eyes. Meaning what? Fear?

I said, "It doesn't necessarily mean that the cards had anything to do with Gianetta. A lot of the furniture here, especially the stuff up in the battlements and the attics, could have been here for a hundred years or more."

"These are old cards," Mrs. Kessler said, handling them, moving them about in her hand.

"What are they for?" Terry asked. "Why are they supposed to be so wicked?"

"Well, they're part of the occult world, and there are people who consider all of that dangerous." Still holding the cards, Mrs. Kessler sat down in the chair opposite Terry. Opening up the silk cloth, she spread it out in front of her.

"You mean like ghosts? That kind of thing?" Terry asked.

Mrs. Kessler looked up at him. "More or less. Psychic phenomena, the supernatural. Does that frighten you?"

"I don't want anything to do with it," Terry said, and got up so quickly he almost knocked down his chair.

"Is something scaring you?" Oliver said.

"No, of course not." Terry was red-faced and looked unhappy. I think I'll go down to the music room and play the stereo," he said, and made what was obviously an escape.

"Something *is* frightening him," Mrs. Kessler said.

"Well if his mother put the hex on these cards and told him they were spooky, it's probably that," I said. "Although I'd think a healthy fifteen-year-old would be more curious than frightened."

"It's something more than that." Mrs. Kessler was laying out the cards, looking at them.

I stared at the brilliantly colored pictures, thinking of Stacey and her fright. Undoubtedly she was behind the far wall in her little alcove, sleeping or reading. Then there was that odd thud I had heard . . . But I forgot about the assorted fears as my attention focused on the cards.

They were vivid and strange and evoked feelings in me that I couldn't quite define. I picked up some and looked at them. "What do they all mean?"

"Different things, and also certain cards themselves can have different meanings depending on whether they're right side up or upside down."

"Why do you suppose Terry's parents were so full of warnings about them?"

"Because they come out of myth, much of it pre-Christian, although no one really knows their origin. But the great psychologist Jung wrote of them, and some of the psychic and spiritual elements that the cards represent coincide with the mythic forces that Jung deals with. To those for whom everything outside the Bible is of the Devil, they would be frightening."

"You seem to know an awful lot about it. I mean," I added hastily, "that . . ." My voice trailed off and I could feel the blood coming into my face. There was no way I could finish off that sentence in an acceptable way.

"That's all right. I know quite well what you mean. You find it astonishing that such a product of Yankee New England and Boston should have such an esoteric interest. My study of it started with Jung, as a matter of

171

fact." She had most of the cards laid out now. I put my hand out and turned one or two, looking at them. "What does that mean?" I asked, pointing to a picture of a woman with wings, with the Roman numeral XIV on top and the word "Temperance" underneath.

Mrs. Kessler smiled. "Well if looked at this way it can mean a certain kind of success, and harmonious partnership. Reversed, it means something destroyed through bungling."

"And this?" I was holding a picture of a crumbling tower and people falling out of it.

She looked up at me quickly and then down again. "That's one of the most powerful cards in the pack. According to one of the major authorities it can mean the suffering of an individual through the forces of destiny being worked out in the world, or, reversed, the calling down of a disaster which might have been avoided. Unnecessary suffering, self-undoing." She paused. "In metaphysical terms it can mean the impact of divine revelation, or, if the conscious mind is too weak to deal with that, it could be catastrophic, the division of the mind against itself."

I shivered. And then asked, "Do you believe in this?"

She smiled. "It depends what you mean by believe. I studied Jung for a long time. Have you ever read his theory of synchronicity?"

I shook my head. "No."

"Well, briefly put, it means that everything that happens at a given time is connected in some way, whether apparent or not. Which is why there are Jungians who believe, for instance, that while astrology has been abused by the superficial and the quacks, it cannot be dismissed as total nonsense. So, do I believe in what I see in the cards when I give someone a reading? Yes, I suppose in that context I do."

I was still trying to make sense of this coming from this descendant of New England rationalists. She looked up

172

at me and smiled again. "I used to catch the same expression on my husband's face, at least at first." She paused. "Would you like me to give you a reading?"

Suddenly I thought of Stacey's fright. Of my own terrible unease in the bedroom where I had first been put. Of Terry. Were his parents right? Would I be playing with something potentially dangerous?

"It's all right," Mrs. Kessler said gently. "I won't if you don't want to. But there's nothing to be afraid of."

"There isn't?" The question came out more sharply than I intended.

"No. I called up one of my greatest friends, the monsignor of a nearby church, and asked him. And he said it would be wrong only if I used the cards to foretell something instead of putting my trust in God."

"Are you a Catholic?" That a Truesdale of Boston could be Catholic was almost as shocking as her interest in the Tarot cards.

"Yes. I converted thirty years ago. I don't talk about it because it deeply offended my sister."

"Hasn't she forgiven you yet?" I smiled, because I couldn't help being amused.

Mrs. Kessler smiled back. "She thinks she has. And she is the dearest person I know. But it still bothers her."

"How does she feel about the Tarot?"

"She doesn't like it any more than Terry's parents, but for different reasons, I think. She feels it's unworthy of the descendant of Puritans and the granddaughter and great granddaughter, on both sides, of Unitarian ministers."

I looked at Mrs. Kessler's roundish, pleasant face, and a sense of peace, something I hadn't felt for a long time, came over me. "How did your husband feel about them?"

"He found them historically and artistically fascinating. But he wasn't greatly interested in the psychic or spiritual world. His faith was very simple and very powerful."

"He was Jewish?"

"Originally, of course. But he was a convert before he met me. It was through him that I went into the Church."

"Curiouser and curiouser . . ." I quoted.

"Alice in Wonderland," Mrs. Kessler said promptly.

"Correct." I watched her gather the cards up. "Did you say you were going to give me a reading?"

"Yes. Shuffle these seven times."

"Why seven?" I said, taking the cards.

"Because that means a fair amount of handling, and will enable me to sense your vibrations."

I'd heard the phrase, of course, before. I didn't know what I thought about it. I took the cards, which were larger than regular playing cards and felt awkward in my hands. "I can't do a proper shuffle," I said. "My hands won't get around them."

"That doesn't matter. Just move them around with each other."

So I shuffled the old-fashioned way, which simply meant picking up a few and slipping them elsewhere in the pack. After doing this seven times I handed them to her.

"What is your birth sign?"

"Er—Cancer."

She opened out the cards in a crescent. "Now choose seven and give them to me."

I did so, and handed her the seven cards. She put them out in some special kind of order and looked at them, touching some of them from time to time.

After a while I said, "Is it that bad?"

"No. Not for you . . . I don't think. But there is something strange going on around you. And . . ." She looked up. "You've been having some kind of dreams or visions, haven't you?"

That shook me, although after a moment I realized that Dr. Langdon could have gossiped. I felt a surge of resentment towards him. Physicians were supposed to keep

174

their counsel and that of their patients'. "I suppose Dr. Langdon told you. Yes. I have these sudden, well . . . it's like scenes being acted out in front of me. Always the same. And then I dream it at night. But I didn't tell the doctor about the dreams. . . . Did Rupert mention them?" I could hear my voice rise. If I felt resentment towards Dr. Langdon, my reaction to Rupert's loose tongue was fury.

"No, no one mentioned either the vision or the dream to me." The calm gray eyes looked across at me. "You're talking about that scene the other night at the dining table when you broke the glass, aren't you; when the doctor took you out to bandage your hand? He didn't say a word when he came back and not afterwards, at least not in my hearing and no one has reported to me that he did. But I was sitting opposite you, and I was fairly sure you had seen something when you glanced down at Gianetta's empty chair. I've seen it happen to people before. It's nothing to be afraid of, you know."

I looked at her and believed her completely. "And no one told you about the dream?"

"No one."

That also I believed. Mentally I made an apology to both the doctor and my irascible ex-boss and current roommate. Slowly I breathed out. "It's not a pleasant vision or dream."

"There's probably an element of warning of some kind in it."

I thought about Gianetta falling, of the blood spurting from her head; of whatever it was that I just missed seeing at the edge of the picture; of her telling me something about a letter, only not being able to hear it.

"Don't strain. It won't come to you that way. Just relax and be open. I'll go on with the cards." She looked down again.

"I'm sorry if I sound like your gypsy tearoom fortune-teller, which I assure you I'm not, but there is some kind of problem or riddle that is around you and that you are involved in. And there are three or four people who are involved with you, but not for the same reasons. You are closely bound, but in different ways, to all of them. But there are two kinds of bonds here, an inner and an outer. You will solve either the inner or the outer, I can't tell which, but at great cost. There is death and there are celebrations. There is a path and there is a wish, but both are blocked . . . It's a very strange spread. What one asserts, something else contradicts." She glanced up. "Be careful."

By this time I was just as shaken as the most dedicated fortuneteller would have liked me to be. "Very little that you say makes me feel warm and secure. How much faith shall I put in it?"

"I told you. There's no need to worry. Don't be frightened. Nothing is irrevocable. But forces are moving. There are great changes beginning to take place and you are part of them. I'll have you do another drawing." She made as if to sweep the cards up.

My hand seemed to shoot out of its own accord. "Don't —not yet."

She paused, watching me.

"Who else do you see in them?"

"I can't really answer you that way. Do you have somebody specific in mind?"

I saw, in my mind, Oliver. "Yes. I have someone specific in mind." My heart speeded up its thump, thump.

"What is his—or her—birth sign?"

My mind went blank for a moment. Then, "Capricorn, I think."

"What is it you want to know about Capricorn?"

The trouble was, I didn't know what I wanted to know. Finally I said, "Is . . . is he one of the three or four around me?"

"Yes."

I leaned back. Why did I ask that? I wondered. I knew the answer. Mrs. Kessler swept the cards up and said, "Do another drawing, this time of three!"

I got up. "No, I must go to bed." I glanced down at her face, trying to find the peace I'd seen there before. But whatever it was had gone. I not only could not find it, it was hard to recall that I'd ever experienced it. A great restlessness seized me. "I must go to bed. It's late."

"Do my dear. You need your rest." She had laid out the cards again and was staring at them when I left.

I couldn't get the cards out of my mind. Rupert had come to bed shortly after I had turned out the light, undressed in the bathroom and slipped into bed, all within a few minutes and without talking. I was glad of his presence and ashamed of myself for being that glad. Finally I went to sleep. . . . Suddenly the cards were in my hand again in my dream, and I was standing at the threshold of a cave, a cave in which I knew something was going to happen. The trouble was, even though I knew it beyond doubt, I didn't know whether whatever it was was good or bad. While I was standing there, trying to discover, somehow, the answer to that question, a figure appeared from inside the cave. In my dream I stared at him in awe. He was tall, with a gold circlet on his head, a blue robe and a red cloak. In his right hand he carried, point down, a sword. "What do you want?" the figure asked me.

"I want to find the way," I said.

"Then stay with me and follow me."

He turned and walked forward, and I saw then that the cave had passages leading from it, some of them lit, some of them shadowy and one of them dark. The king in front of me—and I knew he was a king—chose the dark path.

"But that's dark," I said.

He didn't turn. His voice came to me. "I told you. Follow me."

But I didn't want to. How did I know I could trust him? "No, stop."

The king turned. His face was barely visible in the dim light trailing in from the brilliant cave that we had left. Curiously, when we were in the cave, he was a complete stranger. Here, far down the tunnel, when I could hardly see him, I was convinced that I recognized him, that he was someone I knew. "Who are you?" I asked.

"You know who I am," he said.

"No I don't."

"Then you will have to follow me to find out."

"Why should I believe in you if you don't tell me first who you are?"

"I'm looking for the Madonna."

"Which Madonna?"

"The one that is lost."

"But she isn't lost. Who are you?" In my dream I felt suddenly frantic, because either the light was fading, or we were, without my realizing it, going further and further into the tunnel. I was convinced now that I knew who the king was because his voice was familiar. But he was completely invisible. "Where are you?" I called out.

There was no answer. At that point the light from the cave vanished altogether.

"Come back!" I yelled. "Wait for me. I can't see."

There was no reply, and my feet refused to move. I felt rooted to the floor of the tunnel, which was totally black, but no longer silent. Far away, in the direction from which we had come, there was a step, and then another, sounding like thuds, but thuds that were coming much nearer. Suddenly I screamed the name of the king, which in my dream, I had just discovered. Unfortunately, I also woke up at that moment and had no idea whose name it was. My eyes opened. "Oliver," I said, and then noticed that the light was on and Rupert was going towards the door.

"Where are you going?" I asked, the panic from the dream spilling over into reality.

"Something's happened!"

"What do you mean?"

He paused at the door. "Somebody upstairs screamed and there was the sound of something—I don't know what. I barely heard it, but I have to go."

"Wait for me!" I yelled, throwing off the covers.

"Well hurry!"

I flew into my robe, tying the belt as I followed Rupert across the stone floor through the first room and then the great hall. We tore upstairs, and I barely took in that someone had turned on the lights. When we got to the top we saw a whole bevy of guests in robes and dressing gowns bent over something at the bottom of the steps leading to the battlements.

"Is he alive?" someone said.

Rupert pushed through the crowd, with me behind. Down on one knee on the floor was Dr. Langdon. He was examining a pajama-clad figure whose face I couldn't see because the doctor was kneeling in front of it. Then I moved. The blood was the first thing I saw, smeared all over the head and upper body. Then I recognized the face. It was Terry MacNaughton.

SIX

"**I**s he alive?" Rupert asked.

"Yes, he seems to be," the doctor said. "Without an x-ray I couldn't be sure, but I'd be surprised if he didn't have a nasty fracture."

"What on earth did it?"

It was the obvious question. There was silence while we considered the equally obvious answers.

"He could have concussed himself by falling down those stone steps, couldn't he?" Oliver said.

"Quite easily. Especially if he tripped at the top."

"Then all that blood on his body isn't necessarily serious?" Mrs. Kessler asked. Her curly gray hair was folded neatly in two plaits lying black and gray against her blue robe. Despite the gray hair and obvious sophistication, there was a child-like quality about her. Her sister was not in evidence.

"No, no. Scalp lacerations bleed copiously. All the blood comes from his head."

"Could I help you to move him?" Robert Orvietta, standing on Terry's other side, asked humbly.

Dr. Langdon glanced up. "No. We have to cover him. But we can try to slip a blanket under him. I'll show you how. We must get an ambulance here and have him taken to the hospital. Head wounds should be kept as still as possible." He looked around. "Perhaps Marco should call."

"Thank you, I am already doing so," Marco spoke rather sharply. He had the receiver of the hall phone to his ear and was busy dialing. "I am calling Dr. Nedi. He is one of the chief doctors of the hospital."

I slipped behind him and went to a large bureau in the narrow hall outside the main bedroom. Luckily, the castle did not have its full complement of guests. There were plenty of blankets folded in the big wardrobe. "Here," I said, bringing them out. "Do you want a pillow, too?"

"No. A folded sheet wouldn't be too bad an idea if you could find it."

I went back to get the sheet, and when I returned, Marco was off the telephone and Dr. Langdon and Robert Orvietta were holding Terry by the shoulders, hips and head, while Mrs. Kessler on one side and Harriet Orvietta on the other were slipping a double blanket under the boy. That done, two blankets were put on top and the clean folded sheet slipped under his head. "I hope the ambulance doesn't take too long," Dr. Langdon said.

Marco, plainly reading North European criticism in this, snapped out, "They will be here very shortly, you will see."

And they were. Less than ten minutes later it was possible to hear the sound of a car coming up the winding road very fast. In an amazingly short time it had come under the archway into the courtyard.

"I'd better go down and let them in," I said, and ran down the steps.

As I was standing, holding the door open for the stretcher bearers, Dr. Nedi arrived in his small Fiat. Jumping out, he followed the attendants up the steps.

Twenty minutes later, the ambulance had left, with Terry strapped onto a bed inside, and Dr. Nedi following in his own car. Ignoring the obvious non-Italians standing

181

around, he had told Marco in Italian that he would call him tomorrow as soon as Terry was x-rayed and they could establish the extent of his injuries.

"What did he say?" Mrs. Langdon asked, when Marco had left to escort the medical party downstairs.

Oliver and I both started to translate. I smiled at him and he smiled back, deferring to me. "He'll let Marco know tomorrow what's going on," I said.

"What time is it?" I asked Oliver.

"About two A.M." He looked at me with concern. "Do you think you'll be able to go back to sleep?"

"I don't know. I was having some kind of weird dream."

"What was it?"

"I can't remember. Something about a tunnel." The rest of the dream seemed to have receded for the moment. "Oliver, what happened?"

"I don't know. I heard this yell or scream, then I came pelting out of my room and found Terry here."

I turned to the doctor. "Did you hear anything else?"

"No. Except for a violent thumping, the kind of thing we've been hearing before. I've always assumed it was a heavy door blowing back and forth. But then as Landau says, there was a scream and a sort of thud. When I got out here, he was bending over young MacNaughton."

We were all standing in a huddle in the hallway. As Marco came back upstairs, I leaned over and picked up the blankets and sheets. "Some of these are going to have to be cleaned. There's blood on them. I'll fold them and leave them on the bench here."

"I think it would be better if perhaps we all went back to our rooms," Marco said.

The group broke up. Oliver gave my arm a pat and went towards the dining room and his own room. The others dispersed in the direction of theirs. It occurred to me as I followed Rupert downstairs that not all members of our party had been there: for example, David and Stacey Brownson.

"Rupert," I said, trying to catch up with him, "some of the people were missing. The Brownsons, for instance. Do you think it's strange they didn't hear?"

"They were probably sleeping more soundly."

"Yes, but Stacey's room was right near the hall there. Why are you running? Why don't you wait for me? Here, I'm trying to catch up with you!"

Rupert stopped where he was, one hand on the stone bannister. I caught up with him and glanced at his profile, which looked unusually severe. "You look cross. What about?"

"Nothing."

"There's no use saying 'nothing' in that snotty voice when you look black as a thundercloud."

By this time we were downstairs, with Rupert striding ahead through the main hall into the smaller hall and then into the room we shared.

"Rupert—" I started.

"I don't know about you, but I want to get some sleep. A bedroom is for sleeping, not chatter. Good night."

I slid down into bed. "You're a bad-tempered, mean-minded, parsimonious, unsympathetic and altogether un-attractive human being."

"Thank you. Anything else?"

"Yes, but I'll wait until I'm no longer sharing quarters with you. It'll be safer."

"Don't let me frustrate you in any way."

"I won't."

Why, I pondered, lying with my back to Rupert's bed, was he so difficult? With the idea of lulling myself to sleep and keeping my mind off all the implications of what had just happened, I started to list possible reasons: he was more worried than he let on? Possible. But that would imply that he knew things he hadn't told me. Guilt? Over what? He could, of course, have killed Gianetta and Ricardo. If he was in Geneva he was near enough to have done so. I veered away from such a distressful thought. Anyway, whatever had happened to Terry had not been done by Rupert unless he had set it up ahead of time. And what had happened to Terry?

The obvious answer was the most likely: He had come downstairs, tripped at the top step and fallen all the way down. It could have happened to anybody, particularly with the castle's dim lighting. But the lights in that particular place in the hall were not dim. In fact, they were probably the brightest in the castle. Also, were the lights on, or had Oliver turned them on as he came out? I would have to ask him. Either way it was reasonably certain that Terry had suffered a bad, but not mysterious, accident. My eyes started to close and then flew open again.

But why was he coming down those stairs in the middle of the night? To sleep in the sitting room? Going to the bathroom? But wasn't there a toilet in the battlements? Not, as I remembered, a very efficient one, and certainly not adequate for anyone who might be suffering an onset of diarrhea. Given that possibility he would, of course, seek one of the downstairs baths. My eyes started to drift closed again. Just as I slid into sleep it occurred to me that given my relative willingness even to consider the possibility that Rupert might be the murderer of Gianetta and Ricardo, it was passing strange that I should feel so secure sleeping in the same room with him that I should go back to sleep in the middle of the night on this frightening floor of this frightening castle. . . . But before I could think any more on the subject, I was asleep.

While we were at breakfast the next morning the telephone rang and was answered by Marco. When he came back he said that Dr. Nedi had reported that Terry had a severe concussion as the result of a skull fracture, and was in critical condition in the Intensive Care Unit. He also added that the matter had been reported to the police, who would be getting in touch.

When Marco returned to the table and told us that, he looked worried, more worried at this point than on his dignity. "You will please all remain here this morning," he said.

"Isn't the funeral this morning?" Dr. Langdon asked.

"This afternoon at one. But you will please stay at the castle this morning." And he stalked out.

"I don't know what he thought we were all going to do," Rupert muttered, "kick up our heels at a picnic on Monte Subasio?"

"No, but we have gone for rides and walks," Oliver pointed out. "If the police are coming, then I suppose they'll want us around."

"It will give me a chance to do my laundry," Miss Truesdale said. "I shall ask Maria for some detergent." She got up and left.

"I wonder where Ludovico is," I said. "He hasn't put in an appearance since he arrived."

"I think he stayed with people he knew in town, and, of course, his position here is a bit awkward," Mrs. Langdon said.

"You'll probably see him this afternoon at the funeral mass," Oliver said, reaching for some more coffee.

"Isn't the mass for both Gianetta and Ricardo?"

"Yes," I said. "At least that's what I understand." Oliver got up. "I think I'll follow Miss Truesdale's example and go do some laundry. God grant that in addition to everything else, there isn't a water shortage."

Shortly after Oliver went into his small room at one end of the dining room, Rupert got up, slammed his chair back under the dining table and stalked out. As he reached the door he turned. "I'm going to be using our bathroom

185

for the next hour, so perhaps you could stay out of the bedroom." And left.

"It was bad enough having him as a boss," I said, taking some more coffee. "Having him here is impossible, except —" At that point I wondered what Mrs. Kessler would make of my sharing a room with him.

"Except?" Mrs. Kessler said inquiringly.

"Well, I don't know what you'll make of this, but he and I are sharing the main room downstairs. This is not love or sex or romance. It's because I can't sleep in the small room opposite his, so Andrea, who officially shares the room with him, offered to switch beds. That's all I do, sleep in there."

"My dear, you don't have to explain yourself to me. Even if you were doing more than just sleeping, as you put it, we *have* heard of such things in Boston."

"I always think of it still as the home of the Yankee Puritan."

"Obviously you haven't been there lately."

Why do I care? I thought. I, who had lived for years, openly if not always happily, with David? Because of Gianetta? No, even if she were alive, and I were sharing the room with, say, Andrea, I'd be more amused than eager to set matters straight. . . . And at that point I remembered my strange dream.

"Mrs. Kessler," I said suddenly, "I had a weird dream last night."

"Yes, I know. You have these dreams. We discussed the matter yesterday."

"But this dream was different. I dreamed I was in a cave, and I saw someone who looked like . . . well he looked like a king . . . like one of the cards you showed me yesterday. He told me to follow him into a dark passage leading out of the cave, but he wouldn't tell me where it led. Just wanted me to follow him blindly. I refused, and he disappeared and then it was dark and I was lost. . . ."

186

Curious, I thought, even describing it brought back the sense of suffocating fear.

Mrs. Kessler was watching me. "Come along into the other room and show me the card you're talking about."

We went into the sitting room, which appeared rather deserted, and sat down at the table. Mrs. Kessler took the pack from the table where it had lain, wrapped up in its silk. "Now, which one. Show me."

I took the pack and spread it in front of me. "That one," I said, pointing to a king on a throne, holding a sword, a gold circlet on his head.

"The King of Swords," she said. "Interesting."

"What does it mean?"

"It means that one of the men I saw you surrounded with wants you to trust him, even though you can't see where he is leading. But at the moment you're not doing so."

My mind went to Oliver. "But I do trust him."

"Then it's someone else. But whoever it is. He is the one you *should* trust."

"How do you know that?"

"Because I remember the cards."

"But you can't tell me who he is."

"No, only you can do that."

"That's not very helpful—" I looked up. "No criticism intended."

In the middle of the morning, before even the first mourners arrived for the funeral, Gianetta's London solicitor, Sir Humphrey Barrett, arrived.

I had heard Gianetta speak of him often when I visited her flat in London, but I had never met him. Therefore my mental image of him as a sort of cross between George Roper and Sir John Gielgud had remained unimpaired. I was therefore stunned to find myself being introduced to a short, stout, bald man with a bristling salt-and-pepper mustache and twinkling hazel eyes. "How do you do?" he

187

said. "I've heard Gianetta speak of you often."

"How do you do?" I was trying to keep the surprise out of my voice. "And she spoke a lot about you, too."

"With affection, I hope, at least some of the time."

I must have shown astonishment at that, because he went on.

"She and I used to have grand battles."

"I didn't think one fought with one's solicitor."

"That's what she thought, too. Which is why we had such terrific fights."

He turned away then to meet the others grouped around the sitting room.

"I always thought that one told one's solicitor what to do and he hemmed and hawed and then did it," I murmured to Oliver, who was standing beside me.

"So did I. But I do remember the contessa would sometimes have a phone call with him from London and then come back into the dining room or sitting room with her nose held unusually high."

"I wonder what they fought about?" I said.

"I always wondered that, too." Oliver's voice was dry.

"Ah Carmichael, good to see you," Sir Humphrey was saying. "When did you get here?"

I watched Sir Humphrey and Rupert converse with some indignation. Obviously they had known each other before. Why that should give me a sense of grievance I wasn't sure. But it did. I felt that Rupert had, as usual, held out on me. "You didn't tell me you knew Sir Humphrey," I said to him after the introductions were over and we were waiting to go down to the funeral.

"You didn't ask me."

"Well it's not the kind of thing you ask straight out of the blue. On the other hand, since you knew I was related to Gianetta, you might have mentioned it the other day when George Roper said he was coming, for instance."

Rupert stared out of glinty blue eyes. "I see. I should

have banged on the glass at the table and said, 'Attention everyone, I know Sir Humphrey Barrett. Has everyone fully grasped this fact?' "

I turned and walked away, going out into the hall and staring out the window that led straight onto the courtyard. I had forgotten, momentarily, the power Rupert had to arouse in me a rage out of all proportion to what he had done, or to the basic formality of our relationship. I had not felt rage like this in years—many, many years. As that thought emerged into the upper and conscious reaches of my mind, I wondered when it was in the past, and inspired by whom, I had felt it. But before I could give the matter my attention, I saw a large black car swing under the arch and into the courtyard. It was still half an hour before the burial mass was to begin, but obviously people had begun to arrive. I noticed then an unusual number of smaller cars parked around the edges of the courtyard.

This particular group stood talking for a moment, then Marco appeared from the front door and went to greet them, kissing the women and touching cheeks with the men. So, I thought, these must be some of Marcello's relatives from Castiglione and other towns. I wondered if they would come upstairs, and rather hoped they wouldn't. Somehow I did not feel up to meeting numbers of distinguished people I did not know.

"Who are they?" somebody asked from behind me.

I turned and saw Sir Humphrey staring out the window over my shoulder.

"I don't really know. But I'm pretty sure they must be Monaldis of one kind or another. Marco came out to greet them as family members."

"Ummmm," Sir Humphrey said.

A thought occurred to me. "Did you come out for the funeral, or because of the will?"

I encountered a sharp look. "What do you know about the will?"

"Nothing. Except that George Roper said the other day that you were coming today with a copy of the will. It infuriated Marco, who felt that Gianetta should have used a local lawyer."

"She probably would have except for two things. One is that for all her Italian name and heritage, she's always felt more English hyphen American than Italian, and for another, it would have been difficult to find a lawyer in Castiglione that was not already either representing some branch of the Monaldi family or was related himself. The ramifications of the Monaldis are enormous."

"Somebody—I don't know who—told me they're listed in the *Almanach de Gotha*. Is that true?"

"Quite true. And there are one or two branches of the family that can trace their ancestry back to people in Rome who were important in the old Roman Empire of the fourth and fifth centuries."

I looked down at the descendants of ancient rulers. The women looked to me no different from perfectly ordinary, unexceptional, unremarkable women that could be found in any country in Europe or countries settled by Europeans. The same could be said of the men. Idly I wondered what it was like to bear the consciousness of such a burden. What did it do to the person who carried it?

"You know, I'm glad I don't carry that burden. It sounds like anti-snob snobbery, which I really don't think it is. Fancy having to live up to that! I wonder how Marco copes with it?"

"By being a revolutionary, I expect."

I glanced quickly at the Englishman. Obviously he knew a lot about the state of affairs at Civitella, but of course he would. "He doesn't act the revolutionary very much now. Once or twice he's been as stiff and pompous as all get out. From revolutionary to *ancien régime* in one leap."

"That follows. The aristocracy has always had yearnings

towards the peasantry—look at Tolstoy! And so has Marxism. The one thing they all have in common is loathing of the middle class—the only class they can't bewitch or control."

I thought about it. "Yes, you're right. Why is that?"

"Because the middle class is moved along by the individualistic desire to get ahead. It's pragmatic and practical. It's not interested in ideological theories. It's not idealistic, in the sense that it's not motivated by concepts of government. The middle class wants to have law and order so that people and property will be safe, and after that it wants to be left alone."

"It sounds horribly selfish. No wonder everybody hates it."

"Yes, but think about it a little more. How gloriously unselfish is the motive of either the aristocrat or the intellectual-revolutionary? As someone once said, if the intellectual who is a liberal-leftist did not have the underclass, the poor, on whom to lavish his liberalism, and to use as a weapon in his fight against the middle class, and to make himself feel noble, then he'd not be able to function as a liberal. If all poverty were to be wiped out tomorrow, where would your idealists go? There's no victim. And without a victim, their justification for tearing up governments and blowing up institutions disappears. It's a symbiotic relationship, that of the intellectual and/or aristocrat and the underclass whom he is supposed to serve. Their common enemy is the member of the middle class who wants to make enough money to open his own business."

I listened to him and then said, "I can't argue with what you've said because I haven't really thought about it. But I'd love to hear a debate between you and—well, not Marco, perhaps, he doesn't strike me as articulate enough —but somebody who is, with his views."

"Then it's a pity you weren't around to hear my battles

with Gianetta, because that's frequently what they were about. That and related subjects."

"But Gianetta wasn't, really, an aristocrat. Her mother was from Boston and her father was an Italian journalist. It's true that Marcello was, but then that's only by marriage."

"Yes, and no. Her father was a journalist, but he was very much an intellectual, and was a grandson of one of the older Roman families, although not on a level with the Monaldis. Her mother was a Boston aristocrat, a Mac-Nair. And while the old Yankee aristocrats don't have titles to help the poor European to identify them, don't think for a minute they haven't got the identifying spots and stigmata of your true patrician. With, of course, an enormous extra helping of Yankee Puritan–Protestant guilt about their money. But the saving grace of people like the MacNairs, as long as they don't disappear into Ivy League academia, in which case they seem to lose most of their good American common sense and try to become European theorists . . . what was I saying? Oh, their saving grace is hard, native practical sense. And after Gianetta had soared high enough with her splendid social theories and what her money should do to facilitate them, we'd have a huge fight, and she'd suddenly come down and be a MacNair of the MacNairs. She'd be as canny then, as her old great grandfather."

He hesitated. "Back to the unhappy present: How is the police investigation going? I tried to reach the chief of police on the telephone before I came here, but he was out. Has anything come to light?"

"No. Not really. I take it you know about Ricardo, too."

"Ricardo Natale?"

"Yes. You know who he is, then—was?"

"Of course. What do you mean by was?"

"He was killed, too. Probably by the same murderer—or terrorist—who killed Gianetta."

There was a silence. Then he said, "Tell me about it—everything you know."

So I did. When I was finished Sir Humphrey stared out the window. Finally he said, "That might put a different face on things."

"In what way?"

But he didn't answer. Then, "Poor Mary."

It was a shock to hear her called by her English name, yet that's what she was, English.

"I sat with her for a while," I told him. "And asked her if there was anything she wanted to talk about. She said no. But I had the feeling that there was more in her mind than just grief for her grandson. Do you know anything about him?"

"He was, I'm sorry to say, something of a bad lot. Part fake revolutionary, and part opportunist. His father, you know, is the real thing—an absolute, dedicated Marxist. I can't imagine Ludovico throwing a bomb at anyone. That isn't his style. But in his own, quiet, austere way, he is a passionate ideologist."

"Doesn't he teach at the University of Milan?"

"Yes. Political science or economics."

"I met him. He didn't look at all my idea of a son of Maria, which I put down to snobbish reasons. But he was also rather off-putting."

"There's a forbidding quality about him. I only talked to him once, when he was here visiting his mother on some occasion. It took me a while to decide what it was about him that bothered me. Finally, on the plane back to London, it came to me. His ideology, is fueled, I believe, by an extraordinary degree of personal anger and resentment. That's often the case with ideologists of any kind. With him, though, it was palpable. There were moments when I could feel it."

I considered that. "I'm not sure whether that was what I was feeling. Only once did he seem, even briefly, a grieving father. Maria was far more stricken over Ricardo's death. Although, as I told you, I think there was something else bothering her."

"Young Ricardo was in a fair amount of trouble one way or another. I had told Gianetta to refuse to have anything to do with him—not to help him out, because half the time he was in trouble with the law and she'd never know where her money was really going. But you know your grandmother, particularly where recipients of her generosity were concerned."

"Was she that fond of him?"

"No. I think it was for Maria's sake. But from something that Maria once said, I don't think she approved of Gianetta's bailing him out any more than I did. Mary Fletcher is a very tough lady brought up on the streets of London. She's not what we English call soft."

"I wonder what Ricardo was doing here."

"It could have been anything from wanting a handout to blowing up the castle, or various things in between." He paused. "You say the police think he was killed at the same time and by the same method as Gianetta, but struggled along that passage before dying?"

"Yes. Incidentally, I didn't know that lower basement or dungeon or whatever it is existed, and I certainly never knew about that passage. Did Gianetta know about it?"

"Oh yes. It was probably made long after the castle was built. Popular myth has it that it was created by an illicit lover. I'm much more inclined to think that it was made to hide something or somebody involved in smuggling or some other kind of illegal trade." He glanced at his watch. "The mass will begin soon. Gianetta telephoned me the day before she died. I had the feeling that she wasn't entirely private so she couldn't talk freely. But she said she had received two letters that distressed her, and that she was sending them on to me with something of her own. Also something about a bill."

"That was a little strange, wasn't it? Bills were something she didn't have to worry about."

"Even Gianetta had her budgetary limits. And she had strong feelings about being overcharged. But it wasn't that."

"But you didn't get them?"

"No."

"The mails are terrible. Everyone here takes it for granted, so things were rarely posted either to or from Civitella. She usually sent the stuff out by somebody who was returning to England or France or Switzerland or Germany or the States, and could mail them from there. Anywhere, rather than Italy. And if anyone wished to write here, she always told them to send it by somebody who was about to come here. In fact she had a very reliable courier service."

"I know. Which is why I'm surprised I don't have the various items she was sending."

"Did she say who she was sending them by?"

"No. But it could have been anyone. You know what a way-station it is, with people going in and out."

All the time he was speaking I had been trying to make up my mind as to whether I should tell him about my strange dreams and visions, so many of them concerning a letter. He seemed so prosaic and I did not want to be laughed at or put down. And yet . . . I decided to go at it obliquely.

"Marco had a funny phone call from Venice. That was about a letter, too."

"Who from?" Sir Humphrey's voice was sharp.

"That's the odd part. Whoever it was was female, and was old, deaf and had a thick accent. With the result that Marco couldn't make head or tail of what she was saying, beyond the fact that it had something to do with a letter."

"I shall have to ask him."

"He'll probably give you a huffy answer."

"That may be. I'll try for as much tact as possible. But

I think I should find out."

"Do you have any idea what it could be about?"

"No. None at all. But with things as they are, anything could be important."

"Sir Humphrey," I said. "What exactly do you think is the connection between the deaths of Gianetta and Ricardo?"

When he didn't answer I said, "You know, she—Gianetta—and I did have our differences. But I was terribly fond of her. . . ." My voice faded as a queer pain hit me. For the first time I was thinking of her as dead.

Sir Humphrey put out a pudgy hand and patted my arm. "I know you were, and she was of you. She always said she was sorry you weren't her real granddaughter, and thought you were enough like her to be related. The answer to your question," he went on, as I got a tissue out of my pocket, "is that I don't really know. But as I said before, Ricardo was half revolutionary and half criminal—and wholly out for himself. His name came up in police reports almost a year ago when some Red youths—I'm speaking of their political color—made off with some valuable drawings from a small museum near Arezzo, and the drawings haven't turned up since. Some investigators paid a visit to the castle to find out about Ricardo's whereabouts, which was how Gianetta and Maria discovered it, and they were very upset. But when the police finally located Ricardo and questioned him he swore up and down he had nothing to do with the theft, and they couldn't prove he did. Any connection he might have had with the drawings was never established, but the shadow remains. How many people here knew about it I'm not sure. Probably no one. I can't imagine either Gianetta or Maria talking about it. But it's one of the reasons I've spent the last year trying to persuade Gianetta not to come back here. She was a very rich woman and, given Ricardo's associations, a natural target. But she wouldn't listen. . . ."

"And you think this call from Venice could have anything to do with that?"

"I told you. I don't know. The first thing I'm going to do is find out whether there have been any art thefts up there or near there. If so, then it's possible somebody traced it to Ricardo, and from him to here. It's by no means impossible. And even then I don't know what it would have to do with his death. I'm just groping."

"What's weird," I said, taking the plunge, "is that I've been having strange dreams about Gianetta in which she's telling me about a letter and saying that I must look for it. In fact, in one dream she was telling me what it was about, but something drowned out her words, and then I woke up." I glanced at the lawyer quickly, to see if his reaction would be that I was either a lunatic or making the whole thing up. But he merely looked interested.

"Did you know," he said, "that your grandfather, Marcello, had dreams that were sometimes clairvoyant, and that he had some odd psychic qualities?"

"No," I replied. But vividly, once again, I saw him holding my hand and asking why I was sad. "Yes," I said, contradicting myself, "I did. Only I didn't think of . . . what happened between us as psychic." Then seeing Sir Humphrey's inquiring expression, I told him about Marcello's holding my hand in the hospital and asking me why I was sad, and my telling him about Samson.

"Yes. That sounds just like him. And now, apparently, you have the same. It's a pity you couldn't hear what Gianetta was telling you in your dream."

"Yes. Oliver and Rupert said maybe they should hire a hypnotist so I could remember it."

"That might not be such a bad idea. They say the human mind holds somewhere everything it ever heard or saw." He paused. "So you told Rupert and Oliver."

"Well—Rupert was there when it happened. We're sharing the room downstairs, the one with the bath in the tower, not, as I keep telling everyone, for reasons of passion or romance, but because of what happened the night before, when he and I found Ricardo and because I can't sleep down there. I suppose that sounds highly stupid to you?" I looked challengingly at him.

"Not at all. And anyway, it's none of my business. You mean you had the nightmare and then woke up and told him?"

"More or less . . ." I paused, momentarily confused. "I seem to have had a series of nightmares. It was the following night I dreamed about some sort of rhythmic thuds —they were all mixed up in the dream—and I woke up to find Rupert at the door. We went upstairs and found a clutch of people around Terry MacNaughton, who'd fallen down the stairs leading to the battlements."

"I didn't know about young Terry. Where is he now?"

"In the hospital. He cracked his head and was completely unconscious."

"When did this happen?"

"Last night. Or, more accurately, around one-thirty this morning."

Sir Humphrey was looking at me intensely. "Gianetta is dead—murdered. Ricardo is dead—also murdered. Terry MacNaughton is in the hospital with a cracked skull—all this within what? Five days?"

That chill I had felt sometimes quivered through me. "I hadn't thought about them in such a . . . a connected way."

He didn't say anything for a moment. Then, "I meant to ask, when did you arrive?"

"Last Tuesday—the day Gianetta was killed. Oliver called me at work and told me what had happened. Maria had called him. Anyway, Oliver and I flew out here that afternoon and arrived here in time for a late dinner around nine."

"Five days ago."

"Yes." Somehow it seemed like a fortnight.

Marco's head suddenly appeared as he came up the stairs. "The mass is about to begin," he said sternly, looking at me. "We are waiting for you."

I glanced guiltily towards the sitting room. "Have the others gone down? I didn't hear them."

"They are downstairs. It is astonishing you did not hear them, but you were perhaps absorbed with Sir Humphrey."

"Yes, my fault, I'm sorry," Sir Humphrey said quickly. "We'll come down."

I had indeed been absorbed listening to the solicitor. Many more cars were parked in the courtyard and I could see the backs of more through both archways. As Marco took my arm to lead me into the chapel, I slid a black lace scarf over my head.

The two coffins, end to end, took up almost the entire center aisle of the small chapel. On both were flowers. On Ricardo's were sprays of the yellow *planta genista*—broom plant—that covered the Umbrian hillsides. On Gianetta's were roses from her garden. I recognized them as coming from her beloved rosebushes and could see they had been freshly cut. I could not bring myself to believe that it was her body in that long wooden box. But the flowers on top, cut off from the branches that gave them life, seemed themselves to be grieving. Don't be sentimental, I told myself, but without much effect. The dying roses appeared to me to have more to do with the dead Gianetta than the incense, the candles and the hastily muttered Italian of the mass for the dead.

I had been to few Catholic services in my life. To please her father, Marcello, my mother had me baptized in the Church. But I had never made my first communion. She had died before that took place, and my father's abhorrence of all forms of religion and religious observance had brushed off on me. I sat unmoved by the ritual and the liturgy. The priest's surplice did not look particularly clean, and I found the way he licked his finger as he turned the pages of the big prayer book unappealing. How could this strange, mechanical, unmoving ceremony say anything about, or do anything for the soul of Gianetta? Perhaps the spirit of my agnostic or atheistic father lived in me more than I had realized. Yet, I knew I was not consistent in my aversion. Once, when I was passing by, I had, on impulse, stopped in London's Westminister Cathedral and stumbled into a Latin mass. I sat there, in one of the uncomfortable straight chairs, overwhelmed by the beauty of the mass and the powerful sense of transcendence it conveyed. Perhaps there was something about this chapel and these people that was bothering me. To distract myself I looked around a little.

My feeling of isolation, even alienation, was made more complete by the realization that among her close friends and in-laws I was, among those I could see, one of only three who sat tearless. Marco was crying openly; so were Maria and Oliver. Others had tears in their eyes. Only the Langdons and I sat stoney-eyed, like some bleak tribute to Protestant restraint. Only I'm not a Protestant, I protested to myself. I'm not anything.

It was then I noticed something I didn't immediately take in. I looked back and then stiffened. The Madonna was gone. The space above the altar was empty, with only a few roses resting on the place beneath where the Madonna had been.

The mass continued. We stood for the gospel and sat down for the homily. I knew I could, if I made an effort, understand what the priest was saying. Making the necessary effort, I caught some words here and there, then sentences: Gianetta's gracious generosity, her kindness, her sympathy for the poor and those less fortunate, et cetera, et cetera. The portrait he was building was almost unrecognizable and filled me with indignation. Gianetta was both kind and generous. No one knew that better than I. But this saccharine word picture had nothing to do with the frequently imperious, dominating woman whom I had loved and fought with, who could be arbitrary to the outer limits of anyone's patience, but who could also, quite suddenly, reveal a humility of spirit that had on more than one occasion shaken me to my bones. What that rather oily little man up at the main altar was talking about was as removed from Gianetta as . . . as the contents of the elongated wooden box a few feet from me.

At that thought, as though a bolt had gone through me, I felt her presence near me so strongly that I thought surely other people must be as aware of her as I was. She must be palpable, if not actually visible, to those around me. It was disturbing and quite frightening. And yet, most curiously, if this was the supernatural that one read about, its impact *felt* totally within the realm of the natural. Gianetta was there, near me, and there was something I knew she wanted me to know. And then, equally suddenly, she was gone.

I could feel the sweat on my face even as I felt the chill in the stone chapel. Quickly I glanced around. No one seemed to be any different from a few minutes ago. The priest had gone back behind the altar and was holding his hands out over a chalice. Quickly, noticing that others were kneeling, I slid to my knees.

After the mass was over, I walked out with the others, hoping to have a word with Oliver about the missing Madonna. Her absence bothered me. In a few short days she must—more than I realized—have come to typify for me something about Gianetta herself. I thought of the long face, the oddly tender eyes, the hands holding the baby. I was not usually susceptible to fifteenth-century paintings. Often they struck me as unreal. Yet before Gianetta had moved the Madonna to the chapel, I had looked for it more eagerly than anything else when I had gone to the little museum. She had been on a wall by herself, with a few vestments of the late fifteenth century in a case at one end and some fragments of a fourteenth-century manuscript in another case at the other. It was not a large work, yet even among the other six Mantoris on the remaining walls, it dominated the room. The Virgin had always been for me rather unbelievable. I'd never been able to make a flesh-and-blood young woman out of the miracle-working saint of Lourdes, Fatima and a dozen other reputed appearances, and the fifteen-year-old Israelite girl who gave birth to a Being who changed the world forever. But this painting had come nearer to conveying her reality —whatever that had been—than anything else. I was more upset than I knew.

But before I could speak to Oliver I learned that Marco, George Roper and various cousins from Castiglione were going in the funeral cortège to the Monaldi burial plot, located on a low hill a mile away just within the Monaldi property, and that I was expected to go with them.

"But I'm not really related," I said quickly to Marco.

His brows rose and then descended in a frown. I saw immediately that I had offended, and added quickly, overcoming my secularist's dislike of burial ceremonies, "But of course I'd be honored. It was just that it hadn't occurred to me, since I'm not really related."

"Neither am I, and neither is Maria, who is, of course, going," Marco said rather coldly. "Nevertheless, you are a Monaldi."

What demon entered my head at that moment I don't know. But I found myself remembering that though she tried in every way she could not to show it, Gianetta did not like Marco. "My mother was a Monaldi," I said, as coldly as he. "I'm a Winthrop. And what about Oliver? He was closer to Gianetta than anyone else."

202

"He is not in any way a Monaldi." The intensity with which he said that was astonishing.

"But . . . the museum, it's named after your grandfather."

"He did not wish for a memorial. And there are those who think that the name has not been honored by it." And Marco, his eyes as hard as brown stones, turned and walked over to some distant cousins who were getting into their car before returning to Castiglione.

If he had slapped me across the face I could not have been more stunned. I opened my mouth to speak, but nothing came out.

"Close your mouth, Julia," Rupert's sardonic voice sounded from one side. "It's unbecoming half open."

I turned and looked at him, irritated as usual at his jibe, but curious as to whether he had heard and what his reaction was. "Did you hear what he said?" I asked.

"I did."

"Don't you find it weird?"

"Not particularly."

"But the museum was his idea originally, not as a memorial, of course. But he wanted it for Castiglione."

"True."

"And the whole memorial thing was because Marcello was the one person in Gianetta's entire life whom she adored."

"Which made things easier for Landau, in a way."

"What on earth do you mean?"

"I'll tell you what I mean, but not now and not standing right here within hearing of everyone in the courtyard. And for heaven's sake," he paused, "leave the subject alone until you get back and we can have a quiet chat. I know you . . . I know how you feel about Landau, but it's a tricky area. Truly, Julia. Take my word for it." I was still staring at him when he said, "Perhaps that's too much to ask, to take my word for something concerning your precious Oliver. But then take Barrett's."

"Sir Humphrey's?"

"Yes. Sir Humphrey's. He's a canny man. Now, they're obviously waiting, so you'd better get in the car and go."

I liked the graveside ceremony little better than I did the mass. This was probably because it seemed to me a charade. Perhaps, I thought, watching sweating men lower the coffin with ropes into the grave, it would have more reality for me if I felt the weight of Gianetta's body. I would know, then, that it was Gianetta in that long box. As it was, I was still bothered by the sensation that came and went that she was still alive and somewhere near. Along with the others I took a handful of dirt and threw it onto the coffin. The dirt felt real, as did the sunlight and the slight wind and the sound it made blowing through the cypresses. But Oliver should be here, I thought, glancing around at the faces. George Roper, Gianetta's cousin, looked properly subdued but hardly stricken. To be fair, although cousins, they had never been close. Marco had tears in his eyes, but I couldn't rid myself of the feeling that those were easy tears, easily evoked by ritual, rather than by grief. Apart from Maria, there was no one here for whom Gianetta was all-important.

Then Marco looked up and saw me watching him, and there was, again, the flash of hostility I had seen before. It was surprising and a little disturbing. He and I had never been one another's greatest admirer, but on the whole we had had a reasonably pleasant surface relationship. Why now did he feel the enmity that I saw in his face? Because of the museum? Because of my affection for Oliver? The discomfort I had been feeling since I arrived suddenly increased. Which would indicate, I thought, that it might have its origin in more than ghosts and bad dreams and "visions."

Once or twice I glanced towards Maria, looking oddly stolid and English in a black hat and black coat. But she kept her red-rimmed eyes on the coffin, and I knew, without being told, that along with the wooden box and its contents, an important piece of Maria was being lowered also into the dirt.

Back at the castle Sir Humphrey gathered those of us who were related or involved in Gianetta's will: George Roper, Marco, a quiet man from Castiglione whom Marco introduced as his lawyer, Oliver, Maria, Rupert (to my surprise), and me, in the sitting room. The others went off tactfully to pack.

"Why is Carmichael here?" Oliver whispered to me.

"I don't know."

I tried to catch Rupert's eye, but he was staring down moodily at his hands.

Sir Humphrey took his stand in front of the empty fireplace. Oliver and I sat on the sofa facing him, with Marco and his lawyer to our right and Maria, George and Rupert to our left.

"The will is fairly simple," Sir Humphrey said. "Out of Gianetta's estate Maria will be paid a yearly income for life amounting to some twenty thousand dollars. Julia is left Gianetta's flat in London and the outright sum of fifty thousand. There are one or two charitable bequests amounting to another fifty thousand. The rest of her estate which, after taxes, is something over two and a half million dollars —I'm giving the figures in dollars since the money derives from American holdings—the bulk of it will go to establish a residuary trust with the Monaldi Museum in Castiglione as the beneficiary. From the income will be paid the maintenance and expenses of the museum, Oliver Landau's salary and sufficient funds for the purchase of items at the discretion of the trustees. Until Gianetta's death the trustees were Gianetta, Oliver, and myself. Rupert Carmichael and

Julia Winthrop will now take Gianetta's place so that there will be four trustees in all."

There was a silence after Sir Humphrey finished speaking. Then Oliver said, his voice harsh, "Why Carmichael?"

Rupert looked up, his eyes narrow and very blue under his black brows.

"Well I don't know much about art," Sir Humphrey said. "And with all due respect to Julia's job, I'm not sure how much she knows of the period the museum mostly covers."

"I know enough for all of us."

It was curious. I had known Oliver well for a long time, and loved him, but I had never heard that particular note of rancor in his voice. Rupert, I noticed, said nothing.

"I'm sorry if it disturbs you," Sir Humphrey said equably. "But that is the way Gianetta wanted it." He spoke with good humor, but there was a note in his voice too that I hadn't heard before. Underneath that rotund amiability, I decided, there was steel.

Sir Humphrey turned towards Maria. "You knew what she was leaving you, of course." It was a statement rather than a question.

There was an odd, intense look on Maria's face. "Yes. But—" She started and then stopped. Then she looked around.

"Yes, Mary? What seems to be the trouble?" The implacable note had gone from the solicitor's voice, which was now kind and reassuring.

"That's . . ." Suddenly Maria, still wearing her coat and hat, stood up. "Sir Humphrey," she said. "That's not the right will."

It was as though she had exploded a bomb in the room. We all stared at her, not moving.

"What do you mean?" Sir Humphrey said, no longer warn and reassuring, but sharp.

206

"She wrote another one. At least, she wrote something to be added. A cod . . . cod—"

"Codicil?" Sir Humphrey said.

"Yes, sir. That's what it was. She wrote it a few days before she died and had Ruggoni and me in to watch her sign it and then witness it."

Sir Humphrey let out his breath. "So that was what she was sending me."

"Didn't you get it?" Marco said.

"No. I never got it."

SEVEN

Oliver was the first to speak. "Well she may have added a codicil, Maria, but that doesn't mean that this will is invalidated."

"But she changed it."

"She told you?" Sir Humphrey asked.

"She said everything would be different, except my income. I think—bless her heart—she thought I'd be worried about that." And the tears started coursing down Maria's olive cheeks. "Not that I was. She paid me well. I have money put by."

"She reassured you that your legacy would be all right but that she'd changed the rest?"

"That's right. That's just what she said. "Don't worry, Maria. Your part isn't changed. It's the only part that isn't.""

"There's no proof of this." Oliver spoke calmly.

"No, there isn't." Sir Humphrey looked at us. "Only that she said she was sending me two letters that had disturbed her and a bill and something else. Those were her words." He moved towards the door. "I think I'll just put a call through to my office to see if anything's arrived since I left."

I turned to Maria. "Did Gianetta send them by somebody, Maria? I mean to post in England or one of the other countries?"

"Yes, just the way she always does."

"Who did she send them by?" Rupert asked, speaking for the first time.

"That's the trouble, I don't remember. A number of people left that day—the day before she . . . she died. And she'd saved up a lot of mail to go back, some of it to France and some of it to America. I know that because I saw her handing some to Master Philip Roper who was flying back to New York after he got to Rome. . . ."

Everybody looked at George.

"Did you know about it?" Marco said.

"I knew she'd added something to her will because she asked me about some legal terminology and the valid way to express herself."

"Just a minute," Sir Humphrey said. "Wait until I put the call through." Then, half way to the door he stopped. "I've overlooked one small detail," he said drily. "I don't speak enough Italian to make the call. Can someone do it for me?"

Oliver got to his feet. "I'll do it," he said. We sat there silent, hearing his voice from the hall as he talked to the operator. After that it went quickly. As Oliver came back in the sitting room we heard Sir Humphrey's voice. "Ah, Jerry, yes, do you know if any mail from the contessa—posthumous mail, of course—has come in since I left? It hasn't. You're sure? Yes, do check. I'll wait." There was another pause. "Very well, thank you."

He came back in.

"Nothing has come in the past day. That doesn't mean it positively won't. But if the letters for England were mailed in England two to three days ago, it would be highly unlikely that they hadn't arrived. The English mails are rather good. Maria, do you know what else the contessa sent to go to England?"

Maria shook her head. "No, Sir Humphrey, I don't. I know that she had letters she was sending to America, to England and, I think, to France. But then a lot of guests were leaving that day, one way or another, and she was sending mail by all of them. I know, because she came into the kitchen with the letters in her hands and asked me if I had any mail for abroad." Maria sat down again.

There was a silence. Then George Roper spoke. "In any case, I know she had a copy made."

Everyone turned to him. "She did?" Sir Humphrey asked.

"She did indeed. That was my doing. When I was giving her the benefit of my legal training I asked her if she was having a copy made. My lawyer's hair rose when she said it hadn't occurred to her. So I drove her into the town myself and waited outside while she went into one of those photocopy places and came out with three extra sheets of paper, which she folded as she walked back to the car. When she got back in I told her she was to keep one with her. She said she would and thanked me."

"But you don't know where?" At least three voices asked that question.

He shook his head. "I'm afraid not."

Sir Humphrey turned to Maria. "Do you have any idea where that would be?"

"Sir Humphrey, it could be anywhere. That desk over there, another desk in her room, some files that she carried back and forth. . . . It's always such a commotion getting her and all her luggage back to England . . . but that's over now. . . ." And the tears started down her cheeks. "I can't get used. I just can't."

"I know, Mary. I'm sorry. I can't get used to it either." Sir Humphrey waited a moment, while Maria searched for and found a handkerchief and mopped her eyes. "Do you know where this file you speak of is kept?"

"Well, usually it's in her room, the room where Count Marco is now."

"I can assure you I have seen no such file in the room,"

Marco said belligerently. "And there would be no reason why—"

The Italian lawyer, who plainly understood English, spoke to him in Italian, and even I was able to understand that he was trying to soothe him, to assure him that no offense was intended by the question.

"No, no, please don't be offended," Sir Humphrey said quickly. "It's just that you might, perhaps, remember seeing it in a cupboard or something."

"I have not seen it," Marco said firmly. "I have never seen it."

"Well," Sir Humphrey said. "We'll just have to inaugurate a search." He hesitated, and then said, "Mr. Roper, Signore—" he bowed to the Italian lawyer, "perhaps the two of you would assist me in the search."

"Of course," George Roper said.

The Italian lawyer bowed in return.

"Oliver," I said. "What about you? Do you have any idea where she could keep that file?"

Oliver was sitting on one of the straight chairs, his hands thrust deep in his trousers pockets. "I've been trying to rack my brain. I remember the file well. It's the kind of thing I've seen often enough not to notice, if you follow me. I've also seen it in Gianetta's flat in England, usually after she's just arrived back and is in the process of unpacking. But I can't remember when I last saw it."

"Did you know about the change in Gianetta's will?" Sir Humphrey said. "I know you and she often talked on the phone."

He shook his head. "Not about the will, no. We did talk frequently, of course—daily, when some purchase she was particularly interested in was coming up at Christies, say."

"Is that where you bought her stuff?"

"Most of the best of it, yes. Some, of course, we got here."

Suddenly I remembered the Madonna. "Oliver, The Madonna—it's not in the chapel."

"No. I thought it might be wiser not to have it with all those people flocking in and out—"

"You are speaking of our relatives?" Marco queried, reminding me strongly of a growling dog.

"No, of course I'm not. But the entire farming community and nearby village have been in and out since Gianetta was lying in state. The chances are most of them wouldn't know the Madonna from the latest kitsch at Assisi, but there might always be one who did, or someone pretending to be a local. And the Madonna was, without question, the most valuable piece in the museum."

"Where is she?" Rupert asked, speaking up suddenly.

"In the Monaldi Museum. I took her back yesterday afternoon."

I saw Marco's already stiff face grow tighter. "With Gianetta dead, who is in charge of the museum and its art pieces?"

It couldn't have been a plainer slap at Oliver, and I held my breath. Oliver could be extremely volatile. Sir Humphrey said hastily, "Well, as you have just heard, Landau and the contessa were co-trustees with me, so—"

"But Gianetta is dead." Marco's voice, rasping, cut across Sir Humphrey's polite tone.

"As you heard, in the most recent will we have, Gianetta's place on the trust will be taken by Julia and Rupert Carmichael."

"But we know now that will is phoney baloney. That there's another."

The strange, out-of-date slang sounded ludicrous, especially spoken in Marco's thick Italian accent.

"I'm afraid I acted out of force of habit, Marco," Oliver said. "Gianetta always left the transport and security measures up to me. I just didn't think. If I did wrong, I'm sorry."

212

I was feeling nettled at Marco, not only for this gross incivility, but for the things he said about the museum. So I said "And there's nothing to make us believe that you would have any authority over the disposition of the art objects in either will."

Marco glared at me, his tan, long-fingered hands clenched in his lap.

"I'm sorry if I stepped out of line," Oliver said.

"You didn't, Landau." Sir Humphrey paused. Then, "Sometimes we have to ignore family tensions at a time like this. Feelings have a way of expressing themselves in odd disguise."

It was at this point that we all became aware of male voices in the hallways outside the sitting room. Just as our heads turned, the chief of police appeared, followed by one of his underlings.

"Yes. Good afternoon," he said. "A sad affair, a sad affair. The contessa was much beloved."

"Have you made any progress?" George Roper asked.

"A little. We now think it most likely that Ricardo—" the police chief sent a quick, speculative look at Maria. He started again. "We think it probable that Ricardo killed the contessa first and was then killed by someone unknown."

Everyone spoke at once. "But you said you thought the same person killed both," I finally said.

"I said I thought it was possible." The police chief spoke carefully. "I did not offer any firm diagnosis. I said I would have to wait for the coroner's report and laboratory tests. They are now in." He hesitated again. "There is also Ricardo Natale's political record."

"He really was a bad lot," Oliver said. "Sorry, Maria. I know he was your grandson and you loved him. But it doesn't alter the facts."

Maria sat in her chair, her ankles squarely together, her feet shod in sensible black tie shoes that could easily have come from Selfridge's in London. "It's all right. I know. I've known Ricky since he was a child. It's not devotion to him, when I say I don't believe that. My son, Ludovico, could, for a reason, kill someone. I could. But not Ricardo. He would talk and strike attitudes and make speeches. He used to do it to the contessa. I know, because sometimes it upset her but more often it amused her. But I do not think he could kill."

"Natural affection . . ." George Roper murmured.

"It's nothing to do with natural affection. I was far fonder of the contessa than I was of anyone, even Ludovico, who refused to live with me in the house the conte provided after he was seventeen. He ran away and he has never lived with me since. Visited me, yes, occasionally. But never stayed. Always with friends in the town. But Ricardo," she shrugged. "He never stood for anything. Just took what he wanted where he could. The contessa—" Maria's tears started to flow again. "She could be difficult, and she liked things to go her way. But she was never anything but kind and considerate to me. And for all I told her not to send Ricky any money, she would do so sometimes. Because she was afraid he'd ask me, and then I wouldn't have enough."

I stared at Maria, thinking that young people now would call that feudal patronage. Yet Gianetta's consideration for Maria went far beyond that. Today Maria would have health insurance and guaranteed income and state care for as long as she lived, at least she would in England. But a bureaucracy can only give benefits, not love, and what Gianetta gave Maria was love. I came to realize my name was being mentioned. "You should go back to bed and dream again, Julia," Rupert was saying, a sardonic look on his face. "Perhaps this time what's in the letter will come."

"Or perhaps a hypnotist?" Oliver offered. And then, "I'm serious. The information is there somewhere in Julia's head. What a pity we can't get it out."

"I'm not a safekeeping box," I answered crossly. The idea of having someone try and put me into a trance (which is what I thought would happen) gave me an unpleasant sensation.

All this time the police chief, as silent as mountain, had stood listening to our talk. "What is this about a dream?" he asked.

Marco made a sound that sounded like "Tcha!" He took his hands out of his pockets, and I could see them, clenched. "We do not need to worry ourselves about such nonsense. We need to find the second will."

The police chief answered him in Italian. The Italian lawyer said something, also in Italian. Marco replied in a flood of Italian.

"Put us in the picture, won't you?" Sir Humphrey said.

"I am sorry," the police chief said. "I was just pointing out to the conte that anything that anyone could tell us about the letter to the contessa would help us in our investigation."

"There were two letters," Sir Humphrey said. "She told me that over the telephone. She said she had received two letters that had upset her, and she told me that she would be sending them to me, along with what she described as something else, which I now think was the will, plus something about a bill."

"A bill? A bill for what?"

"I'm sorry. I don't know."

The police chief stared at Sir Humphrey for a moment, then turned back to me. "And in your dream, which of these documents were you dreaming about?"

"A letter from Venice, I believe, although I have a feeling that there is another piece of paper involved."

"This is ridiculous," Marco said.

"What is in the mind can be found, if one knows how." The police chief looked at me steadily. And there was something about the way he was peering at me that made everyone else stop and do the same. A queer, uncomfortable feeling came over me. Somewhat to my own astonishment I heard myself say, defensively, "I'm not willingly holding something back. I can't help what I dream."

"Perhaps," the police chief said, "she told you a little, eh?"

"What do you mean?"

"You talked, perhaps on the telephone? She told you of these letters. They slipped your mind. You now think—"

I stood up. "Signor Birazzi. I'm not sure what you're getting at, but it sounds to me like you're suggesting that I'm playing some kind of game."

"Are you?"

"No she is not," Maria said indignantly. "Miss Julia does not lie or play games."

I was touched and completely astonished. "Thank you, Maria."

Sir Humphrey seemed to gather the threads in his competent hands. "So where are we? The general consensus is that Gianetta—the contessa—was killed by Ricardo, who was in turn killed by someone else, or who died accidentally. But why?"

At that point Ludovico walked into the room. He stood, tall and thin, his gray-blond head thrown back. "I have heard you think my son committed the murder."

"Yes. We do."

"It is not true."

"Why do you say that?"

"He was my son and I loved him. But he was worthless."

"You have no right to say that, Ludo," Maria said. "If he is worthless, it's you who made him that way, with your political views and theories. Always pumping him full of a lot of nonsense that he's a victim of the ruling class. If it weren't for the ruling class—the contessa—he'd have been in jail for petty thievery long ago."

216

"And that's all you did," Ludovico exploded. "Paid court to and waited hand and foot on a woman who exploited you from start to—"

Open-mouthed we watched as the short, stocky Maria rose, reached up and slapped her tall son with her open hand. "You ungrateful wretch. I should have taken a belt to you when you were a trouble-making boy. The count and contessa would have done anything for you—sent you to school and through university and given you money to travel, but all you did was backbite and bad-mouth them from the time you were twelve."

"I did not appreciate being a servant."

"You were never their servant."

"Oh yes I was. Eating in the kitchen—"

"With me—your mother. What's wrong with the kitchen?"

"That entire system should be abolished. If Ricardo had had the guts to blow this monstrous reminder of a monstrous class up I should have been proud to visit him in prison. Instead, he snivelled around, wheedling money, trying to use the blackmailing devices of a criminal—"

"What blackmailing devices?" the police chief broke in.

"I didn't waste my time asking," Ludovico said, but he hesitated a moment too long before speaking.

"Oh yes you did. You knew."

Ludovico drew himself up. "And what if I did? It was nothing to do with me. And you cannot possibly prove that I knew. You have no legal claim on me whatsoever. You will never solve this case. One day this whole castle will go up—poof!—and will take the parasites with it." And with that Ludovico stalked out.

There was a pause, then Sir Humphrey said drily, "Is he right? That you don't have enough to hold him for questioning?"

"Yes. Quite right. I'm not sure what mischief Ricardo

217

was up to. But even if I were sure, I'd need a lot more to hold his father."

The policeman left shortly after Ludovico removed himself, and, as though by common consent, the rest of us drifted out of the sitting room, avoiding one anothers' eyes. I took a walk down the long path behind the castle, finally ending up in the town, where I went to the local ice cream parlor and had a dish of *gelato*, sitting in the little piazza, staring at the townspeople strolling past and watching the cars turn in from the *autostrada*.

I didn't know what I thought about the scene that had taken place. My mind seemed to be a series of uncoordinated pictures: Gianetta opening a letter, and the still, almost paralyzed, expression on her face. Then I saw her opening another . . . from whom? . . . And then a bill. And then going to the telephone in the hall and putting a call through to Sir Humphrey. Pieces of paper that disturbed her peace sufficiently to make her change her will. And speaking, or thinking, of the will, there we all were, not knowing where or how her considerable estate would be distributed. And what would happen if the second will were never found . . . ?

"Are you thinking about the will, the letters, or what Ricardo may or may not have been up to vis-à-vis Gianetta?"

I jumped so much I almost knocked over my dish of ice cream. "Where did you come from?" I asked rather crossly, as Rupert sat down.

"From the castle. Where else?"

The waitress passed by and Rupert ordered two ice creams.

"I don't want any more," I said.

"Not to worry. I'll eat both."

"You'll get fat."

"If I thought it would put weight on me, I'd sit here until tomorrow morning, consuming all the ice cream the shop had. I've been trying for years to put on ten pounds."

"All the world's trying to lose weight except you," I said. "Why is it that you have to be so different about everything?"

"Meaning?" Rupert picked up his spoon and attacked his mound of chocolate dessert.

"Meaning that at a time when everybody else is thinking in international terms—everybody who has the world's good at heart, that is—you're one block of xenophobic prejudice. And just as the ecumenical movement is taking real hold, you attend the Church of England as though it were the one true faith."

"That's because I'm contrary. It must be my Irish great grandmother. 'Name your giver'ment and I'm agin it.' But my dedication to Canterbury does not mean that I discount dreams, psychic phenomena, and other supernatural happenings. Are you sure Gianetta didn't discuss any of those things with you? The policeman has a point, you know. They may all be tucked in your mind somewhere and be popping out in dreams."

"As you very well know, since I was stupid enough to work for you, I have been in England steadily this entire summer, holding together your establishment while you disport yourself elsewhere. How could I possibly have talked to Gianetta about Ricardo or anyone else?"

"There's that strange modern instrument, the telephone."

"Gianetta and I never talked on the telephone, or rarely. She always wrote me letters."

"I notice that you've eaten your ice cream after all," Rupert said now. "I think I'll have some more." And he beckoned the waitress. "Want some?"

"No thanks, I'll have a *cappuccino*."

We sat in silence for a while.

"Don't bite my head off," Rupert said, finishing off his third ice cream. "But did Gianetta ever say anything significant to you about Ricardo?"

I shook my head. "Not that I remember. Not unless it's hidden in my unconscious, just as that wiley cop suggested. But if it is, why would I have suppressed it? Surely to God that rather stupid and unwashed brat didn't. represent some deep emotional drive I've been running away from."

Rupert frowned. "No, I don't think so. Unwashed was only one of his many unsavory qualities. Nevertheless, I sometimes felt sorry for the poor worm."

"Good heavens—why? Since he was fifteen, whenever Maria could be found in tears in the kitchen, it would usually be because Ricardo was in trouble and touching her for money or help, or trying to get it out of Gianetta—if he could get to her, that is, past Maria."

"Or past Oliver," Rupert said emphatically.

And then, suddenly, from nowhere, the suppressed memories resurfaced. Oliver folding a letter and putting it in his pocket and my catching sight of the scrawled return address: Ricardo Natale; Oliver talking to a seventeen-year-old Ricardo out in the courtyard, and Ricardo pocketing some lira bills that he had slid from Oliver's hand.

I put down my *cappuccino* cup as the memory unwound.

"Why on earth are you giving Ricardo money?" I'd asked indignantly. There was something about the look on Oliver's face that had upset me. I couldn't understand the intensity of my feeling about it.

"I feel sorry for him, Julia," Oliver had explained. "His father keeps him on an awfully tight string, wants him to be a brilliant student—the usual story of the self-made man. And Ricardo hasn't a bean for just ordinary fun."

"I just suddenly remembered something," I said. Why had I pushed that memory so far down? The answer was clear: everything that scene implied threatened my image of Oliver as I so much wanted him to be. "Oliver told me that he was sorry for Ricardo."

"Well, I can agree with that. Though perhaps not for the same reason." He glanced up at me. "And let's not have another fight about it, Julia. I accept—I've always had to accept—your feeling for Oliver."

"It was David I was in love with, remember?"

"It was David you turned to in childish rebuttal when you couldn't have Oliver."

"That's a pretty long childish rebuttal—a four-year affair with a married man."

"You were always nothing if not stubborn. You wouldn't have had the affair if he hadn't been married."

"No, I would have married him."

"No you wouldn't. You wouldn't have given that second-rater the time of day. His great attraction was that he was unobtainable, i.e., a perfect instrument with which to pay back Gianetta and Oliver. Because you were jealous."

"Of Gianetta and Oliver? You must be raving."

"Oh I'm not implying there was anything improper there. But they were devoted, and you resented his dancing attendance. And don't get up and walk away, that's what you always do. Take flight. When things upset you, you run. Just the way you did when you left London and the gallery. Why not try confronting them, and yourself, for a change."

I stared at him open-mouthed, every muscle and nerve braced to do just what he said—run. And then another memory sprang, vivid as a painting, into my mind. "My dear," Gianetta was saying, as we stood outside a church in Spello, while Oliver parked the car, "you can't bear to let Oliver pay attention to an old woman. That's why you're sulking. It's most unattractive. And although you don't think so, I'm not taking anything away from you."

That was the first summer after he had paid so much attention to me the year before, and I was expecting the same this year. But, aside from an occasional smile, he was making it plain that not only did he not have the time to spend on me this year, but the lavish attention of the year before had come, not because he had fallen in love with me, but because Gianetta had put him in charge of my art education. The realization was so devastating that I had manufactured an excuse to leave the Civitella the following day. I never again spent as much time there, and never again completely trusted Gianetta even when she reached out, which she did, more often than I wanted to acknowledge.

I looked up to see Rupert watching me. He gave me a rather crooked smile. "You've had ill luck with your men, Julia—your father, Oliver, David. But then I think you picked David, as I said, because he wasn't free. Now that he is and plainly wants you, what are you going to do about it?"

"Nothing. I don't want him." There was a long pause. "How absolutely awful to think that you might be right."

"Unthinkable."

My mind slid back to something else he had said. "Why were you sorry for Ricardo?"

"Because Ludovico was trying to make an ordinary, not very bright son into an intellectual and revolutionary. All he succeeded in doing was to destroy any respect for law and society the boy might have had, without imbuing him with any principles about building another kind of society. So that he simply became an anarchic dropout, a petty felon."

"Why would he kill Gianetta?"

"I'm not entirely sure he did, despite what our cop says, but if he did, then he did it out of fright. She must have caught him *in flagrante* in some way or other."

My mind seemed to be operating at two levels: On one I was attempting to imagine what possible story Ricardo could be using with which to blackmail Gianetta. On the other I was pursuing the strange memory that had just erupted into my mind, and why it had been so buried.

222

"Rupert, do you think something's wrong with my mind?"

"No, why?" He looked at me. "Because you dream and discover you know things you didn't know you knew?"

Despite my more or less ongoing irritation with my ex-employer, I felt a wave of gratitude. "You make it sound ordinary."

"It is, given all the reactions and emotions you've never allowed yourself to look at."

My gratitude vanished. "What does that mean?" I flared up.

He grinned. "Sometime when you're feeling calm and relaxed and undefensive I'll discuss the matter with you. We can pull our wheelchairs together under the tree."

"Wheelchairs?" And then I saw what he meant. "It shouldn't take that long, unless, of course, you're right about my touchiness."

Sir Humphrey strolled up. "Ah, here you are! May I join you?" He pulled up a chair. "What is everybody having?"

After the waitress returned with his ice cream and *cappuccino* he said, "What a pretty kettle of fish all this has turned out to be."

"You mean the will?"

"Yes. Although it could apply to almost everything that has happened for the past week, beginning with Gianetta's death."

"Do you think Ricardo killed her?"

"I don't know. I don't think it's impossible. Despite his loving father's comment, I don't think he was a weak nothing. I think he was, as we've said, a thoroughly bad lot and quite capable of killing Gianetta or anyone else. Whereas his father, who could in theory rationalize wiping out an entire village if he thought it would advance the people's revolution, would not, himself, be able to pick up a gun or rock and kill an old woman."

223

"Funny," I said. "I can see him eliminating Gianetta as a political act with no trouble at all. In fact, I wonder if he did."

"It could, I suppose be decided easily enough whether or not he was in Milan at the relevant hour of the morning," Rupert said. "Like Julia, I think if he could canonize something as a political act, he could carry it out."

We all sat there, staring at the cars, the church, the people when suddenly Rupert said, "Did anyone except me notice that when you, Barrett, asked Roper if he knew what was in the new will, he never answered?"

Sir Humphrey, who had ordered himself some strawberry ice cream, paused, spoon in air. "Bless my soul. You're right. He didn't."

"What would be the legal position if he did know what was in the will, but the will itself never turned up?"

"There is a presumption that the will has been revoked, which, in nonlegal terms, means there could be the devil of a legal row over who inherits what."

"You don't seem enormously surprised," I commented to the portly solicitor.

"That she made a new will? Or that I never got it?"

"I suppose I meant that she made a new will."

"According to Maria," Rupert said, "it was a codicil—not a new will."

"I hadn't thought about your being surprised at not getting it. I'm so used to the bad Italian mails and the almost as bad mails in New York that I didn't think about it. Do you think there's something sinister in the fact that you didn't get the will?"

"Or the letters, whoever they were from, or the bill," Sir Humphrey said. "As a matter of principle I'm rather slow about imputing sinister reasons for strange happenings. But I must own to an uncomfortable feeling about this. There's a fair amount of money at stake here."

"How much?" Rupert asked.

"Before taxes, about ten million. After taxes, somewhere between two and three."

"I have a hard time getting my mind around that sum."

"You would not believe the amounts she's given away."

"Oh yes I would," I said. "I've been a recipient of some, and I know others who have."

"And not just individuals," the solicitor said, finishing up the last of his ice cream. "Hospitals, foundations, other worthy causes. To say nothing of the museum."

The word was like a firecracker that went off in my head. "Rupert, did you know that Marco and some of the Italian relatives have been resenting the museum?"

"Yes. That fact trickled in a while ago."

"Sir Humphrey here said it was because Gianetta preferred London to Perugia and an English lawyer to an Italian one, so they take it out by pooh-poohing the museum. In other words, ruffled feelings."

Rupert didn't say anything.

"Well," I said, beginning to get cross again. "What are you holding back?"

"It's not just that, Julia. Some of the pieces in the museum *are* really good—the manuscript fragments, the chests, one or two of the tapestries and several of the paintings. But . . ." he glanced up at me. "Others of them are questionable."

"What do you mean by that?"

"If you're going to leap to the defense like a wounded mother every time anybody looks as though they were going to question Oliver's judgment, then I'm not going to go on with this. Your old love for Oliver, which I suppose now has never really died, may be having a second incarnation—"

"I am not, repeat NOT, in love with Oliver."

There was a dead silence after I'd said this. Everyone seemed startled. Especially me.

"Then I can only say," Rupert said drily, "that you've

been giving a really convincing performance for the past several years."

"Yes, I'm bound to agree with that," Sir Humphrey said judicially. "It used to worry Gianetta a lot—your infatuation with him. All right, all right," he said hastily as I started to protest. "We stand corrected."

Something strange was happening. It was as though a whole series of scenes were being enacted in front of my eyes, jumbled together, out of order or time: Oliver giving me a playful kiss on the cheek, my throwing my arms around his neck, his disengaging me, and my sudden awareness that Gianetta was watching . . . Gianetta's voice, upraised behind the closed living room door, "You must not encourage her, Oliver. After all, she doesn't know . . . she has no idea that—" And then the imperious voice suddenly dropped. I had been coming out of the bathroom next to the sitting room, and had stood, transfixed, my robe clutched around me, my sponge bag in my hand. Then I heard steps and flew along the dark red tiles into the dining room and into my small room opening off of it. . . . Those were all memories, vivid and incredibly real, but memories, nevertheless. Then, in my mind, came another kind of scene, not a memory, born of my own senses, but something I had never seen before, though I knew it had happened: I saw Gianetta getting out of bed and slipping something white into her skirt pocket, a big, square pocket that sagged with the weight of its contents, and then the blood flowing out of her head. . . .

"Are you all right, Julia. Julia!"

It was like coming out of my own head into the sunlight. I had been away, somewhere. But where? The two men were staring at me, Rupert on his feet.

"I think we'd better get back," Sir Humphrey said. "Julia doesn't look too well."

"What were you seeing, Julia?" Rupert asked.

The sun was still shining. People were strolling back

226

and forward. My eye riveted on a woman with a child. The child was wearing a scarlet skirt. When I had noticed her before, they had been crossing the street. They were now stepping on the curb. So only a few seconds had elapsed. Yet I felt as though I had been in a strange world for a much greater period of time.

"Are you ill?" Sir Humphrey said.

"No," Rupert replied. He came over and gently took my arm. "I don't think she's ill. But she's had one or two of these . . . episodes. It's all right Julia. I'm sure it's nothing to be frightened of."

"What episodes?" Sir Humphrey's bristling gray-and-black brows were frowing.

I took a breath. "Ever since I got here I've been having queer . . . well sort of visions, or, if I'm asleep, dreams. They're all about Gianetta. I keep seeing her in the garden, with the blood flowing out of her head. . . ."

"Couldn't that just be grief and shock?" Sir Humphrey looked as uncomfortable as most Englishmen would when confronted by something outside of the familiar three-dimensional world.

"Quite possibly," Rupert said rather crisply as he returned to his chair. "But that doesn't mean that they therefore have no meaning outside Julia's anxiety. What did you see, Julia?"

I took a breath. "I'd like to have something cold to drink. A ginger ale or a Coca-cola or something."

A pained look came over both men's faces. Rupert beckoned the waitress. "*Limone,*" he said firmly, ordering lemonade. "Much better for you. Now, what did you see?"

"The trouble is, it's all a jumble."

"Well—spill it out. We'll try and unravel it."

So I told them about Gianetta, the overheard conversation, the blood flowing from her head and the skirt with something sticking out of her pocket.

"What?" Sir Humphrey asked.

I half-closed my eyes, trying to see what it was that Gianetta had slipped into her pocket. For a second, or half a second, I had seen it, the knowledge of what it was lay at the edge of my mind, just beyond where I could reach it. "I can't quite get it. It's like Gianetta telling me what was in a letter, which in my dream I heard and understood, but couldn't get back when I woke up."

We sat there in silence while I sipped my lemonade.

"Barrett," Rupert said suddenly. "Do you think you could make an educated guess as to how Gianetta changed her will?"

"I could. But I'm not going to. That kind of speculation would be insane and dangerous. Why?" He looked keenly at Rupert.

"Because I have a feeling that until we know, Julia's not going to be safe."

"Why me?" I asked, jerking my head up.

"Because I think you are the key to this whole thing, and I also think at least one other person knows that and will take every step to remove you."

"Who?" Sir Humphrey and I asked together.

"That's the part I don't know," Rupert said.

Dinner was a glum meal. No one talked much, and the guests, between bites, eyed each other nervously, trying to direct glances when no one was watching.

"By the way," I asked Marco. "How is young Terry? Have you heard?"

"He is better. But not well enough to see anyone. Besides, a policeman is there on guard."

"Why should a policeman be there? Wasn't it an accident?"

Silence. Then: "They seem to think that someone might have . . . helped him to fall," Marco said. He was still angry, whether about Terry, or the museum, or the continuing presence of the guests, or the old will that had been made public, or fear of what the new one might hold, I couldn't even begin to guess.

"Poor boy," Mrs. Kessler said. "I do hope he won't suffer any ill effects."

"The doctor says he is doing well," Marco almost snapped.

After coffee in the sitting room Mrs. Kessler got out the Tarot cards and started laying them on the table, looking closely and at length at some of the vivid pictures. I went over.

"What are you doing?" I asked, smiling a little. "Telling your own fortune?"

"No. Sometimes I just like to play with them, looking at them, even use them as an aid in meditating." She glanced up. "Why not sit down and let me continue telling your fortune?"

I sat down, not because I particularly cared about my fortune, but because I was filled with a foreboding. Damn Rupert, I thought. He had inserted the idea in my head that I wasn't safe. Was my foreboding from that? Or something else? Letting Sarah Kessler tell my fortune might distract me from—what? That was the odd part. I didn't know. But I had a very strong desire to keep my mind busy, and not to be left alone. I was about to say, "All right," when I glanced up and saw Oliver across the room. He smiled, and I became aware of a strange pain around my heart.

He strolled over, his lanky, elegant figure moving with the grace that had always been a part of him. "Come out for a walk," he said, and put his hand on my shoulder. Something—some kind of energy—passed through his hand into my body. I felt like a steel shaving responding to a magnet, as my body gathered itself to rise up at his request. Yet beneath that compulsion, some part of me of which I had only lately been aware withheld itself.

"Let her have her fortune told," Mrs. Kessler said.

"You don't believe in that nonsense, do you?"

It was that that broke his spell. Not because I was such a believer myself, but because it was a rudeness towards Mrs. Kessler. I shrugged my shoulder pushing his hand away. "Not now."

I had then the strange suspicion I often had before, especially in the mediaeval hill towns of Italy: as though, if I rounded a corner quickly, I would find the thirteenth century still going on; that the past was not a terminated segment of the unfolding time ribbon, but a place still happening, as indeed the future is also—somewhere happening.

Ignoring his discourtesy, Mrs. Kessler handed me the cards. "Now shuffle," she said.

"Go away," I said silently to Oliver. I felt that he—and what he was feeling—would interfere with the cards. Then I must believe in them more than I realized, I thought, shuffling and reshuffling the cards. Or would it make any difference whether he were there or not? Were the cards already told? Were they laid out somewhere so that what would happen had already been set?

I watched the cards starting to quiver in my hands, and saw then that I was shaking. "It's cold in here."

Mrs. Kessler put her own hands out and placed them around mine. "It's all right," she said. "Everything's all right."

My sense of warmth came back. The cards lay still in my hands and Mrs. Kessler's small, square hands were like bookends around mine. I glanced up. Oliver had moved to the window and was staring out.

"It's all right," Mrs. Kessler repeated softly. "He won't affect the cards. Now, shuffle them again."

Strange, I thought. I had said this afternoon before Rupert and Sir Humphrey that I was not in love with Oliver. But it was only now, at this moment, that I knew it was true. How long had I not been in love with him without knowing it? And why had I not known it? I

230

thought then about David, and our years together, and I knew then that what Rupert had said was true: David, celebrity journalist and writer was soothing balm to my ego after having to swallow how little I meant to Oliver. And Gianetta admired his books, that helped, too. Most of all, he was married. . . .

"You stopped shuffling the cards. Would you prefer not to go on?" Mrs. Kessler's gentle, well-bred Boston voice brought me back.

"Sorry," I said. And I shuffled the cards a third time, this time thoroughly.

"Now draw seven."

I studied the brilliant pictures that she finally laid out in rows.

"Well," Mrs. Kessler said after a moment, "your King of Swords is there and in a dominant position." She looked up at me and smiled. "You remember, you thought you knew who he was? Do you still?"

I had thought he was Oliver. Now I knew he wasn't. I shook my head. "No, I was wrong."

She nodded, looking a little bird-like. After another moment she said, "What I see here is confusion."

"That could well describe my feelings at the moment," I agreed.

"No. Not that kind. "But there is something you have to do or find out, and until you do, nothing else will come clear."

"I have a vague thought, a depressed sort of feeling, that perhaps the cards had already been laid out somewhere, the plot set."

"It's hard to explain how it both is and isn't. It has to do with our concept of time, which is limited. God sees time in a different way."

Mrs. Kessler, I decided, was the only person who could talk about God in that casual way who didn't embarrass me. Perhaps because she wasn't embarrassed herself.

She frowned. "There's property here, a strong, powerful woman who owns—or owned—the property, a search, celebrations and a death. But the center of it is the mystery that you have to look for or find the answer to."

My head started to ache. "I don't like mysteries," I said, sounding to my own ears rather like a cross child. "They . . . disturb me."

"You are wise to be disturbed. Take care of yourself. Try not to be alone."

That was so much what Rupert had said in the afternoon that I jumped. "Somebody else said that." I paused, then tried to say lightly. "I hope mine is not the death you see there."

"No, or I wouldn't have told you. But it is close to you. The only thing; it may have already taken place. Sometimes, in cards or clairvoyance, it's almost impossible to tell whether something has or is going to take place."

"Funny," I said. "That's what I often think when I'm in something like the mediaeval Underground City in Perugia, or in the old town in Gubbio: that if I move fast around a corner I'll find the thirteenth or fourteenth century going on. As though it were a place, still happening. And that the future's like that, too."

Mrs. Kessler gave me an odd look. "Have you always thought that way?"

"No. I don't think so. But I can't remember when I first thought it. Maybe when I first visited Gianetta and Marcello. I think about it more in Italy than anywhere else. Why?"

"Well it's a concept a lot of people have: that time is not linear, but a spiral—people in the East, especially. The linear concept is very Western."

I looked down at the cards. "Is there anything else?"

She put her hand on one of the cards. "I'm not quite sure what the sun card is doing here, but it seems to be related to the priestess here. And the priestess represents

232

the mystery I was talking about."

"It's all very strange and baffling. And now that you have told me all this, what do I do about it?"

"I expect you will be told in one way or another."

"What do you mean?"

"Don't you have dreams?"

"Yes. Do you mean you think they are messages of some kind?"

"People used to call them messengers of God."

"How about messages from the unconscious?"

"Well," Mrs. Kessler said, sweeping up the cards, "I heard a great Jungian psychologist once say that if you really wanted to understand what the Book of Job is about, read it, substituting the word 'ego' for the name Job, and the word 'unconscious' for the name God. In other words God frequently dwells in the unconscious."

"I thought other things, usually unpleasant, lived there."

"Everything lives in the collective and individual unconscious, but that doesn't mean that God doesn't live elsewhere. You look tired."

I felt suddenly overwhelmed with the need to sleep, and gave a huge yawn. "I'm going to bed." I got up. "Thank you."

Mrs. Kessler smiled. "We'll have one more session before we part. We haven't finished yet."

As I started to leave the sitting room Oliver came up. "Let's have that walk."

"I can't, Oliver. I'm asleep on my feet. I'm going to bed."

"You'll sleep better if you take a short walk."

"I couldn't sleep better than I feel I'm going to." I reached up and kissed him on the cheek.

He put his arm around me and held me, and something of the old yearning for him came back. "It's going to be all right," I said, repeating Mrs. Kessler's magic formula.

"Afterwards, after all this dreadful thing is over, we'll be together," he said. And gave me a passionate kiss.

How often, I thought, as his mouth pressed on mine, had I fantasized this moment. But I had always felt that Gianetta's tall, regal form stood between me and Oliver's kiss.

"Good night, darling," he whispered, and went back into the sitting room.

I went slowly downstairs, still thinking about Gianetta standing between Oliver and me. Curiously, that thought had not before defined itself. Now that it had, I could only wonder that I hadn't seen it. I had thought Gianetta was being ludicrous to think I was jealous of her: the vanity of an old woman. Now her intuition about that did not seem so absurd.

I walked through the great halls turning on the lights and leaving them on. It was no longer Gianetta's cost—the estate would have to pay. Would it come out of Oliver's future salary? The money that was left for the museum? Then I grinned to myself. Somewhere in those two and a half million dollars would have to be found the money to keep the lights on so that I, in bed, would not be surrounded by the dark, at least not until Rupert came to bed himself. And a feeling of gratitude washed through me. Rupert's presence comprised, for me, the difference between safety and danger.

That was my final thought before I went to sleep within a few seconds of my laying down.

As I had known I would, I dreamed of Gianetta. And in my dream I was aware of my dreaming. But Gianetta was not actually in my dream. I did not see her. I simply knew that I had to get up and find her. That she was somewhere and was waiting for me to come to her. Then I opened my eyes. The room was dark, unusually so. The moon must have risen and disappeared, or perhaps it was a

234

small moon. I sat up and felt the cold around me, and knew then, beyond a doubt, that Rupert was not there.

"Rupert?" I said, but no sound came out. Rupert was not there.

Terror is a terrible thing—a pounding heart, a clammy sweat on the skin. "Help me," the words formed in my mind. Who was I praying to? I didn't know. What was I afraid of? I did not know that either.

Some of the terror receded. I decided that the best thing I could do was not to fight the fact that I was afraid. Simply accept it. Oddly, doing so made me less fearful. I was still overwhelmingly sure I was not alone. "Who's there?" I said, my voice sounding cracked and high.

There was no sound except the shutter creaking back and forth in the night breeze.

"Rupert?" I said aloud. There was still no answer. Yet I could not shake the feeling that I was not alone, or perhaps I simply feared I was not alone . . . and my imagination had taken off, as it was wont to do in this ancient keep.

Every kind of childish and supernatural fear held me to the bed. I did not want to put my feet on the floor, to move around the room. Yet I made myself do just that. Groping tentatively, I put my feet on the side of the bed, then leaned forward to turn on the light, which was just out of my reach when I sat up in bed. My finger pushed the switch. Nothing happened. Then I pushed it back the other way. The darkness remained unbroken. Damn! I thought. I stared at the shutter and was not surprised to see the reflection of a slight flickering through the slanted louvres. Sometimes the slightest of storms was all that was needed to knock the castle electricity out of whack.

Without light, even less did I want to get up. Yet something was pushing me, or rather pulling me. The dream from which I had just waked was still vivid and fresh in my head, much more vivid than my senses, which felt almost drugged. My feet found my bedroom slippers and mindlessly, without thinking, I stood up. Where had Rupert put the flashlight? On his night table, on the other side of his bed.

Pushing my feet in front of me, I slid over the short space to his bed. Then ran my hands over its surface. As I knew, without having to confirm it this way, Rupert was not there. The bed was flat and by the feel of it, had not been slept in.

I took a deep breath and decided to visit the bathroom before I did anything else. Assuming that the light would be off there, too, I did not even bother with the switch, but shuffled my way across the room, used the toilet, and flushed it. Then I came out, felt my way to Rupert's night table, groped for his flashlight, found it and switched it on. Its beam revealed an empty room. So much, I thought, for my powerful intuitions. I was probably as psychic as a sheet of plastic.

But where was Rupert? I turned the flashlight beam onto my bedside clock. Three-fifteen. An eerie hour and an hour when Rupert should have retired. A niggle of worry, like a dark stain, slid through my mind, followed again by fear.

Gripping the light, I went over to the window, reached up to the fastening and opened the blinds. A pale, thin, high moon shone a feeble light over the front lawn of the castle, far below. The stars were distant points. At the very edge of the horizon, where clouds were visible in the lower sky, flickers of lightning still made vertical patterns on the ground. Was the storm retreating, or on its way over to the castle? Retreating, surely, I thought, and hoped. Putting on my robe, I decided to go and look for Rupert.

EIGHT

Rupert was not upstairs in the sitting room. I stood there, contemplating the general state of disarray that would, I know, be put right early in the morning before the guests had time to assemble. The room looked strangely abandoned. I suddenly felt wide awake, anxious, fearful. Sitting down on the sofa, I stared at the portrait of Gianetta over the fireplace. I had never thought it was particularly good, either as a portrait or a painting. A friend of Oliver's had done it, and I had been surprised that it hadn't shown more quality. Yet now, looking at it, it seemed incredibly real. Almost alive.

"Well, Gianetta," I heard myself saying. "What is it you want me to do?" The words hung in the air.

"What are you doing up, Julia?"

I spun around. Oliver's tall figure, draped in a dark floor-length robe, stood in the doorway.

"I couldn't sleep. And Rupert seems to be missing. So I came up here to see if he was up here."

"You seem to have become rather attached to him—in view of the dislike you expressed with such fervor on our way down here a week ago."

"Oh well . . ." I knew what he said was true and was embarrassed. I could give no reason for it. "What are you doing up?"

"Couldn't sleep. Then heard your voice."

"You must have acute hearing. I was talking to Gianetta's portrait over there, and your room is right on the other side of the dining room."

"My hearing is pretty acute. And your voice is fairly carrying. Added to that—" he paused.

I got up. "Added to that, what?"

He stood in front of me, his hands jammed into the pockets of his robe. "Added to that, the fact that my hearing—and all my senses—are particularly sensitive where you're concerned. I think if you called my name a continent away from me, I would somewhow know it."

I stared up at him. "Why now, Oliver? I know you said it was Gianetta's death that made you realize how you felt about me. But if that's really the way you felt, it's hard for me to understand how you could have been so oblivious when I was doing everything short of buying space in the London newspapers to announce how I felt about you. I was hardly subtle. You must have known it. But, after that first year, you always made it abundantly clear that you weren't interested in me, at least in that way. And Gianetta warned me off, too. Rupert once said I was jealous of the two of you. I thought it was a lot of nonsense. Now I'm not so sure. Gianetta was in her seventies. But perhaps I'm being naive. Was there something I should have been jealous of?"

As I said that my eyes slid over to the portrait again. Gianetta was, right until the end, a remarkably young-looking woman for her age. Her figure had remained firm and slender. Her neck muscles had held. The bones of her face, always beautiful, had remained. There were lines and other marks of aging, but Gianetta could have passed for a woman in her early sixties.

Oliver moved forward, the skirt of his robe making a soft shushing sound on the carpet. "If you mean was there something physical between us, then the answer is no.

238

But not all bonds are physical. You should know that also, because of the bond between you and me."

"What are you talking about? There's no bond between us. That was my secret sorrow all those early years, the thing Rupert was talking about and that Gianetta alluded to in guarded terms from time to time, as though it were a malaise that was taking a boringly long time to go away. All I knew was that I had fallen head over heels in love with you that summer when I was nineteen. How could I help it? You took an ignorant, raw school girl, and talked to her about art, really talked. Not just gave classes. You made me see paintings as I had never dreamed they could be looked at. And I fell so hard that I was never able completely to pick myself up. But the next summer I was here, you managed never to be there when I called you, never to be around when I wanted to see you. You were charming and distant. Eventually I got the message and left. Years later Gianetta accused me of being jealous. I thought it was outrageous vanity. Now I know it was the truth. I was jealous. But only because you were friends with her in a way you would not be with me."

"How could I be? Gianetta was not one to brook a rival, not even a beloved one."

There was something about this conversation that was upsetting me. "You're being absurd. Gianetta was nothing if not realistic. How could she consider me a threat?"

"You're young, Julia, very young for your age. You still think that all love stories end with the bride and groom at the wedding on their way to their little home in the west. Well it isn't always like that. Yet the tie can be ferocious."

"What are you telling me? That there was an affair going on between the two of you?" I found myself furiously angry, although I could not, in the welter of emotion, be quite sure why.

"I told you. There are more ways than just one of

having a passionate relationship. Gianetta knew that I had fallen in love with you. She let me know very forcibly that if I did not separate myself from you, making quite sure that you recovered from your . . . your maiden attachment, that she would make the both of us suffer."

"And how could she do that? She had no power over me. Did she have some hold over you?"

"Of course: position, money, reputation. None of these was secure in my life until she asked me, after Marcello's death, to take over the museum."

"Maybe not, but, given the museum, you have a worldwide reputation. You could go anywhere."

Oliver was silent for a minute. "It's not as easy as all that. Once, some years ago—during that summer we were together—you asked me if there were any iffy pieces in the museum. I cut you off pretty abruptly. But in any museum there are pieces thought to be fully authenticated that turn out not to be. Sometimes fresh evidence comes to light, people change their stand on various items—look at the Giotto panels! Until a few years ago practically nobody questioned that they were by Giotto. Now they're universally considered to be by his students plus God knows how many restorers!"

"I don't understand what you're saying. What does this have to do with Gianetta's power over you? She could be imperious and domineering, but she wasn't cruel and she didn't play cat-and-mouse."

"Oh didn't she! Letting me think all these years—!" He stopped.

"Think what?"

"Nothing. That's all over—"

"Oliver, what are you talking about?" There was a queer, fevered look about his eyes that disturbed me. "What happened between you and Gianetta?"

I could see his hands in the pockets bunch and then relax. "You didn't know her. Not really. No one else did."

Oliver walked closer to me. "There's no way I can describe those years. I would try every now and then to break away. Do you think I wasn't ashamed of my dependence on her? Do you think I didn't know that her Italian relatives—Marcello's relatives—didn't look on me as a glorified gigolo? Oh she had her ways. It's true, I procured various items that were somewhat in dispute. That school of Perugina that hangs in the museum's big room, also the della Quercia. But the museum had a double purpose. Certainly it was meant to be a monument to Marcello. But it was a cage for me. . . . Then it came to her ears . . . somebody told her . . . that one of the pieces wasn't . . . wasn't genuine. She's never spoken to me like that before —never. All those wonderful democratic principles! She talked to me as though I were some jumped-up messenger boy who had forgotten his station. Oh yes, that was when I saw the real Gianetta. No Prussian baroness could have been more arrogant. That's all I could think about, all the words I could hear, when I flew to London that Tuesday morning. . . ."

"Oliver!" Everything was topsy-turvy. I found it hard to follow what he was saying. But, perhaps because he was talking about Gianetta, the dream about her that had receded when I had come upstairs was back in my mind, and in some way was mingled with what Oliver was telling me.

He put his hand out and gently pushed my hair back. "Julia," he said, "let's leave and get married. We could be back in London by tomorrow noon and get married by special license and have a glorious honeymoon motoring down here again through France. There are parts of Provence I don't think you've seen."

"Oliver—you must be raving! Gianetta's been murdered, not to mention Ricardo. We don't know what's going to happen to the museum and you want me to elope with you in the middle of the night!"

He pulled me closer. "What's strange about that? I've always wanted you."

I pushed away. "Oliver, don't!"

"Why not?"

"Because it's too late."

"No it isn't. I'm free now. We can have one another. It's what you've always wanted. I've known that, even when I also knew there was nothing I could do, no matter how much I wanted it, too." He kissed me again, his mouth, warm, full and tender resting on mine.

It was true this was what I'd dreamed of. Night after night it had been the fantasy I had put myself to sleep with. In my imagination I had stripped him naked and put him into the bed beside me, run my hands over the lean flat planes of his body, felt his fingers on mine, as they were exploring my body now. Had he indeed shared in the same fantasy? Was he now giving us both what we had so wanted?

My body was relaxing under his skilled love-making, but my mind, apparently living its own life, was urging me away. There was some task I was compelled to perform, and all the soft words and erotic stroking could not eradicate that annoying voice in the middle of my head, telling me over and over again that I had to get up and go and do it. It was a curious struggle, and I was aware of my own passive role as a kind of battleground. The prompting, urging, nudging to action was beginning to win out, and I knew it, but for a moment I sank into Oliver's embrace, letting it close over me, telling my mind to leave it alone.

But it wouldn't work. Suddenly I broke away. There was a curious tight feeling in my chest. "I'm sorry, Oliver, it won't work. I don't know why. You're right. Once—once I would have given the sun, the moon and the stars, to say nothing of all my possessions to have you do this. But the time for that is gone, and neither of us can bring it back. I have to go downstairs."

242

He stepped back and looked at me a while. "All right. If you're sure that is your choice."

I started to move away, aware of something nagging at me, something he'd said.

"Where are you going?"

My words came out of nowhere, certainly out of no thought I had been conscious of. "I'm going downstairs to look for Rupert. I'm afraid something might have happened to him." And I turned and went to the door, leaving him standing there.

Throwing the flashlight beam ahead of me, I went down the dark steps, wondering if Oliver were following me, unable to remember whether he had on bedroom slippers or if he were in his bare feet and could therefore be right behind me without making any noise. But I didn't turn around. I went back into the great hall, through that, into the girls' dormitory and over to the door leading to the room below. Why was I doing this, looking here? I didn't know and didn't stop to investigate. But, I did turn on the light in the dormitory and close the door behind me, first taking a swift sweep of the flashlight to assure me that my imagination was as usual, working over time. Oliver was not following me. Was I happy about this or sorry? I didn't know. I did know that a strange sadness, almost desolation, had filled me. But I couldn't think what the immediate cause was. It also occurred to me that for anyone as fearful as I, I was behaving in an oddly uncharacteristic fashion, and that I should examine this more closely.

Instead, I went over to the door leading to the stairs going down, opened it, aimed the flashlight in front of my feet and started to descend.

With the removal of Ricardo's body most of the un-pleasant smell had gone. But a remnant remained, trace-able, undoubtedly, to the big stain of blood still in the middle of the dirt floor. But the presence of the police had left its mark in trampled cigarette butts, a match or two, and the imprint of several pairs of shoes. I threw the light around, looking for—what? I didn't know. Why on earth am I down here? I wondered. Did I think I would find Rupert here?

His name came into my mind like a key unlocking a door. It was Rupert who had discovered this passage, ergo, if he was missing, then this would be the first place to look. It seemed a perfectly logical assumption, so why was my heart pounding and my hand beginning to shake? Was it my own fear? The fear that had kept me awake the first night and other nights of previous years when I had found myself alone in the great floor of the castle. What did I think was here that was so terrifying?

"I must go along the passage." I was astonished to realize that I had spoken aloud. But my voice had an odd, muted quality that came from the thick, earth-buttressed walls that were so close around me. How many prisoners in past centuries had been kept here? How many had died?

I shivered and cast the beam of light around the edges of the walls again, assuring myself there were no skeletons or bones. To my horror I realized the light was beginning to weaken. That meant the battery must be giving out. If I were going to go down the passage I'd have to do so right away, or wait until I could find Rupert to replace the batteries with new ones. I hesitated. It would not take me more than a few minutes to follow the passage to the end of the tunnel. I remembered Rupert going down there and returning fairly soon, although he did admit he had not pursued the tunnel to the end. Well, I could hardly get lost. The passageway was a bare three feet across. I walked as quickly as I could, trying to outrun the fading batteries in the flashlight. Once I stumbled against a hard clot of earth incrusted with pebbles. Another time I gave a muffled shriek as three scorpions, invisible against the dark earth, suddenly took fright and scuttled in front of me. They

244

were neither large nor deadly, but they could give a nasty string. My hand shook and the light quivered. Taking a harder grip on the handle of the light, I pushed forward.

The passage was longer than I had thought it would be. I should have realized that when Rupert, not wanting to leave me alone too long, had not gone to the end of it. My intelligence and my common sense kept telling me to go back, to retreat now: to remember my pathological fear of the dark and of enclosed places, all good reasons to go back while there was yet time. Yet, pulled by a force that I was aware of but had no power to understand, I kept going. At about the same time I became aware that the passage was tilting down, that the air was getting closer, and it was becoming a little harder to breathe.

Then, several things happened at once. The passage tilted up, the air suddenly became fresh, and a faint gray-gold dappled wash seemed to pour down from somewhere. I pressed forward, switching off the even fainter light from my flashlight.

The dappling, I discovered, came from leaves growing out of a bush that hid the exit of the passage. The light, of course, was from the dawn which was painting the eastern sky in great stripes of pink and rose and gray. The flowers looked dark, many of the blossoms drooping. I paused, struck overwhelmingly by the realization that it must have been at this hour that Gianetta had come to visit her beloved roses. It seemed such an obvious thing to be overwhelmed by. For almost a week we had known that Gianetta died in her rose garden shortly after dawn the previous Tuesday. Yet it was as though the death she had died had had no reality. I had seen her body, yet that, too, was unconnected with the death she had died. Was that why I had suffered so little grief? Was it really, in effect, for me, as though she had not died?

I heard someone give a cry, and realized a second or so later that it was I. I felt filled with a terrible grief and a terrible anger . . . the anger of someone who had been betrayed.

The light in the garden grew stronger and more gold. The roses were not dark now, but red, the dew on their petals glistening and winking. Down in the town the early morning bells were summoning the faithful to the first mass on Sunday. Walking away from the bush I reached out my hand, touching the petals, feeling their velvety surface, the moisture still on them.

"When I see these roses I understand eternal life," Gianetta had once said to me. "It's about the only time I do."

"But they die in a day," I had protested. It was one of the rare times, in more recent years, that I had yielded to her invitations. Requests, she had called them. Commands I had said to myself.

"The individual flowers do, of course. They have a glorious day and then die, but more blossoms come. The branches that gave them life don't die. The petals crumble and fall on the ground and become part of it. But the thought that became rose—all roses—remains and all roses return to it." And then she had moved off, the handle of her flat basket looped over her arm.

I knew now, as I had never known before, why she came out here, although I could not have put it into words. "Dear Gianetta," I said aloud, "wherever you are, I hope there are a million roses."

And then it happened again. The sense of peace vanished. The pain and the anger were back. A great restlessness seized me, the sense of a task I had to carry out. I had come here for a purpose. What was it? I glanced around. The shadow of the sun across the top of the sundial was long, but there was something odd about it. I stared at the stone face, with its hand, placed in such a way that the sun would always cast its shadow over the correct hour. Except that it was off. The shadow pointed through nine o'clock.

246

It was not, I was quite sure, even seven. How strange. Marcello, the summer I was first here, boasted about the accuracy of his sundial.

I walked over to look at it. There were little bits of dirt on the platform below on which it rested. Yes, it said a little past nine. Without even thinking my hand went out, grasped the slanted bar that formed the clock hand and pulled. The top moved, just as Marcello all those years before had said it would. It was a secret place, he had said, that he had used when a little boy to send messages to friends in the time honored way of small children.

Moving a little to get a better grip, I lifted the top off. There, underneath, in the hollow plinth, was a bulky white envelope. And it was at that moment, as my hand touched the envelope, that I remembered something that had been bothering me. Tuesday, Oliver had said, *My flight to London Tuesday*. Surely he had meant, to Rome. That was the day he and I flew down here, and he had mentioned in passing that he hadn't been to Civitella for a month.

And then I caught my breath as everything fell into place.

There was a slight sound. The envelope in my hand, I glanced up. It was curious. I knew the blow was coming before it actually fell, and for a second I thought I saw Gianetta smiling at me. Then everything went black.

I woke up with a sore head and a feeling of nausea, and found myself staring at a white ceiling. Then I turned my head a little. Rupert was standing by the end of the bed.

"Rupert!" I said. "What happened?"

"You got clouted on the head by Oliver."

I closed my eyes. After a minute I said, "He killed Gianetta."

"Yes. I've been pretty sure he did. But what convinced you?"

My head was aching ferociously, but I decided to try

247

to sit up. After I'd settled myself against the pillows I said, "He made what I thought was a slip of the tongue. He said he'd flown to London Tuesday morning. I thought at first he was talking about our flight to Rome. But later, I knew, suddenly, that it wasn't a slip; he meant what he said, and that he had killed Gianetta. Always before the idea had been impossible because he was in England." I put my hand up to my head. "I don't know why I was so stupid. I always knew there was that nine-thirty flight from Rome, and that early in the morning he could have gotten there from Civitella in two hours." I paused. "I suppose I didn't want to believe it."

Rupert was watching me with an uncharacteristically kind expression. I blurted out, "He wanted me to elope with him last night, in the middle of the night."

"Why didn't you? Or did you know he was the murderer?"

"No, I just knew that I didn't feel that way about him any more. That it was past. I felt sorry for him. But I couldn't . . . I couldn't love him in that way." After a minute I went on. "He said awful things about Gianetta —about how she'd humiliated him over some painting or other. That was the reason—" I stared at Rupert. "Was that why he killed her?"

"Partly. I'm sure that Gianetta, feeling betrayed by having the memorial to her beloved Marcello exposed to ridicule or disrepute, could be devastating. She was an aristocrat. And no matter how egalitarian their ideas may become, the ruling classes, when pushed, always show that *au fond* they never forget that they are the rulers. Just as Oliver never forgot that he was a bright boy up from the bottom."

"Oliver? He never said much about his family. I always thought they were teachers or something."

"His father was a cook and his mother a waitress. He

248

got where he did by scholarships, grants and hard work—the more credit to him! But he was a fearful snob and that was the chink in his armor. Gianetta probably didn't mean to run her needle through it, but, in what must have been a terrible scene, they undoubtedly both reverted to their worst types: she the arrogant, insensitive lady of the manor, he the insulted servant."

"Poor Oliver," I said. And then, "Poor Gianetta—and all because some of the things in the museum were a little shaky in their authentication."

"No. I think she might have been able to live with that. It's because of the Madonna. It's a fake. A lovely fake, but a fake, painted not from four to five hundred years ago, but about a hundred and twenty-five. It's a copy of one that actually existed, but it's not by Mantori."

"Good heavens! How did she find out?"

"I'm afraid through Andrea and me." Rupert looked at me gravely. "We ran into her in Florence in May—as you know. I'd met her before, of course, but I'd never been here. Anyway, we saw her at an art gathering and discovered that we were going south at about the same time. So she invited us to stop by and see her museum. She was as proud as she could be of it, endearingly so. And I think she felt that, according to what she'd gathered from you, I didn't give it enough credit. I'd heard vague rumors about some of the stuff Landau had got for her, and anyway, in view of your relationship to the place, I was curious. So was Andrea. So we came.

"It was a much better museum than I thought it would be, so that shows where prejudice can lead you. And she was a wise old bird in her way. She knew there were areas of doubt as to whether such-and-such a piece—the della Quercia, for instance—was by the artist or mostly by his students. But they were none the less valuable to her because of that. I'd heard of the Madonna, of course, who hadn't? When I didn't see it in the museum, I asked about it. She said it was in the family chapel at the castle and she was saving the best to the last.

"So she took us in there just before lunch and we all sat in the front pew and admired it. It is indeed exquisite. Nor can I say that I took one look and suffered doubts. It did strike me that it seemed a lot more *finished*, in some vague way neater than the rest of Mantori's work. His faces and hands were always lovely, but sometimes his fabrics and materials were a little slap dash. And the Madonna's dress had almost as tactile a quality as some of Piero's. On the other hand, the model was obviously the one he always used, so, beyond 'ohing' and 'ahing,' I didn't say anything and didn't really think much. I did notice that Andrea was pretty silent. He's a fairly taciturn chap so that didn't seem too unusual. Then, during lunch, Andrea asked casually about Oliver's adventures in finding the lost Madonna, and Gianetta trotted out the saga, as pleased as though she'd done the detective work herself.

"Andrea asked what was, I suppose, a pretty obvious question: Why was such a valuable painting in an unguarded chapel? And Gianetta said that Oliver thought Marcello would have liked it there, because he loved the chapel and was deeply religious."

"That's funny," I said. "Oliver said it was Gianetta who wanted it there."

"Yes," Rupert replied. "I remembered you'd told me that at some point. And I suppose that was the first element of doubt I had. Not enough to say anything to Gianetta, but enough to make me wonder. Because the chapel was a damn silly place to have it.

"Following lunch Andrea and I drove down to Rome where some of his paintings were going to be on exhibition. After about seventy miles of silence Andrea suddenly said, 'There's something about that painting that bothers me.'

"I didn't even have to ask which painting. But I almost

told him to leave it alone. Not that it would have had the slightest effect on him. But I somehow felt that the whole thing spelled trouble. The critic and dealer in me wanted it settled and cleaned up. But . . . well . . . never mind that—"

"No, Rupert. Let's have no more shadowy corners."

"I was afraid it might involve you," he said bluntly.

"Oh. I see." Then another aspect struck me. "You mean you thought I'd had something to do with whatever hanky panky was going on?"

"No, of course not! Don't be so defensive. But if what Andrea was vaguely hinting at was right, then you could get caught in the backlash."

"Oh. Well, thanks."

"And, as you observe, I was right. Anyway, Andrea set out to investigate the painting's pedigree and how Oliver found it and who sold it to him. It's a long story, and I won't bore you with the step-by-step details. But it seems that the painting—the original—did indeed end up with an old and wealthy noble family near Venice. Then, about a hundred and thirty years ago or so it was badly damaged in a fire in the family chapel, irreparably so. The then-owner was devastated. He'd always loved it more out of religious sentimentality than artistic sensibility and was neither too bright about the ethics of art nor too scrupulous. Anyway, he had it copied by a clever young painter who was under his patronage. It was such a good job, the owner never bothered to mention that it had been copied. A lot of the chapel contents had been sent away for cleaning and restoration, so when the copy came back, along with the other stuff, no one thought anything about it. After all, we have to remember that Mantori's work was not considered that important at this time—was not 'discovered' until after that, notably by Oliver. So it wasn't like copying a Raphael or a Botticelli or a Piero. Anyway, the family pretty much died out, the last member going about twenty years ago, and leaving only a widow. She'd been a second wife and before that, German *Fräulein* to his children, all of whom were also dead. Well, you know the rest of that. Oliver ran it down there."

"That was the German woman, I bet, who was on the phone."

"Almost certainly . . . It seems that, about three years ago, long after she'd sold the painting to Oliver, she was going through some old family documents and came across a letter from the copier to the owner, thanking him for his patronage and, incidentally, for his generous fee for copying the Madonna. There was absolutely no mistake; the painter spelled it out. So she wrote to Oliver, explaining, which was pretty gutsy of her, since she was living very modestly indeed and had to offer to refund the money Gianetta had paid through Oliver. To have had to give it back would have been a miserable hardship. You can imagine her delight when Oliver told her to keep it, and you can also imagine that she wouldn't press the point.

"All of this Andrea found out quite easily. When Oliver produced Mantori's famous lost Madonna, he wasn't backward about recounting the adventure; how he'd followed one lead after another through documents in libraries, museums and private collections, and so on. And Gianetta told the tale far and wide, too. All Andrea had to do was look up interviews, articles, and snippets in the back issues of art magazines and newspapers. There he found the name of the German baroness, the one on the phone, and he went to see her. She's as old as time and deaf as a post, but he finally made her understand what he was interested in—without telling her why, of course. So she quite happily told him the entire story, expressing much gratitude towards Oliver, but especially towards Gianetta, for their generosity in letting her keep the original purchase price. She's lived completely retired for the past two decades and had almost no knowledge of the world today.

"Andrea asked tactfully if he could see the letter from the painter. The baroness said of course, all he had to do was ask Oliver. He had asked her to send it to him after explaining to her that all important paintings had to have their histories well documented. So Andrea left, came to see me in Paris, where I happened to be at the time, and laid this nest of scorpions in my lap."

Rupert plunged his hands in his pocket. His shoulders were stooped over, making him look like an undistinguished scholar. "Sometimes I think the only thing worse than taking action is not taking action. I decided not to call Gianetta and blurt out the unsavory mess over the telephone. Perhaps if I had, if I had prepared her—" He shrugged. "But what's the use of thinking about that. Events beat me to the draw. Evidently Andrea's visit reactivated the old lady's sense of gratitude. She decided she didn't have much longer to live and wanted to express her appreciation to Gianetta for enabling her to live comfortably in her last years. So she wrote a letter of abject thanks. You can imagine the effect it had on Gianetta. She went up to Venice and had the whole story from the old woman in nothing flat. And what it showed her, of course, was not only that the painting—the Madonna—was a fake—I think Gianetta could have taken that in her stride —but that Oliver had known about it and had said nothing, had let her go on thinking and telling everyone that it was genuine and a great find. That was what was unforgivable, because deception was the one thing she could not endure. Further, his silence would cast doubt on the other, genuine Mantoris in the museum. If he'd said, immediately, that he'd learned the Madonna was a copy, then the art world would have assumed that he'd be equally forthcoming about the other Mantoris if there was any controversy surrounding them. But what aroused her rage more than anything else was that Oliver, whom she trusted, had made a fool both of her and of Marcello.

253

"All of this she poured out on the telephone to me. She was so infuriated that she scared even me, so I can imagine what effect she must have had later on Oliver, tearing strips off his skin as she went. I sympathized with how she felt; he really had behaved appallingly. But I tried to calm her down and told her that for her own sake she should consult some experts in Rome to get their opinion. Then I gave her Stephano Luciano's name and suggested strongly that she get in touch with him immediately."

"How long ago was this?"

"Two or three weeks ago. She and Stephano must have moved rapidly. Apparently, according to what she told me later on the phone, she had him up here practically the next day. He looked at the Madonna and said yes, he thought it was a fake, but if she'd like more opinions, backed by the latest scientific investigative equipment such as infrared spectroscopy, then he'd take it to Rome, which he did. She asked him to consult three other experts without telling them first what he knew, and only implying there was some question. Two of them thought it was a copy, and the spectroscope confirmed that it was painted not five hundred years ago, but more like a hundred and a quarter. Stephano returned the painting with their signed statements, a copy of the scientific report, and his bill. Copies of all that were with the will in the sundial."

"Isn't it odd that nobody had picked that up before?"

"Not really. It was almost three years ago that Oliver decided it should hang in the chapel. I think that was his way of keeping it out of the public eye as much as possible."

"I remember thinking it was funny, because Gianetta practically never went into the chapel, and when I commented on this, he replied that she rarely went to the museum, either, which, of course, was something of a *non sequitur*. She was proud of it. Anyway, wouldn't the truth come to light eventually?"

"I think Oliver was like a juggler who was confident he

could keep all those balls in the air without dropping them. He played his luck. As long as Gianetta was alive he could keep the thing going. Afterwards, well, I'm sure she told him the contents of her original will: that he'd be in charge of the museum and have an income for life. And he could arrange another tragic accident to the Madonna to get rid of the whole thing."

I rubbed my head a little. "Poor Oliver. It didn't work." I paused, suddenly remembering my vision, the blood flowing from Gianetta's head, and this time (to my great relief) it was the memory of the vision, not the vision itself. "No, not poor Oliver. He killed Gianetta. Brutally."

"Yes. I can understand his rage; not because she'd found out, but because she'd humiliated him. So in the end it was the most deadly of the deadly sins: pride."

"What exactly happened after Gianetta found out, I wonder? I suppose she called Oliver and gave him hell on the phone."

"And she must have told him that she was altering her will and leaving him out. That was probably the final straw. He came to Italy and lay in wait for her—I gather everyone knows about her early morning strolls—and then killed her. Since Oliver got away, I don't know. It's only a guess."

"He did get away?"

"Unfortunately, yes. We were so busy trying to make sure you weren't dead, we didn't have time to alert the police. We'd managed to stop him from hurting you very badly by yelling just after he started to lower that rock. It startled him and deflected his arm, so you didn't get too much of a blow on the head. But he succeeded in getting into his car and drove away."

"Never mind. Lucky for me you were there. How on earth did you come to be in the right place at the right time?"

"Because we heard a noise. Barrett and I'd spent the night in the music room—just beyond the girls' dormitory

255

—plotting how to get Oliver to betray himself. Then we heard this sound, which turned out to be Oliver pursuing you down the dungeon stairs. We followed, trying not to make too much noise. But how he managed not to hear us I don't know, except that I think he was beyond taking in anything at that point except silencing you."

We were quiet for a minute or two. I sat there, leaning forward, my head in my hands, not because my headache was worse, but because I was trying to make sense of what happened.

Finally I burst out, "I can understand—I suppose—why Oliver decided he had to try to kill me: After all, he let slip something that made it obvious he killed Gianetta. But I don't understand why less than an hour before that he was making declarations of love all over the place and asking me to leave all and run off with him that minute. And I still don't understand how Ricardo came into this."

"I should think it's pretty obvious why he was trying to make passionate love to you. He knows you fairly well, and if he succeeded in getting you into bed, I think he figured it would be a short step for you from there to the altar. Despite your flutter with David Brownson, you do radiate what I'm sure he would think of as middle-class morality. And the reason he wanted to tie you up in matrimony with the greatest possible speed—I'm afraid this is going to do nothing for your vanity—is the new will, which you don't seem to have given a thought to."

I took my hands away from my face. "You mean you found it?"

"Yes. Or rather you did. In the sundial."

"Oh my God!" That part had disappeared from my mind. Now I saw, as though in an unfolding film strip, Gianetta slip something—a bulky white envelope—into her skirt pocket before leaving her bedroom, and the same envelope lying in the hollow narrow plinth of the dial, after I'd taken off the face. "That was where it was. Why on earth did she put it there?"

"Who knows? It was a safe enough place, and not one that anyone would think of, with the possible exception of Maria. Barrett, who's been here several times, gave himself a tour of the castle yesterday, and in some of those storage rooms up in the battlements, found various chests open and their contents strewn around. Without anything else to go on, that doesn't mean too much, except that Gianetta ran a rather tight ship here with her staff, and I don't think she would have tolerated such sloppiness, if she knew about it, and I don't think Maria would have, either. But Barrett called Birazzi, the police chief, and found they already knew about it. One of their men came and snooped around yesterday, after Terry's fall. Marco knew, of course, but didn't think it worth telling anyone else. Anyway, they speculate that someone—Oliver—was searching high and low for something, which could account for some of the noise people heard and which people were inclined to put down to supernatural agitations, since apparently banging from the upper floor had been heard before. A more mundane explanation is that Terry, who was already nervous, heard, got up, found Oliver, was going to get help, and was pushed down the stairs. Again, it's speculation. Until and if Oliver is caught and cares to enlighten us all, it will have to remain so. By the way, young Terry seems to be showing every sign of recovering."

"I'm glad," I said mechanically. Then I took a breath. "What's in the will?" I was fairly sure by now what I was going to learn and was astonished at my reluctance to hear it.

"Apart from one or two bequests—such as Maria's—you inherit the whole shooting match—all two and a half million dollars after taxes."

I sat there for a minute, curiously unsurprised. "Why

aren't I feeling delirious with joy?" I said finally.

"Because it's probably becoming abundantly clear to you that it's one hell of a responsibility. It's by no means all joy, and that by itself—quite apart from who and what you are—it will create both enemies and friends, and while being rich will make certain things—material things—much easier, it will make other things permanently more complicated."

"Fanny Brice said, 'I've been rich and I've been poor and rich is better.'"

"It sounds like basic wisdom, but who is Fanny Brice?"

"An American entertainer in the twenties and thirties."

"In that case, you should feel happy."

"I should, shouldn't I? But, as of the moment, I don't. I feel anxious and . . . and as though something . . . something were unfinished."

"There's a lot unfinished," Rupert said rather grimly.

"I wonder why she left it to me?" I burst out.

"She probably thought you were the best person to leave it to. Apparently there's also a letter asking you please to allot some of the money to the care and upkeep of the museum, and, if you can, to add to its collection. Which shows, by the way, not only that she trusted your integrity and intelligence, but also your good business sense. It was, if you care to look at it that way, a gesture of atonement-*cum*-humble pie."

I sat there, pulling my knees up to my chest. The sense of urgency was still driving me, yet I knew that before I would respond to it, there were pieces that had to be picked up and put together. "When I called you and told you Gianetta was dead, did you think Oliver might have anything to do with it? I mean, I didn't even know then it was murder, but did it cross your mind that it might be?"

"In view of what I knew about the painting, he seemed an obvious choice of villain or evil agent, if there was one, except for the unavoidable fact—from what you said—that he was in London, waiting for you at the airport. That was a bit puzzling. It wasn't until later that it occurred to me that he could have flown in from Rome that morning."

"Was that why you were so funny on the phone? Why you were so insistent that I wait a day to go?"

"Yes. I felt that he had something to do with it, no matter how unlikely, at that moment, it seemed. But I certainly couldn't let you know why I thought that, and have you trot off and tell Oliver."

"I apologize for calling you Scrooge and a few other unpleasant names," I said.

"Think nothing of it. It wasn't the first and it probably won't be the last. Gianetta, by the way, had phoned me with the outcome of her investigations. I have a feeling she wanted someone beside herself to know, and now that I know what was in her mind about her new will, she chose someone connected with you. In addition to which, of course, Andrea and I were the ones who first tripped her suspicion."

"I'm surprised she didn't tell Sir Humphrey."

"He's not part of the art world. And she may not, at the time she called me, have wanted to make what Oliver had done a piece of legal knowledge."

"But she altered her will."

"The will was dated three days before her death. Her telephone call to me was several days before that. She was undoubtedly thinking about it when she rang me, but may not have made up her mind."

"The way you fly around, I wonder she knew where to reach you."

"I sent her an updated itinerary, along with my bread-and-butter letter. Something told me she might want it."

I said, a little sadly, "I notice she didn't tell me any of this."

Rupert didn't say anything.

"All right," I said. "You don't have to say it. I'm sure

259

she thought I'd get on my high horse about Oliver."

"Would you?"

"I don't know. Poor Gianetta," I continued after a minute. "She took such pride in her collection, especially the Madonna."

"Yes. That's what makes it bad, although the rest of the collection is perfectly acceptable. But the whole thing about the Madonna must have been agony for Landau, too. He certainly didn't start out to be a fraud. But Gianetta wanted so much for her museum to be highly regarded, and he wanted so much to please her."

"Considering that you've never liked him, in fact, what was it you called him?—a bogus lapdog—you're being very charitable."

"You said it was jealousy."

"I apologize again."

We didn't say anything for a moment, then I continued. "It's funny. You were right in a way. All my life I had wanted Oliver and when I couldn't have him, took David as a sort of substitute. But when Oliver started, at long last, making love to me, I couldn't go through with it. Whatever I'd had for him had gone."

"That's probably just as well," Rupert said drily, "Since if he ever is caught he'll have to go to jail for quite a while. Also—" He stopped.

"Also what?"

"It doesn't matter now."

"You can't start something and not finish it."

"Yes, I can. However, I'll go on. I think the nearest thing to genuine affection he ever felt for anyone was Gianetta. In a curious way, I think he did love her more than he'd ever cared for anyone. There are more ways to love than is generally acknowledged."

"He said something like that himself. Something about there are more ways of loving than just the physical kind."

260

"He should know. The only physical kind he wanted did not involve women."

"I asked Gianetta once if she thought he was a homosexual and got one of her put-downs by way of an answer."

"That was probably something she didn't want to think about herself. But certainly Ludovico knew it. He had known it from the time they were both at Cambridge."

"You don't suppose Ludovico was involved in this, do you?"

"I have no reason to think so. But I'm not sure the story is entirely over yet. And I do agree with Ludovico's estimate of his son, Ricardo. I think Ricardo was only a revolutionary when it suited his financial purposes to be so. I think he was interested in the main chance for himself and any opportunity to promote it, and that's all. What I don't know is what he was doing in the garden, and why Oliver killed him, because it's fairly obvious now that Oliver killed both Gianetta and Ricardo.

"By the way, the will in the sundial was a copy. Timothy Randall, one of Gianetta's numerous godchildren, called late last night after you'd gone to bed. Gianetta had given him the English mail to post when he arrived in London, but he did a detour in France and only just reached England last night, where he heard about Gianetta's death. He hadn't posted the letters yet so he called here to see if someone could tell him if he should go ahead and mail them. When he heard Barrett was here he asked if he could speak to him, told him about the letters, one of which was to Barrett, and at Barrett's request, opened the envelope. It turned out to be the original of the will, the signed document from Luciano, and his bill." Rupert straightened, stretching and yawning. Then he said, "I'm going off to the museum now with Barrett. He's going to close it officially till everything gets straightened out and properly probated. I don't think there's any further reason to feel that you should not be alone, so I'll leave you."

"No. I'm coming with you."

"You've just had a blow on the head. You're supposed to be quiet."

"There's nothing noisy about going to the museum."

"You shouldn't—"

But I was out of bed and standing on the floor. "You can't stop me. If you won't let me go with you, I'll nag Marco to take me there. Besides . . ." A brand new thought struck me. "It's my museum now!"

"I can't believe that you're not related to Gianetta. You're getting more like her every day, and I suppose all that money will make you worse."

"I thought you approved of money. It's only ideologists like Ludovico who don't."

"Don't you believe they don't like money! They just want it in *their* hands, not some rich capitalist's. Especially not Gianetta's"

"Yes, I heard him talk to Maria. But I still can't completely understand why he hated Gianetta so much!"

"Ludovico was a natural repository for revolutionary resentment. He was brought up in, but not of, the household of one of the oldest of the Italian aristocracy. And, thanks to Gianetta's American fortune, it was a wealthy household. Curiously, if Gianetta and Marcello had been of the old school and kept Maria and her offspring in the peasant's quarters so that they mingled only with other peasants, which was what would have happened if Ludovico's father had been alive, I don't think this would have happened. But Ludovico was practically like a son of the house, except that he wasn't. And that thin but impassable barrier was what goaded his soul. He hated Gianetta and he hated Marcello, and the kinder they were, the more he hated them. One of the curious bits of gossip in the art world when Oliver's star was on the rise was that he had been once, in his Cambridge days, the lover of the son of one of the contessa's servants. This tidbit was remembered

262

by some Cambridge contemporary who was later at Christie's or Sotheby's or somewhere. Anyway, the tale was that Oliver threw him over for some more highly placed companion, which would be typical. I think the objects of Oliver's erotic impulses were very much sublimated to his social ambition."

I thought for a while. "It's an odd circle, isn't it. Everything seems connected with everything else."

"I'm sure Mrs. Kessler would tell you that that's the way it is."

"Do you believe her . . . well, strange theories?"

"Yes, I think I do."

"But I thought you were an orthodox, Church of England, church-going Christian."

"I'm not sure the two are as irreconcilable as people used to think. Are you sure you want to go to Castiglione with me?"

"Yes. I'm certain. I'll be with you in a minute."

Before we could leave we had to run the gamut of two police cars and several *carabinieri* grouped together around the courtyard. Rupert spoke to the police chief as we were going out. Birazzi looked coldly at me. "You are coming back?"

"Yes, of course I'm coming back. Why?"

"There are questions I would like to have you answer."

"All right."

"Why do I feel all of a sudden that he doesn't approve of me?" I asked Rupert as we were getting into the car.

"Because he probably doesn't approve of you inheriting all that money. Most likely he is, to some degree or other, a Communist. Many Italians are. Which doesn't in any way prevent them from being Catholics."

Three of us—Rupert, Sir Humphrey and I—drove in Rupert's car. Now that I was in the car, I found I couldn't get to the museum fast enough. It was as though there were a hand in the middle of my back, pushing me. "Can you go any faster?" I was amazed to hear myself ask. I was always a pantywaist about driving, and Italian traffic usually filled me with terror.

"What's the rush?" Sir Humphrey inquired. He was sitting in the back.

Rupert, who was driving, glanced at me out of the corner of his eye, but didn't say anything. Obediently, he speeded up the car.

"Why are you indulging this speed demon in her foolishness?" Sir Humphrey asked querulously. "This is an idiotic pace on a foreign road driving on the wrong side."

"Did it ever occur to you," I said, "that since all countries except Britain drive on the right, then the British might be driving on the wrong side?"

"Impossible!" Rupert murmured. "We British are never wrong."

"That's the stuff," Sir Humphrey said. "And I still don't understand why we're going at seventy miles an hour."

"Are we in a hurry, Julia?" Rupert asked.

"Yes. Don't ask me why; I don't know. But—all of a sudden—I think it's important to get there as soon as possible."

I saw Sir Humphrey glance at me in the rear view mirror. "Does anyone have a key to the museum? It's still early in the morning." He glanced at his watch. "Eight forty. It won't be open, will it?"

I answered after a minute. "There's usually a caretaker on the premises. Oliver, of course, always had a key."

"I wonder where Landau is now?" Sir Humphrey said thoughtfully.

"Running hell for leather for the nearest frontier, I should think," Rupert said.

I glanced back at Sir Humphrey. "I take it you know all about l'affaire Madonna?"

"Yes, we had a chat yesterday evening. That German baroness called again while you were out, I think, or downstairs, and since I was the only one in the castle who could speak German, I talked to her. She'd heard about Gianetta's death and wanted to express her sympathy et cetera, and also wanted to know whether Gianetta had received her most recent letter, thanking her yet again for her generosity. When I respectfully inquired what generosity she let loose a flood of German about the Madonna and who painted it and Gianetta's kindness in letting her keep the money. Further questions got me nowhere, so I asked Carmichael here what he knew about it and got the full story. I must say the whole thing's ironic. I'd been trying for years to get Gianetta to have some of the items in her museum properly authenticated by some outside expert or experts."

"You mean you entertained doubts about Oliver?"

"Well . . . I'd never met him, of course, but he sometimes sounded a bit too good to be true. I don't know. I suppose it's the lawyer in me: always have everything signed, preferably by six witnesses."

"Can't you go any faster, Rupert?" I said suddenly.

Rupert glanced at me again. "Have you any idea what's giving you this anxiety to get there? This is fast enough."

"No. I don't. But I know it's important."

"Have you had breakfast?" Sir Humphrey asked, soothing and pragmatic.

Rupert grinned. "First things first, eh?"

"No, but I'm not hungry."

"It'll only be a few minutes now," Rupert said.

We arrived shortly before nine. I was out of the car almost before it stopped and turning the handle of the big double door. It was locked. I went to the side and raised my hand to push the bell. What prevented me, I'll never know. But my hand stopped just short of the bell, hovering there.

"Well," Rupert said, coming up behind. "Why don't you push it?"

I didn't say anything. He put out his hand, but I pushed

it down. "Oliver's in there," I said. "Don't ask me how I know, but I know. I don't think we should ring the bell."

"Then how do you plan to get in?"

"Let's see if we can find a window," I said.

"My cat burglar days are long gone," Rupert said sarcastically, "quite leaving apart the fact that the lowest window is above my head, and far above either yours or Barrett's."

"I can stand on your shoulders."

"You do realize, don't you, we could be arrested for unlawful entry?"

"Rupert, Oliver's in there. I don't know what's going on, but my feeling of danger is overwhelming."

"Then why don't we call the police?"

"Why don't you stop arguing and help me to find an open window?"

"Because I'm a mouse in a mouse suit. I have no desire to be shot at. Oddly enough, I have even less desire to see you shot at."

"I'll ask Sir Humphrey," I said, deliberately using it as a ploy. I knew the lawyer would reject it out of hand.

"Will you let me get on your shoulders to see if any of these windows can be opened?" I said.

"Certainly not. I'm not up on Italian law, but I'm reasonably sure that unlawful entry is the same here as anywhere else."

"But Oliver is in there and the matter is urgent."

"What evidence do you have for saying that?"

"None," I said. What was the use of trying to explain my own powerful feelings?

Then the round lawyer surprised me. "Are you having one of your psychic shoves?"

Even at that moment of urgency I couldn't help grinning. "I wouldn't put it that way myself. But, yes. I am."

"All right. I'll squat down, near the house wall right

under the window, you climb on and then I'll straighten up."

"No," Rupert said, with a note of resignation in his voice. "I'll do it. I was trying to figure out a way that I could stand on something. I certainly couldn't on Julia, and I don't think I could on you. I may be thin, but I'm as heavy as you are."

"No need to be so smug about it," Sir Humphrey said.

"All right, Julia, come on." Rupert had gone up to the wall of the house, the one away from the road, and lowered himself to a squatting position. "Now get on, brace yourself against the wall, and I'll try to rise slowly. If you start to totter, for God's sake call out."

Perhaps it was because of my enormous urgency, or because my mind was totally preoccupied with getting in, but the whole thing seemed to happen with ease. I took off my shoes, stepped on the shoulders of Rupert's blue pin-striped suit, and kept my hands on the wall as we rose slowly. When Rupert was standing at his full height I was waist high above the window ledge.

The first thing to do was to see if the shutters would open. We were in luck, I thought. They were. But the tall windows were locked from the inside. Rupert went down as slowly as he came up, and we tried the whole thing all over again on the second window. This time the shutters were locked. But at the third window everything worked. The shutters were open, and the windows, although pulled together, were not latched. I pushed gently one side and then the other. One of the sides swung open and I was able to push the other open.

"I'm going in," I whispered down to Rupert.

I suddenly felt his hands like iron on my feet. "Not until you promise the first thing you do is to open the front door. Barrett and I will be standing there, waiting."

"I promise," I said. I had already smelled something familiar and frightening.

Rupert clung to my feet. "I mean it, Julia, unless you want us to go and get the police, I want you to get to the front door and open it."

"All right, I promise," I said, and with that heaved myself up on the ledge, hung for a moment, then got my legs over and into the room.

The smell of gasoline was overwhelming, and I could see the trail of oily fluid like a stream in the middle of the floor.

Later I had time to think what an irrational thing Oliver was doing. At the moment, I didn't question it's degree of insanity. All I could wonder was why I hadn't known before that this was what he would do. There was a lot of the angry child about Oliver. He might bring himself down, but he wanted everyone to be very sorry. My courage quailed at that moment. All it would take would be the striking of a match for this tinder box to go up. There would be no escape for anyone. Yet I looked at the La Spagna madonna across from me, remembering how Gianetta had loved her face, and at the fragments of illumined parchments in the glass case next to her. They were, for those who cared, literally beyond price and were among the few remains of an almost illiterate age. The written word was thrown away by the ton, daily, in every Western city. If the twentieth century was nothing else, it was articulate. But these finely, carefully wrought missals were the loving work of thousands of hours by patient men and women, to whom this was a lifework given by them to God. Once gone, the missal pages would be gone. They might live somewhere, in some dimension or consciousness. But the paper to look at and the ink to read would be gone. As would the triptych on the wall, in all its brilliant and illumined colors. I took a deep breath, then, in my stocking feet, went forward, avoiding the greasy petrol, moving as quickly as I could to get away from the fumes.

Remembering as well as I could the layout of the museum, I envisioned going through the door facing me, then turning left, passing through two more rooms, and then veering right. This would bring me to the corridor around the inner courtyard or patio. If I could follow that around, I would come to the double doors. All I had to do was to make no noise and to avoid Oliver.

My luck held for the next two rooms. On silent feet I walked as quickly as I could down the center, noting that the strip of gasoline circled the room, a few feet from the paintings on the wall and around the display cases or chests. Then, in the third room I saw Oliver, standing there, staring at a small piece of mediaeval sculpture portraying the crowned virgin.

He turned and looked at me, and then looked back. It was hard to pick out her face in the dim light filtering through the louvers, but I remembered the oddly tender look in the elongated features.

"She's lovely, isn't she?" Oliver said. "I always liked her best of all, better than that damned Mantori—or pseudo-Mantori."

"Don't do this, Oliver. It would be such a waste." He was standing between me and the far door, and there was no way on earth I could get past him.

"Not according to some of the bloody critics. Second-rate stuff, one of them said."

"That's only about two or three of the items, and only because . . ." My voice faded. I did not wish to exacerbate his feelings, so I did not finish as I meant to: *because of your inflated claims for them.*

"Because I pressed their authenticity? That was Gianetta's fault. She wasn't just willing to buy a piece because it was beautiful and certainly of a given period. It had to be an authenticated piece by an authenticated painter or sculptor of the first rank."

"That's because she didn't know herself. And anyway, she wanted to have proper honor for Marcello."

"That was her idea to begin with. I told you, by the time she died, and a few years before that, it was honor to herself."

"I don't think you're being fair, Oliver." I was straining to keep my voice as even as possible. To keep out of it any trace of the panic I felt. I was now well and truly trapped. I could not get past Oliver to the front door. Nor could I get back to the open window fast enough to escape the flames if he should drop a match in any part of the oily fuse he had spilled. "Nobody's motives are entirely pure and unmixed. I know mine aren't."

Oliver turned. "You!" he said. There was loathing in his voice. "You could have prevented all this. With Gianetta's money we could have gone on to make this a first-rank museum of the smaller, private variety. But you were so busy panting after your boyfriend you couldn't see it."

"I told you, you were right. I don't love David."

"I know that. I'm not talking about David. He was just an excuse. I'm talking about Rupert. Bloody-minded bastard. He and his friend Andrea. They couldn't mind their own business. They had to snoop around and then tell Gianetta that the damn Madonna was a fake and I knew it!"

He looked at me. Even in a half-dark room, standing several feet away from him, I could see the rage in Oliver's dark eyes. He stood there, his petrol can dangling by its handle from his hand. "And the old bitch summoned me as though she were some queen and I her lackey." He almost spat the words.

"I thought you loved her," I said. "Weren't you the one who said there were more ties than just the physical ones?"

"She should have trusted me. I would have made it right in the end. As I got hold of better and better pieces I could have fudged the claims on the others."

"Why didn't you tell her that?"

"Because for her there was no later. Every piece had to be a gem."

"Didn't you care for her?" I was trying to keep his attention on his affection, hoping it would get him to put down that terrible weapon he was swinging around.

"Yes, the way I did my mother, who also in the end tried to destroy me."

"You never told me that. I thought she died."

"Oh she did. Eventually. Some twenty years after running away with another man and leaving me to be brought up by my unyielding, unbending monster of a father. But I never saw her after I was eleven."

"But what happened, Oliver. Why did you have to kill Gianetta? She would have listened to you. I'm sure of it. She loved you."

Oliver's free hand was opening and closing. "I kept hearing her voice on the phone, the words she used, the contempt. I can't describe it to you. A master at school in England once talked to me like that. Years later I went back to the school and waited for him in an alley. I was younger and stronger than he was. I left him alive but only just."

Oliver turned and stared at me. "You wouldn't understand. When she got through talking on the phone, I pleaded with her, begged, crawled. She was going to tell everyone how I suppressed the letter . . . she was changing her will. . . . By the time she was through I would not only have no job—I'd have no hope of getting another. I'd be the joke of the art world . . . I begged her again, loathing myself. Finally she said all right. She'd mailed the new will but she'd listen to me one more time if I wanted to come to the castle.

"The only flight I could get from London went to Milan. I got off there and hired a car. Then, on some damnable impulse, decided to visit Ludovico. . . . When the devil wants company! Ludo was the one person who loathed Gianetta. I thought he'd commiserate with me without my having to tell him everything. But he was out, and I found Ricardo there instead. . . . A lovely boy, eager to sell anything that would bring him money—including his own body. Unfortunately, in an excess of . . . of affection, I talked too much. In fact, I told him everything. When I woke up, the little scum had taken off. I could guess where: to get money from Gianetta on some trumped up blackmail or other angle, garnered from what I'd told him. He knew that once I got there, whatever else happened, I'd fix it so Gianetta wouldn't let him have a penny—I'd spike any story or approach he could try. So I got into my car and tore after him. When I got there I parked out by the cypress grove and saw Ricardo's motorbike there, too, half hidden by some trees. It was still warm, so I knew he hadn't beaten me by much and was probably hanging around somewhere. Then I walked up to the castle. The castle door was open, and I guessed that Gianetta would probably be in the rose garden. It was just dawn, and that was always her favorite time. I went down through the passageway." A spasm of pain crossed his face.

Oliver's voice ceased again. He stared at the Madonna, which he had propped against a wall.

"Did you mean to kill her?" I asked. Perhaps if he got lost enough in his story, I thought, I could get away.

"No. Not at first. I was in a rage at Ricardo when I started driving in the dark down the *autostrada* from Milan. But by the time I got there all I could think of was Gianetta. I went down into the rose garden, still meaning to talk, and saw her among the rosebushes, her white head held in that typical tilt. I don't know what happened then . . . I remember fury going through me like a flame. . . . The next thing I remember, she was down on the ground, the blood flowing out of her head, the rock in my hands. I looked up and saw Ricardo. He turned and tried to run away, but I was too fast. . . ."

272

Oliver turned towards me. "And now it's your turn."

"Oliver," I said. "Let me get out. Please. I haven't done you any harm."

He had been looking at the painting. "Haven't you? Yes you have. By omission. I just told you. You could have made everything all right. No, I'm going to destroy this museum and everything that's in it, including you and me. It'll make a fine funeral pyre, Julia—take comfort in that. You'll go in style!"

"Don't you *want* to live?"

"Not behind bars."

"If I promised to help you—"

"Save your breath. I don't believe you."

"What's that noise?" I said, in a stupid attempt to distract him. And then could have chewed my tongue off, because there was a noise, and I wished profoundly that I hadn't called his attention to it. With his free hand he reached into his pocket and took out a matchbox. Then he put the can down, opened the box and took out a match.

"No!" I cried.

"Drop that, Landau." I whirled around. It was Rupert's voice from the door leading to the courtyard. Rupert was holding a gun. Beside him, looking somewhat ludicrous behind a huge fire extinguisher, was Sir Humphrey Barrett. Both men were in their stockinged feet.

"Why should I?" Oliver said. "I've nothing to lose. Besides, if you fire that gun you'll set the whole place ablaze."

"Not if we pour foam on it first. And then you could live without a hand, because I'd blow the damn thing off."

Oliver hesitated. It was curious, I thought. He could face the thought of death. But not of life without one of his beautiful hands. While he was hesitating, Rupert walked forward and took the match and the box out of his hands.

"Damn you, damn you, damn you," Oliver yelled. Agile

as an eel, taking advantage of Rupert's momentary distraction, Oliver snatched the gun out of his hand. Then he pointed the gun at his own head. As he pulled the trigger, there was a hissing behind and Sir Humphrey was pouring the thick foam all over the marble floor.

"How on earth did you get in?" I said a while later in the courtyard of the museum. The police were inside, plus the fire department, who had carefully laid the foam on all the floors and were now busy getting it—and the gasoline—up.

"The same way you did," Rupert said. "After a reasonable time we had to assume you walked into trouble. So we went around to the other side and found another window open. By this time we were pretty sure of what Landau had done. The fumes were coming through the window you'd left open. So we collected the fire extinguisher on the way, after calling the police and the fire department from the office."

Two men came out carrying a covered stretcher. My heart gave a curious pang, but it was, in a strange way, more for Gianetta, wherever she was, than for me. Yet I wasn't sure I would have undone the past hour if I could have.

"I'm sorry," Rupert said briefly.

"Yes, so am I. But given everything, I don't see how it could have ended differently."

He looked at me. "For one recently burning with love, that's a pretty tepid reply."

"I'm not burning with love for Oliver, as you very well know, because I told you. All I meant was that given everything about Oliver, I don't see how it could have ended otherwise. He would have had to be different. And for him to be different you would have had to start again at the beginning of his life, if not at the beginning of the world."

"You've lost me," Rupert said.

* * *

After lunch everyone, including David and Stacey, left. I watched their departure from the upstairs hall window. Just before Mrs. Kessler kissed me goodbye in the hall she said to me, "Well, did you find out who is the King of Swords?"

"Yes," I said. "I did. It's Rupert."

"I thought it would be. Well, the best of good fortune, my dear."

When all the cars had driven away, I went across to Maria's room in the passageway over the courtyard and knocked on the door. After she told me to come in I entered and saw her sitting in the same chair she had sat in when I was last there, staring out at the courtyard as she had been doing that previous time.

I sat down opposite her in the straight chair and remained silent for a minute. Then I said, "I wanted to tell you what I learned about . . . about how Ricardo died."

"That snake killed him. I always hated him, sucking up to the contessa the way he did!"

"And yet you telephoned him in London when you found Gianetta's body."

She shrugged. "Ruggoni—the agent—said I should. The young conte wasn't here, and Ruggoni didn't speak English enough to put in the call to London—you know how much trouble it is, sometimes, getting through from here—so I did." She paused. "What happened to Ricardo?"

I told her, trying to make it a little less tawdry by leaving out the sexual exchange between Oliver and Ricardo. But I might as well have saved my breath.

"I know you're trying to save my feelings, Julia, but don't bother. I know what Ricardo was. He'd sell himself to anyone. And Mr. Landau—" She paused again. "I don't care that he liked boys. That was his business. I didn't like him making a fool of my lady, which he did."

"You knew about the Madonna?"

"No. Not any one picture. But he'd pretend pieces he

brought to show her were so valuable and then some of them would turn out not to be. I'll say this for the contessa, she had a pretty good eye. I've heard her say, 'You're not going to tell me that painting's by so-and-so, because I won't believe it.' And then that piece would never go into the museum. . . ."

I didn't know what to say so I sat there in silence.

Then Maria spoke again, "I knew she was murdered. That's why I called the police and told them that. I wasn't going to have her buried and have the murderer go away like it had never happened."

"Did you think it was Oliver?"

"How could it be? He was in England. Nobody thought he'd be here that same morning, even at six-thirty and in his flat in London at eleven. Which is silly, when you come to think of it, and all the people who've come and gone from there to here. But then the police thought—the way I did—that it was Ludovico, or some other Red."

"You thought that, Maria? And you still called the police and said it was murder?"

"She came first, Julia. She always did. You know that. Yes, I thought my son was behind it, if he didn't actually do it—him and his fine political ideas. May God and Ludo forgive me! Then they found Ricardo. But I knew he didn't kill my lady. I still thought it was political and maybe he was mixed up in it. But he wouldn't do it!"

People's loves and loyalties, I reflected, were odd.

"You know I found the will—or rather a copy of it—in the sundial, don't you?"

"Yes. I heard people talking about it when I was serving lunch."

"Would anyone have known to look there if something had happened to the original?"

"Oh yes. I would. I was too upset to think of it at the time. But I would have remembered. The contessa always put notes there. It was a joke between her and the old conte. And sometimes, especially if she was going away for a few days and wanted to leave me private instructions, she'd say, 'there's a note for you, Maria, in the usual place,' and I'd know it was in the sundial."

"I wonder if she had . . . well . . . a kind of premonition of what was going to happen."

"We all know more than we think we know, Julia."

Much later that night I was sitting in bed, reading. Rupert knocked and then walked in. "What are you doing here? There are plenty of vacant rooms upstairs. Practically everybody's left."

I lowered my book. "Are you throwing me out?"

"I'm merely pointing out that there's no need for you to continue to occupy my room." Snatching up his robe and pajamas from the chair near his bed, he disappeared into the bathroom.

When he came out in his pajamas he looked like a thundercloud. Then he got into bed, switched off the light and turned his back. "Good night," he said angrily.

I got out of bed, went over and slipped in beside him.

He sat up like a spring. "What the hell do you think you're doing?"

"It's called leading you on. Where is your baser self?"

Much later, we lay watching the Italian moon stare at us through the long window. To my delighted surprise, Rupert had turned out to be a tender and considerate lover. And, despite all the tragedies, I was feeling happier than I had ever felt before. Which, I pondered, was amazing. With David, sex came well down the list of things I enjoyed with him on our nights together. Then a slight cloud slid across my mind.

"What about your girlfriend, Rupert?" I said.

"Which one?" He was half asleep.

"The one you told me about who was so perfect in every respect."

"She was mostly in my head. I told you all that to keep my end up. If there's anything I find wholly repulsive it's someone slinking around full of unrequited love."

"You mean you've had a thing for me all these years?"

"One of the qualities I like about you is your elegant turn of phrase. Yes. I've had a thing for you."

"Oliver seemed to think I had a thing for *you*. It came as a shock, but I believe he was right."

"In that case, to quote the late great Winston Churchill, the disguise was perfect. No one, least of all I, would have known it. And while I'm on the subject. I would appreciate your ceasing to call me Scrooge. I'm not Scrooge. I have expenses you wot not of."

"Such as?"

He didn't answer for a minute. Then he said, "Such as a former wife in an institution in Switzerland. And a child in boarding school near there."

"Why on earth didn't you say something about it? You may not be able to bear unrequited love. What I can't stand is silent noble suffering."

"I'm not suffering nobly in silence or any other way. I just didn't think it was anybody's business. The marriage was over a year after it started. I didn't know about her illness when we married, but there's no doubt that simply getting married and having the child triggered off an attack. Afterwards I'd learned she'd had episodes like that as a child and an adolescent. And that's the way it's going to remain, so I'm told. But it's either where she is now or a state place. As long as I have any money at all, I'd rather avoid the latter. Gideon—that's my son—is there in Switzerland so he can see her. In a year or two I'll bring him back to England so he can go to school there."

"Are you fond of him?"

"Very. But he hates me. He believes his mother when she tells him I have locked her away in a prison. At the moment there doesn't seem to be anything I can do about it."

I sat up. "Well there's something I can do about it," I said indignantly. "I can show him I love you and give him an objective opinion and tell him I'd like to be friends with him, too."

Rupert sat up beside me and put his arm around me. "That would be wonderful." He kissed me at length.

"That is," I said, a bit breathlessly, "if you'll marry me."

"You'll have to learn to love Bothwell, too."

"That insufferable hound of yours? You mean love me, love Bothwell?"

"That's right. He's ugly, but his soul is beautiful."

"All right: Put like that, how could I resist?"

"In that case I accept your proposal with pleasure. I'm so glad you asked. You beat my proposal by about ten seconds." After another long minute he murmured, "I feel another attack of basic instinct coming on."

I slid down into bed. "Don't fight it."

Later again, I looked across the room to where the lost Madonna, whom Rupert had brought back and propped up on the bureau, seemed to keep a silent vigil in the dimming moonlight. She made me think of Gianetta. "Arrividerci Gianetta," I whispered. "Godspeed." I was quite sure she was now at peace and on her way.